唐詩明理 接千載
古今抒情詩三百首
漢英對照

rallel Reading of 300 Ancient and Modern Chinese Lyrical Poems：
Tang Dynasty（Chinese-English）

■ 著者：林明理　Author：Dr. Lin Ming-Li
■ 譯者：張智中　Translator：Professor Zhang Zhizhong

著者簡介
About the Author & Poet

　　學者詩人林明理博士〈1961-〉，臺灣雲林縣人，法學碩士、榮譽文學博士。她曾任教於大學，是位詩人評論家，擅長繪畫及攝影，著有詩集，散文、詩歌評論等文學專著 36 本書，包括在義大利合著的譯詩集 4 本。其詩作被翻譯成法語、西班牙語、義大利語、俄語及英文等多種，作品發表於報刊及學術期刊等已達兩千四百餘篇。中國學刊物包括《南京師範大學文學院學報》等多篇。

　　Dr. Lin Mingli（1961-），poet and scholar, born in Yunlin County, Taiwan, master of law, honorary Ph. D. in literature. She once taught at a university and is a poetry critic, and she is good at painting and photography. She is the author of 36 literary books, including poetry collections, prose, and poetry reviews, as well as a collection of translated poems co-authored and published in Italy. Her poems have been translated into French, Spanish, Italian, Russian and English, etc., and over 2,400 poems and articles have been published in newspapers and academic journals.

©林明理專書 monograph、義大利出版的中英譯詩合著
Chinese-English Poetry Co-author published in Italy
© Lin Ming-Li's monographs and co-authored Chinese-English Poetry collections published in Italy

1. 《秋收的黃昏》*The evening of autumn*。高雄市：春暉出版社，2008。ISBN 978-986-695-045-2
2. 《夜櫻－林明理詩畫集》*Cherry Blossoms at Night* 高雄市：春暉出版社，2009。ISBN 978-986-695-068-9
3. 《新詩的意象與內涵－當代詩家作品賞析》*The Imagery and Connetation of New Poetry －A Collection of Critical Poetry Analysis*。臺北市：文津出版社，2010。ISBN 978-957-688-913-0
4. 《藝術與自然的融合－當代詩文評論集》*The Fusion Of Art and Nature*。臺北市：文史哲出版社，2011。ISBN 978-957-549-966-2
5. 《山楂樹》*Hawthorn Poems* by Lin Mingli（林明理詩集）。臺北市：文史哲出版社，2011。ISBN 978-957-549-975-4
6. 《回憶的沙漏》*Sandglass Of Memory*（中英對照譯詩集）英譯：吳鈞。臺北市：秀威出版社，2012。ISBN 978-986-221-900-3
7. 《湧動著一泓清泉—現代詩文評論》*A Gushing Spring-A Collection Of Comments On Modern Literary Works*。臺北市：文史哲出版社，2012。ISBN 978-986-314-024-5
8. 《清雨塘》*Clear Rain Pond*（中英對照譯詩集）英譯：吳鈞。臺北市：文史哲出版社，2012。ISBN 978-986-314-076-4
9. 《用詩藝開拓美—林明理讀詩》*Developing Beauty Though The Art Of Poetry－Lin Mingli On Poetry*。臺北市：秀威出版社，2013。ISBN 978-986-326-059-2
10. 《海頌－林明理詩文集》*Hymn To the Ocean*（poems and Essays）。臺北市：文史哲出版社，2013。ISBN 978-986-314-119-8

著者簡介

11. 《林明理報刊評論 1990-2000》Published Commentaries 1990-2000。文史哲出版社，2013。ISBN 978-986-314-155-6
12. 《行走中的歌者－林明理談詩》The Walking singer – Ming-Li Lin On Poetry。臺北市：文史哲出版社，2013。ISBN 978-986-314-156-3
13. 《山居歲月》Days in the Mountains（中英對照譯詩集）英譯：吳鈞。臺北市：文史哲出版社，2015。ISBN 978-986-314-252-2
14. 《夏之吟》Summer Songs（中英法譯詩集）。英譯：馬為義（筆名：非馬）(Dr. William Marr)。法譯：阿薩納斯·薩拉西（Athanase Vantchev de Thracy）。法國巴黎：索倫紮拉文化學院(The Cultural Institute of Solenzara)，2015。ISBN 978-2-37356-020-6
15. 《默喚》Silent Call（中英法譯詩集）。英譯：諾頓·霍奇斯（Norton Hodges）。法譯：阿薩納斯·薩拉西（Athanase Vantchev de Thracy）。法國巴黎：索倫紮拉文化學院(The Cultural Institute of Solenzara)，2016。ISBN 978-2-37356-022-0
16. 《林明理散文集》Lin Ming Li's Collected essays。臺北市：文史哲出版社，2016。ISBN 978-986-314-291-1
17. 《名家現代詩賞析》Appreciation of the work of Famous Modern Poets。臺北市：文史哲出版社，2016。ISBN 978-986-314-302-4
18. 《我的歌 My Song》，法譯：Athanase Vantchev de Thracy 中法譯詩集。臺北市：文史哲出版社，2017。ISBN 978-986-314-359-8
19. 《諦聽 Listen》，中英對照詩集，英譯：馬為義（筆名：非馬）(Dr. William Marr)，臺北市：文史哲出版社，2018。ISBN 978-986-314-401-4
20. 《現代詩賞析》，Appreciation of the work of Modern Poets，臺北市：文史哲出版社，2018。ISBN 978-986-314-412-0

21. 《原野之聲》Voice of the Wilderness，英譯：馬為義（筆名：非馬）(Dr. William Marr)，臺北市：文史哲出版社，2019。ISBN 978-986-314-453-3
22. 《思念在彼方　散文暨新詩》，Longing over the other side (prose and poetry)，臺北市：文史哲出版社，2020。ISBN 978-986-314-505-9
23. 《甜蜜的記憶（散文暨新詩）》，Sweet memories (prose and poetry)，臺北市：文史哲出版社，2021。ISBN 978-986-314-555-4
24. 《詩河（詩評、散文暨新詩）》，The Poetic River (Poetry review, prose and poetry)，臺北市：文史哲出版社，2022。ISBN 978-986-314-603-2
25. 《庫爾特‧F‧斯瓦泰克，林明理，喬凡尼‧坎皮西詩選》（中英對照）Carmina Selecta (Selected Poems) by Kurt F. Svatek, Lin Mingli, Giovanni Campisi，義大利：Edizioni Universum（埃迪采恩尼大學），宇宙出版社，2023.01。
26. 《紀念達夫尼斯和克洛伊》（中英對照）詩選 In memory of Daphnis and Chloe，作者：Renza Agnelli，Sara Ciampi，Lin Mingli 林明理，義大利：Edizioni Universum（埃迪采恩尼大學），宇宙出版社，書封面，林明理畫作（聖母大殿），2023.02。
27. 《詩林明理古今抒情詩一六〇首》（漢英對照）Parallel Reading of 160 Classical and New Chinese Lyrical Poems (Chinese-English)，英譯：張智中，臺北市：文史哲出版社，2023.04。ISBN 978-986-314-637-7
28. 《愛的讚歌》(詩評、散文暨新詩) Hymn Of Love (Poetry review, prose and poetry)，臺北市：文史哲出版社，2023.05。ISBN 978-986-314-638-4
29. 《埃內斯托‧卡漢，薩拉‧錢皮，林明理和平詩選》（義英對照）(Italian-English)，Carmina Selecta (Selected Poems) by Ernesto Kahan, Sara Ciampi, Lin Mingli Peace-Pace，義大利：Edizioni Universum（埃迪采恩尼大學），宇宙出版社，2023.11。ISBN 978-889-980-379-7

30. 《祈禱與工作》，中英義詩集，Ora Et Labora Trilogia di Autori Trilingue: Italiano, Cinese, Inglese 作者的三語三部曲：義大利語、中文、英語 Trilingual Trilogy of Authors: Italian, Chinese, English，作者：奧內拉·卡布奇尼 Ornella Cappuccini，非馬 William Marr，林明理 Lin Mingli，義大利，宇宙出版社，2024.06。
31. 《名家抒情詩評賞》（漢英對照）Appraisal of Lyric Poems by Famous Artists，張智中教授英譯，臺北市：文史哲出版社，2024.06。ISBN 978-986-314-675-9
32. 《山的沉默》Silence of the Mountains，散文集，臺北市：文史哲出版社，2024.09。ISBN 978-986-314-685-8
33. 《宋詩明理接千載——古今抒情詩三百首》（漢英對照）Parallel Reading of 300 Ancient and Modern Chinese Lyrical Poems (Chinese-English)，臺中市：天空數位圖書出版，2024.10，ISBN 978-626-7576-00-7
34. 《元詩明理接千載——古今抒情詩三百首》（漢英對照）Parallel Reading of 300 Ancient and Modern Chinese Lyrical Poems (Chinese-English) :Jin, Yuan, and Ming Dynasties，臺中市：天空數位圖書出版，2024.11，ISBN 978-626-7576-02-1，ISBN 978-626-7576-03-8（彩圖版）
35. 《清詩明理思千載——古今抒情詩三百首》（漢英對照）Parallel Reading of 300 Ancient and Modern Chinese Lyrical Poems: Qing Dynasty (Chinese-English)，臺中市：天空數位圖書出版，2025.01，ISBN 978-626-7576-08-3，ISBN 978-626-7576-09-0（彩圖版）
36. 《唐詩明理接千載——古今抒情詩三百首》（漢英對照）Parallel Reading of 300 Ancient and Modern Chinese Lyrical Poems: Tang Dynasty (Chinese-English)，臺中市：天空數位圖書出版，2025.02，ISBN 978-626-7576-10-6

譯者簡介
About the Author & Translator

張智中，天津市南開大學外國語學院教授、博士研究生導師、翻譯系主任，中國翻譯協會理事，中國英漢語比較研究會典籍英譯專業委員會副會長，天津師範大學跨文化與世界文學研究院兼職教授，世界漢學‧文學中國研究會理事兼英文秘書長，天津市比較文學學會理事，第五屆天津市人民政府學位委員會評議組成員、專業學位教育指導委員會委員，國家社科基金專案通訊評審專家和結項鑒定專家，天津外國語大學中央文獻翻譯研究基地兼職研究員，《國際詩歌翻譯》季刊客座總編，《世界漢學》英文主編，《中國當代詩歌導讀》編委會成員，中國當代詩歌獎評委等。已出版編、譯、著120餘部，發表學術論文130餘篇，曾獲翻譯與科研多種獎項。漢詩英譯多走向國外，獲國際著名詩人和翻譯家的廣泛好評。譯詩觀：但為傳神，不拘其形，散文筆法，詩意內容；將漢詩英譯提高到英詩的高度。

譯者簡介

Zhang Zhizhong is professor, doctoral supervisor and dean of the Translation Department of the School of Foreign Studies, Nankai University which is located in Tianjin; meanwhile, he is director of Translators' Association of China, vice chairman of the Committee for English Translation of Chinese Classics of the Association for Comparative Studies of English and Chinese, part-time professor of Cross-Culture & World Literature Academy of Tianjin Normal University, director and English secretary-general of World Sinology Literary China Seminar, director of Tianjin Comparative Literature Society, member of Tianjin Municipal Government Academic Degree Committee, member of Tianjin Municipal Government Professional Degree Education Guiding Committee, expert for the approval and evaluation of projects funded by the National Social Science Foundation of China, part-time researcher at the Central Literature Translation Research Base of Tianjin Foreign Studies University, guest editor of Rendition *of International Poetry*, English editor-in-chief of *World Sinology*, member of the editing board of *Guided Reading Series in Contemporary Chinese Poetry*, and member of the Board for Contemporary Chinese Poetry Prizes. He has published more than 120 books and 130 academic papers, and he has won a host of prizes in translation and academic research. His English translation of Chinese poetry is widely acclaimed throughout the world, and is favorably reviewed by international poets and translators. His view on poetry translation: spirit over form, prose enjambment to rewrite Chinese poetry into sterling English poetry.

序言一
Preface

譯筆神遊牽古今

你永遠不可能預測到,兩位詩人湊到一起合作會擦出怎樣的文學火花;特別是當一位寫漢語詩,另一位寫英語詩的時候。這是我接到這本為之寫序的書稿時的感受。

我從上個世紀八十年代開始從事漢語古詩詞英譯,從未想過會把自己寫的古詩詞譯成英語。可是有一天我收到一本寄自美國加州的英漢雙語版精裝書《近體詩300首》(裴陽;2022),那是作者把自己寫的格律詩譯成英語詩,我感到古詩詞英譯已經進展到今詩詞英譯。後來我又翻譯中國現代詩的朦朧詩,也從未想過現代詩可以和古典詩比對性地放在一起翻譯,直到我接到翻譯家張智中與臺灣詩人林明理合作的這部書稿,才又有振聾發聵之感。它的前瞻性與開拓翻譯領域的成功,讓人感覺頗似一騎絕塵。

讀了這部書稿,又讀了其他相關的書稿,感覺這本書與其他幾本書構成一個完整的系列,每一本覆蓋近體詩所經歷的一個或幾個朝代:漢魏六朝、唐、宋、金元明、清。五本書的書名分別為:《漢魏六朝接明理:古今抒情詩300首(漢英對照)》《唐詩明理接千載:古今抒情詩 300 首(漢英對照)》《宋詩明理接千載——古今抒情詩300首(漢英對照)》《元詩明理接千載:古今抒情詩300首(漢英對照)》《清詩明理思千載:古今抒情詩300首(漢英對照)》。其實,早在2023 年 4 月,兩位詩人合作出版《詩林明理:古今抒情詩160 首(漢英對照)》(臺北文史哲出版社),這是他們合作

序言一

　　打通古今詩歌及其英譯的初步嘗試,得到業界的好評和鼓勵之後,便陸續推出如上五種作品。這六本書,若一言以貫之,可謂「詩林明理接千載系列」。

　　翻閱這幾部書稿,我強烈地感覺到,整個系列彌漫著比較文學的氣息。這是詩的比較,是跨越時空的比較。清朝末年的詩距離林明理的詩也已百年,相隔更久遠的唐詩距離林明理的詩已近千年。它不同於比較文學中常說的關係比較,不同地域,不同國別,不同語言,不同民族的文學比較;它比較的是格律詩的靈氣和意蘊是怎樣延展至千年百年之後,融入當代詩的創作;它比較的是當代詩歌的創作如何將其詩美詩情回溯至百年千年前的古代格律詩。這中間是一定有靈犀相通,密碼可循。所以我特別喜歡書名中「接千載」這三個字,在讀者還沒有比較之前,就會感受到這三個字的魅力。誰又能不急於探索呢?

　　張智中博士選出的 150 首唐詩,每一首都是我喜歡誦讀的傳世名篇,可謂篇幅浩繁,已屬難能可貴;更加令我歎為觀止的是詩人林明理竟然從容不迫地從她自己的詩作中也選出 150 首抒情詩與其一一比對,這得從多少詩篇中才能挑出能夠對得上的詩。這六本書告訴我們,林明理博士是一位多產的詩人。我比較熟悉這些唐詩,所以我把注意力放在林明理詩人創作的詩上,細細品讀,看能否讀出銜接上的感覺。結果是每讀完一首林明理的詩之後,總能感受到一些與讀比對的唐詩的感覺相貫通的思緒和詩情。這會使我的思緒飄得很遠,陷入延展和回溯產生的融匯的心動。

　　我讀過較多的翻譯家張智中教授的古詩詞英譯,他的翻譯擺脫了原詩詞格律形式的束縛,致力於展現詩詞的內在美,而且要用英語現代詩歌的形式來展現。他甚至在英語詩

唐詩明理接千載
古今抒情詩三百首 漢英對照

歌的譯文的形式上進行探索，頗有迷人之處。他在翻譯方面的座右銘就是「但為傳神，不拘其形，散文筆法，詩意內容；將漢詩英譯提高到英詩的高度。」（張智中；2023）他在古詩詞英譯方面的探索已經衝破樊籬，卓有斬獲，可圈可點。

這個系列是一部部譯著，在漢語部分經過編選之後，翻譯家張智中教授要同時完成一首古詩的英譯和與其比對的林明理詩人的當代詩的翻譯。在欣賞這兩種的譯文的時候，我一直在尋找他是怎樣在譯文中實現古詩的延展和當代詩的回溯產生的融匯。每當我感受到譯文中也能讀出比對詩之間的銜接與貫通，詩美和意蘊的照應時，我讚賞翻譯家張智中獨闢蹊徑，大幅度甚至跨學科地拓寬漢詩英譯的領域，讓古今牽手，實乃別有洞天。

從這個系列中，我較清楚地看到，翻譯家和詩人是如何配合協作的。詩人盡情揮灑其想像力，展現文字的技巧才能，用情灌注每一行詩；而翻譯家則是謹小慎微，翻譯原詩，即使自己也是詩人也不可失控於創作的衝動而杜撰。

我在《歸舟：中國元明清詩選》（雙語版；2018）的後記裡曾討論過「翻譯家的真誠是至關重要的」。翻譯家要對原語詩人真誠，要對原語詩歌真誠，要對目的語讀者真誠，要對自己真誠。

在這個系列裡，我看到了翻譯家的真誠；看到了翻譯家，一支譯筆神游牽手古與今。

幸運有這個系列，包攬了讀詩，寫詩和譯詩。讀詩是讀心，寫詩是靈魂歌唱，譯詩是對藝術的愛。

王守義

2025 年 1 月 9 日於加拿大

序言一

A Translator's Roaming Pen Connects the Ancient and the Present

You never know what literary sparks will be struck from two poets working together, particularly when one writes Chinese poetry and the other, English poetry. This is how I feel upon receiving the manuscript for which I am to write the preface.

I began translating ancient Chinese poetry into English in the 1980s, and I never thought I would translate this type of poetry I wrote into English. But one day I received an English-Chinese bilingual hardcover book *300 Modern Poems* from California, USA (Pei Yang; 2022), which means the author has translated his own metrical poems into English pieces. It gives me a feeling that the English translation of ancient Chinese poetry has progressed to the English translation of today's metrical poems. Later, I began to undertake the translation of modern Chinese misty poems, and still I never thought modern Chinese poetry could be translated together with ancient Chinese poetry in comparison until I receive the manuscript of this book, which is co-authored by translator-professor Zhang Zhizhong and Taiwanese poet Lin Ming-Li. And I feel somewhat enlightened. Its avant-garde awareness in successfully blazing up a new field of translation leaves the reader in shock as if they saw a horse galloping much ahead of the dust.

After reading this manuscript and other published books in this series, it dawns on me that this book and several other books constitute a series, each covering one or several dynasties of ancient Chinese poetry: the Han, Wei and Six dynasties, the Tang dynasty, the Song dynasty, the Jin, Yuan and Ming dynasties, and the Qing dynasty. The titles of the five books are: *Parallel Reading of 300 Ancient and Modern Chinese Lyrical Poems: Han, Wei and Six Dynasties (Chinese-English)*, *Parallel Reading of 300 Ancient and Modern Chinese Lyrical Poems: Tang Dynasty (Chinese-English)*, *Parallel Reading of 300 Ancient and Modern Chinese Lyrical Poems: Song Dynasty (Chinese-English)*, *Parallel Reading of 300 Ancient and Modern Chinese Lyrical Poems: Jin, Yuan, and Ming Dynasties(Chinese-English)*, and *Parallel Reading of 300 Ancient and Modern Chinese Lyrical Poems: Qing Dynasty (Chinese-English)*. Actually, as early as April, 2023, the two poets have jointly published *Parallel Reading of 160 Classical and New Chinese Lyrical Poems (Chinese-English)* (Taipei; the Liberal Arts Press) as a tentative effort in combining ancient Chinese poetry and modern Chinese poetry as well as their English translations. Heartened and encouraged, they go so far as to elaborate it into other five books chronologically with a view to ancient Chinese poetry. In short, the number totals up to six books, which may be described as "the series of parallel reading of Chinese poems through thousands of years".

Leafing through the books in the series, I strongly feel that the they are permeated with a breath of comparative literature. This is a poetic comparison, a comparison across time and space. The poetry of the late Qing dynasty has been one hundred years away from Lin Ming-Li's poetry, and the poetry of the Tang dynasty has been nearly one thousand years back from Lin Ming-Li's poetry. It is different from the relationship comparison which is common in comparative literature, and from the literature comparison between different regions, different countries, different languages and different nationalities. It compares how the meaning and the ethereal quality of ancient metrical poetry are

序言一

retained and extended thousands or hundreds of years later, to be fused into the writing of contemporary Chinese poetry; and it compares how the composition of contemporary Chinese poetry traces its poetic beauty back to the ancient metrical Chinese poetry written a hundred or a thousand years ago. There is to be a connection, so sensitive like the threadlike core in the horn of a rhinoceros, or there is to be as well as a hidden code. I particularly like the three words used in the title of this series: "connecting over thousands of years" which is enchanting and captivating. And the reader's enthusiasm is thus enkindled for further survey.

In this book, the 150 quatrains are selected from the poetry of Tang dynasty (618-907) by Dr. Zhang Zhizhong, which are my favorite poems and are on the list of my daily reading. The ingenious undertaking is coupled by poet Lin Ming-Li, who impresses the reader with her own 150 lyrical poems to be paired up with the ancient ones. This shows the great number of poems written by her. These six books tell us that Dr. Lin Ming-Li is a prolific poet. Since I am proficient with these Tang poems, I focus my attention on the poems of Lin Ming-Li by careful and close reading, to see if I could get the sense of "through thousands of years". The answer is, of course, affirmative. After reading a poem by Lin, I often have a "through-thousands-of-years" poetic flight of thoughts similar to that in reading the twin ancient piece, which transports me far away, my mind drifting on freely, to be caught in the convergence of extension and backtracking.

I have read a lot of English versions of ancient Chinese poems by professor Zhang Zhizhong, whose translation has abandoned the constraint of the original poem's metrical form, so as to be devoted to reproducing the inherent beauty of the poem in the form of contemporary English poetry. He goes so far as to explore the forms of translated English poetry, which is fairly fascinating. His motto in translation is "spirit over form, and prose enjambment to rewrite Chinese poetry into sterling English poetry." (Zhang Zhizhong; 2023) His exploration in the English translation of ancient Chinese poetry has broken through the traditional barriers to make remarkable achievements in an effective way.

This series is composed of one after another translated work. After all the Chinese twin poems are chosen and ready, it is professor Zhang's labor of love to translate them into English. While appreciating the two kinds of translation — those from ancient Chinese poems and those from contemporary Chinese poems — I have been examining how the translator achieves the integration of the extension of ancient poetry and the retrospection of contemporary poetry in his translation. When I feel the connection and coherence, as well as the meaning and poetic beauty between or in the twin poems, I cannot but admire Zhang Zhizhong as a translator for his unique technique and approach, who has greatly, and even interdisciplinarily broadened the field of C-E poetry translation, particularly in combining the English translation of ancient Chinese poetry and contemporary Chinese poetry, a world all his own.

From this series, I can see very clearly how a translator and a poet can work together. The poet unleashes her imagination, shows her skill and talent in wording, and infuses or charges each and every line with emotion; the translator is careful and cautious in translating the original poem — even if he is a poet himself, he never does it at his own sweet will.

In the postscript of my book *Voyage Home: Poems from the Yuan and Ming and Qing Dynasties of China* (a bilingual version;

2018), I have detailed on "the sincerity of a translator is of vital importance". As a translator, he shall be sincere to the poet of the source language, to the poem of the source language, to the reader of the target language, and to the translator himself.

In this series of "Chinese poems through thousands of years", I see the sincerity of a translator, and I see a translator whose mind is wandering from the ancient to the present, hence ingenious and masterful translations.

The readers are lucky to see this unique series, which includes reading poetry, writing poetry and translating poetry. Reading poetry means reading the mind, writing poetry means singing of the soul, and translating poetry means loving of the art.

Professor Wang Shouyi
January 9, 2025, Canada
(Translated from Chinese into English
by Zhang Zhizhong)

序言二
Preface

北京大學秦立彥教授詩評為序

1. 林明理著：《諦聽》，2018年。

　　從《山楂樹》到《諦聽》，作者的畫作更加空靈清透，構圖變得更簡單，藍色更多地出現。《諦聽》詩畫結合，相得益彰。

　　詩作總體調子偏暖，明亮，平和，追求美好與智慧，沒有現代詩中常見的諷刺、黑暗、悲觀，顯出清澈而堅定的信念。其中很難得的是寫給朋友的詩作，能看出作者非常看重友情，是克服了當代典型孤獨心態的人，因為作者相信「在孤獨之中仍有真正的友誼」（124頁）。其中《致摯友非馬》（106頁）真摯動人，給人留下深刻印象。

　　另一組主題鮮明的詩畫作品涉及生態與環保。林明理博士所畫的動物可愛，浪漫而秀雅。若干首寫動物的詩中，動物常處在生態的危險之中，作者對它們表達了深刻的悲憫。比如《企鵝的悲歌》（44）尖銳地寫出了企鵝的困境。《弗羅裡達山獅》（190頁）從山獅視角來寫，充滿荒野的氣氛，有戲劇性和張力。第80幅所繪的金雕自由自在，展翅翱翔；詩作《金雕》（220頁）從金雕和鷹獵人的兩個角度去寫，兩個角度都有開闊的視野，是一篇傑作。《大熊貓》（224頁）一詩中，熊貓「彷彿夢見了奇異的珍寶」，從中見出作者對動物的溫情。

　　作者在世界各地的旅行，催生了豐富的詩畫作品。畫作《塞哥維亞舊城》（第76幅）、《巨石陣》（第77幅）、《科隆大教堂》（第79幅）中，天空中都有一枚紅月亮，是整體藍調的作品中一點醒目的紅。《塞哥維亞舊城》的繪畫如夢似幻；其詩中的比喻「一座孤獨的城堡／恰似／隨風蕩漾的船」（212 頁），恰切而生動。類似的精妙比喻，再如寫愛情的《夜思》（168 頁）開篇的比喻：「是的，我想的，是你／——褐色眼睛／使我無力地，像只雷鳥／在覆雪中靜止不動」。

林明理博士注重詩歌的音樂性，其詩作常有如歌的氣質。我尤其喜歡《安義的春天》（252 頁）開篇和結尾的歌一般的句子：「金花開了／老村醒著／遠方的雲呵／你思念的是什麼」。

2. 林明理著：《山楂樹》，2011 年。

作者有細膩的目光，尤其是詩中的自然意象相當美麗。我一邊閱讀，一邊做筆記，錄下了許多新奇的句子，常常是比喻或擬人的修辭。

一隻小鳥「正叼走最後一顆晨星」（16）

「遊魚也永不疲乏地
簇擁向我」（22）

「一絲凜然的荷影
夜的帷幕裡的光點」（22）

「阿公背我
為我淌汗
而我滿心歡喜
因為金星繡滿了我紅搖籃」

松針的氣味總是
穿牆破隙
刺亂我的衫袖」（28）

「就像秋葉搖搖欲墜
又怎抵擋得住急驟的風」（30）

唐詩明理接千載
古今抒懷詩三百首
漢英對照

「群峰之中
唯我是黑暗的光明」(62)

「落葉在我腳底輕微地喧嚷」(64)

大冠鷲「似飛似飄地
朝塔林投去」(67)

「夜,溜過原野
踮著她的貓步似的足」(71)

「雲彩是點點孤帆」(96)

「鏽般的天空一片死寂」(102)

「怎忍冬風
把露宿的疏葉一一吹走」(106)

「小船兒點點
如碎銀一般」(108)

「往事是光陰的綠苔,
散雲是浮世的飄蓬」

「即使這秋風也在顫嗦」(120)

「三月的傍晚,我撐著
顛簸的夕陽靠岸」

「群花叢草
向月亮投遞訊息」
「我在暮色中網住一隻鳥」(134)

「我是拒絕失去密度的雲」(146)

序言二

「青煙升了──
一縷縷同爐煙似的」

「貓頭鷹以歌,獨釣空濛」(185)

「電光是雷聲
展開了詛咒」

「可曾將一切痛苦
一針一針地縫合」(196)

「看靈魂如飛魚在光中潛躍」

「我浮蕩的孤帆是單調的言語
發光的月
是我碎成幾塊的江心」

「無視於我的心在到處摸索
直到被銳利的月牙劃破」(212)

「在被淚雨淋濕的記憶中
黎明是多麼緩慢」(212)

「一行白鷺
飛起,如幻夢」(214)

暮鴉「像縷縷飄泊的飛煙」(219)

願林明理博士在詩畫領域繼續耕作,使世人得享其更多成果!

秦立彥
2021 年 12 月 17 日

唐詩明理接千載
古今抒情詩三百首
漢英對照

PS. 北京大學秦立彥教授於 2021 年 12 月 17 日週五於下午 6:53 電郵

明理博士：

　　多謝您的畫和非馬博士的翻譯！您寫出了北國的精魂，與您發過來的花朵對照，能讀到也能嗅到南國與北國的不同氣息。

　　我從學校圖書館借到了您的兩本詩作《山楂樹》和《諦聽》，已拜讀完畢，寫了短評，請見附件。謝謝帶給我閱讀詩歌與欣賞繪畫的愉悅！

　　祝一切順利，安好，

立彥

Poetry Criticism by Qin Liyan, Professor of Peking University, as the Preface

1. *Listening*, by Lin Ming-Li, 2018.

From *The Hawthorn Tree* to *Listening*, the author's paintings are more ethereal and clear, the composition becomes simpler, and the blue appears more. *Listening* combines poetry and painting into one, to complement each other.

The overall tone of the poem is warm, bright, peaceful, with the pursuit of beauty and wisdom, and without the common irony, darkness, and pessimism in modern poetry, showing clear and firm faith. Those poems written for friends deserve special attention, which shows that the author values friendship very much, and is someone who has overcome the typical contemporary lonely mentality, because the author believes that "in loneliness there is true friendship" (124). Among them, *To My Best Friend William Marr* (106) is sincere and moving, leaving a deep impression in the reader's heart.

Another group of poems & paintings with distinct themes deal with ecology and environmental protection. The animals painted by Dr. Lin Ming-Li are lovely, romantic and elegant. In several poems about animals, animals are often in ecological danger, and the author expresses deep sympathy for them. *The Lamentation of Penguins* (44), for example, deals pointedly with the plight of the penguins. *The Mountain Lion of Florida* (190), written from the perspective of a mountain lion, has a wild atmosphere, drama and tension. The golden eagle in the 80th painting is free and flying; the poem *The Golden Eagle* (220 pages) is a masterpiece written from the perspectives of the golden eagle and the eagle hunter, both of which have broad horizons. In the poem *The Giant Panda* (224), the panda "seems to dream of a strange treasure", which shows the author's warmth for animals.

唐詩明理接千載
古今抒情詩三百首
漢英對照

The author's travels around the world have given birth to a wealth of poems and paintings. In the paintings *The Old City of Segovia* (No. 76), *Stonehenge* (No. 77), and *Cologne Cathedral* (No. 79), there is a red moon in the sky, a striking red in the overall blues. The painting of *The Old City of Segovia* is dreamlike; the metaphor of his poem, "a lonely castle/just like/a boat rippling with the wind" (212), is apt and vivid. A similarly subtle metaphor, like the one at the beginning of *Night Thoughts* on love (168): "Yes, I think of you / — brown eyes/make me weak, like a thunderbird/motionless in the snow."

Dr. Lin Ming-Li pays attention to the musicality of her poems, which often have the quality of songs. I particularly like the songlike sentences at the beginning and end of *The Spring of Anyi* (252): "The golden flowers are in bloom/The old village is awake/The distant clouds/What is it that you miss?"

2. *The Hawthorn Tree*, by Lin Ming-Li, 2011.

The author has a delicate eye; particularly, the natural images in the poem are quite beautiful. As I read, I take notes and write down quite a number of novel sentences, often figurative or anthropomorphic.

A little bird "is snatching away the last morning star" (16)

"The fish never tire of
coming round me" (22)

"A glimmer of light in the veil
of awe-inspiring curtain of night" (22)

"He sweats for me
on his back and I
rejoice because gold stars
embroider my red cradle."

序言二

"The smell of pine needles always
breaks through the walls
and ruffles my sleeves" (28)

"Like the shivering autumn leaves
how can they withstand the sudden wind?" (30)

"Among the peaks
I am the only light in darkness" (62)

"The leaves are slightly clamoring under my feet" (64)

The great crowned vulture "is fluttering and wafting
toward the forest of towers" (67)

"At night, gliding across the field
on her catwalk feet" (71)

"Clouds are little dots of sails" (96)

"The rusty sky is dead in silence" (102)

"How to bear the winter wind
which blows away the sparse leaves sleeping in the open one
by one" (106)

"The little ships in dots
are like broken silver" (108)

"The past events are the green moss of time,
and the scattered clouds are the tumbleweed in the floating
world"

"Even the autumn wind is quivering" (120)

唐詩明理接千載
古今抒情詩三百首
漢英對照

"On a March evening, I am poling
ashore on a bumpy sunset."

"Clusters of flowers and masses of grass
sending message to the moon."

"I have caught a bird in the twilight" (134)

"I am the cloud that refuses to lose its density" (146)

"The blue smoke is arising —
a wisp after another wisp like furnace smoke."

"An owl catches emptiness with his song" (185)

"Electric light is thunder
unfurling the curse."

"Did you ever sew up all the pain
one stitch at a time" (196)

"See the soul diving like a flying fish in the light."

"My floating solitary sail is monotonous words
the shining moon
is the heart of my broken river."

"Ignoring my heart groping around
till it is cut by the sharp crescent" (212)

"In the memory of wet tears
how slow the dawn is" (212)

"A line of egrets
fly up like a dream" (214)

序言二

The dusk crows "drift like a plume of flying smoke" (219)

May Dr. Lin Ming-Li continue to cultivate in the field of poetry & painting, so that readers across the world can enjoy more poetically!

By Qin Liyan
December 17, 2021

PS. Professor Qin Liyan of Peking University, on Friday, December17, 2021, at 6:53 PM email to Dr. Ming Li:

"Thank you for your painting and Dr. William Marr's translation! You have reproduced the spirit of North China, and comparing with the flowers from you, we can read and smell the different breaths of South China and North China. I have borrowed your two poetry collections *The Hawthorn Tree* and *Listening* from the university library, which I have finished reading and have written a short comment. Please see the attachment. Thank you for bringing me the pleasure of reading poetry and appreciating paintings! I wish you all the best!"

著者暨編譯者導言
Introduction by the Translator

　　學者詩人林明理從她自己所感覺到的與對唐詩閱讀的經驗回憶裡進行篩選、組合，欲使其創作的詩歌加在編譯的唐代詩作之後，以期望讀者更貼近地感覺和瞭解詩美的世界。而我認為，中國新詩與古詩的最大區別之一，是從聽覺藝術走向了視覺藝術。古詩是口頭可以朗誦的，新詩則是內心體會和感覺的。若能讓古詩和新詩研究同步相輔相成，讓翻譯詩歌的涵義變得更生動活潑，以趨使學生對欣賞詩歌與研讀上產生了更大的興趣，這是此書最重要的價值，也可以加深閱讀時的感性和體悟，這也是我的期許。

張智中
2025 年 1 月 8 日於南開大學外國語學院翻譯系

　　Lin Ming-Li, as a scholar-poet of Taiwan, is a great lover of poetry, and she selects her own poems to be paired up with the quatrains by Chinese poets of Tang dynasty, which have

著者暨編譯者導言

similar themes or sentiments, in order for readers to appreciate more thoroughly the beauty of poetry. It is my belief that one of the most glaring differences between ancient Chinese poetry and modern Chinese poetry lies in the shift from auditory arts to visual arts: when ancient Chinese poetry is to be declaimed, modern Chinese poetry is to be felt and savored in the heart. If the reading and translation of both ancient Chinese poems and modern Chinese poems can be undertaken simultaneously, the understanding of poetry will be deepened, and poetry translation will be more flexible through enlivening — and the readers' interest in poetry, hopefully, will be greatly heightened.

Zhang Zhizhong
January 8, 2025
Translation Department of the School of Foreign Studies,
Nankai University

唐詩明理接千載
古今抒情詩三百首
漢英對照

舊書不厭百回讀，熟讀深思子自知。

——蘇軾（蘇東坡）

Old books are never tired of repeated reading for a hundred times, before you are privy to them.

藝術的藝術，表達的亮點，
文字的光輝，即是樸素。

——美國詩人沃爾特‧惠特曼
（Walt Whitman，1819 年-1892 年）

The art of art, the glory of expression and the sunshine of the light of letters, is simplicity.

— By Walt Whitman (1819-1892), American poet

目錄
Table of Contents

1. 落葉（孔紹安）Falling Leaves (Kong Shao'an)
   秋在汐止晴山（林明理）Autumn in Shixiqing Mountain (Lin Ming-Li) ········ 46
2. 普安建陽題壁（王勃）An Inscription on the Wall (Wang Bo)
   兩岸青山連天碧－陪海基會走過二十年感時（林明理）Green Mountains and Blue Sky on Both Banks—Together with SEF Through the Past 20 Years (Lin Ming-Li) ············· 48
3. 登城春望（王勃）Spring View Atop the City Gate (Wang Bo)
   春日江中（林明理）Spring Days on the River (Lin Ming-Li) ·· 51
4. 詠鵝（駱賓王）Geese (Luo Binwang)
   平魯古城的秋天（林明理）Autumn in the Ancient City of Pinglu (Lin Ming-Li) ··················· 53
5. 送別（駱賓王）Farewell (Luo Binwang)
   小象（林明理）The Little Elephant (Lin Ming-Li) ············ 54
6. 渡漢江（宋之問）Crossing River Han (Song Zhiwen)
   夜航（林明理）Night Sailing (Lin Ming-Li) ···················· 56
7. 邊詞（張敬忠）A Frontier Song (Zhang Jingzhong)
   岸畔（林明理）By the Shoreside (Lin Ming-Li) ············· 57
8. 詠柳（賀知章）Ode to Willows (He Zhizhang)
   一棵雨中行的蕨樹（林明理）A Fern Tree Walking in the Rain (Lin Ming-Li) ··················· 59
9. 回鄉偶書二首（其一）（賀知章）Returning Home (No. 1) (He Zhizhang)
   念故鄉（林明理）Longing for Home (Lin Ming-Li) ············ 61
10. 賦得自君之出矣（張九齡）Since You Left Me, My Lord (Zhang Jiuling)
    給敬愛的人（林明理）To My Beloved (Lin Ming-Li) ············ 63

11. 照鏡見白髮（張九齡）Gray Hair in the Mirror (Zhang Jiuling)
    夜思（林明理）Night Thoughts (Lin Ming-Li) ················ 64
12. 南樓望（盧僎）South-Gazing Tower (Lu Zhuan)
    觀七股鹽田園區（林明理）Watching the Idyllic Area of
    Qigu Salt Mountain (Lin Ming-Li) ·················· 66
13. 涼州詞二首（其一）（王翰）The Border Song (No. 1)
    (Wang Han)
    別哭泣，敘利亞小孩（林明理）Don't Cry, Syrian Child
    (Lin Ming-Li) ··· 68
14. 鹿柴（王維）A Secluded Forest Scene (Wang Wei)
    殘照（林明理）The Evening Glow (Lin Ming-Li) ·········· 70
15. 竹裡館（王維）A Retreat in Bamboos (Wang Wei)
    在遠方的巴列姆山谷（林明理）In the Remote Balmain Valley
    (Lin Ming-Li) ··· 71
16. 辛夷塢（王維）The Magnolia Retreat (Wang Wei)
    楊潔（林明理）Yang Jie (Lin Ming-Li) ························ 74
17. 鳥鳴澗（王維）The Deep Peace of Spring Dale (Wang Wei)
    青藤花（林明理）Sinomenia Flowers (Lin Ming-Li) ········ 75
18. 雜詩三首（其二）（王維）Miscellaneous Poems (No. 2)
    (Wang Wei)
    當白梅花開（林明理）When White Plum Blossoms Are
    Blossoming (Lin Ming-Li) ·· 77
19. 雜詩三首（其三）（王維）Miscellaneous Poems (No. 3)
    (Wang Wei)
    冬望（林明理）Winter Sight (Lin Ming-Li) ······················ 78
20. 白石灘（王維）The White-Stone Beach (Wang Wei)
    流動中的靜謐（林明理）Quiet in Motion (Lin Ming-Li) ···· 80
21. 田園樂七首（其四）（王維）Joy in Fields and Gardens
    (No. 4) (Wang Wei)
    晨野（林明理）The Morning Field (Lin Ming-Li) ············ 82
22. 華子岡（裴迪）Huazi Mound (Pei Di)
    山影（林明理）The Shadow of Mountains (Lin Ming-Li) ······ 83

23. 宮槐陌（裴迪）The Path of Palace Pagoda Trees (Pei Di)
    月光小棧之讚（林明理）Ode to a Moonlit Inn (Lin Ming-Li)・84
24. 宿建德江（孟浩然）Lodging by Jiande River (Meng Haoran)
    枋寮漁港暮色（林明理）Dusk at Fan-Liau Fishing Harbor
    (Lin Ming-Li)……………………………………………… 86
25. 詠風（虞世南）Ode to Wind (Yu Shinan)
    北風散步的小徑上（林明理）On the Trail Where the North
    Wind Strolls (Lin Ming-Li) ……………………………… 88
26. 龍標野宴（王昌齡）Picnic in Liaobiao County
    (Wang Changling)
    旗山老街的黃昏（林明理）Dusk of Qishan Old Street
    (Lin Ming-Li)……………………………………………… 90
27. 送郭司倉（王昌齡）Seeing Off My Friend Guo Sicang
    (Wang Changling)
    大明湖秋思（林明理）Autumn Thought at Daming Lake
    (Lin Ming-Li)……………………………………………… 92
28. 出塞二首（其一）（王昌齡）Out of the Frontier (No. 1)
    (Wang Changling)
    戰爭仍茫無盡頭（林明理）Still No End of the War
    (Lin Ming-Li)……………………………………………… 94
29. 涼州詞（王之渙）A Border Song (Wang Zhihuan)
    甘南，你寬慰地向我呼喚（林明理）Gannan, You Call to
    Me in Relief (Lin Ming-Li)………………………………… 96
30. 登鸛雀樓（王之渙）Ascending the Stork Tower
    (Wang Zhihuan)
    珠江，我怎能停止對你的嚮往（林明理）Pearl River, How
    Can I Stop Longing for You (Lin Ming-Li) ……………… 100
31. 夜宿山寺（李白）Spending Night in a Mountain Temple
    (Li Bai)
    靜寂的黃昏（林明理）The Silent Dusk (Lin Ming-Li) …… 102
32. 玉階怨（李白）Grievances of Jewel Stairs (Li Bai)
    在交織與遺落之間（林明理）Between Interweaving and
    Oblivion (Lin Ming-Li)…………………………………… 103

33. 勞勞亭（李白）The Parting Pavilion (Li Bai)
    思念似雪花緘默地飛翔（林明理）Thoughts Fly Silently Like Snowflakes (Lin Ming-Li) ⋯⋯⋯⋯⋯⋯⋯⋯⋯⋯ 105

34. 早發白帝城（李白）Morning Departure from White King City (Li Bai)
    奔騰的河流（林明理）The Torrential Stream (Lin Ming-Li) ⋯ 107

35. 望廬山瀑布（李白）Watching the Waterfall of Mount Lu (Li Bai)
    南湖溪之歌（林明理）Song of South Lake Creek (Lin Ming-Li) ⋯⋯⋯⋯⋯⋯⋯⋯⋯⋯⋯⋯⋯⋯⋯⋯⋯⋯⋯⋯⋯ 109

36. 黃鶴樓送孟浩然之廣陵（李白）Seeing My Friend Off at Yellow Crane Tower (Li Bai)
    在那恬靜的海灣（林明理）In the Quiet Bay (Lin Ming-Li) ⋯ 112

37. 望天門山（李白）Viewing Tianmen Mountain (Li Bai)
    萊斯河向晚（林明理）The Rio Tarcoles River Toward the Evening (Lin Ming-Li) ⋯⋯⋯⋯⋯⋯⋯⋯⋯⋯⋯⋯⋯⋯⋯ 114

38. 春夜洛城聞笛（李白）Fluting in Luoyang in a Spring Night (Li Bai)
    致貓頭鷹的故鄉－水里（林明理）To Shuili: the Home of Owls (Lin Ming-Li) ⋯⋯⋯⋯⋯⋯⋯⋯⋯⋯⋯⋯⋯⋯⋯⋯ 116

39. 螢火（李白）The Firefly (Li Bai)
    詠撫順（林明理）Ode to Fushun (Lin Ming-Li) ⋯⋯⋯⋯⋯ 118

40. 夜下征虜亭（李白）Heading for Zhenglu Pavilion in the Moonlight (Li Bai)
    漫步在烏鎮的湖邊（林明理）Walk by the Lake in Wuzhen (Lin Ming-Li) ⋯⋯⋯⋯⋯⋯⋯⋯⋯⋯⋯⋯⋯⋯⋯⋯⋯⋯⋯ 120

41. 憶東山二首（其一）（李白）Two Poems about the East Mountain (No. 1) (Li Bai)
    冬憶－泰雅族祖靈祭（林明理）Winter Memory: Tai Ya Ancestral Sacrifice (Lin Ming-Li) ⋯⋯⋯⋯⋯⋯⋯⋯⋯⋯⋯ 122

42. 宣城見杜鵑花（李白）Azalea Flowers in Xuancheng (Li Bai)
    蓮（林明理）The Lotus (Lin Ming-Li) ⋯⋯⋯⋯⋯⋯⋯⋯⋯ 125

43. 送陸判官往琵琶峽（李白）Seeing a Judge Off to the Lute Gorge (Li Bai)
    北風（林明理）The North Wind (Lin Ming-Li) ⋯⋯⋯⋯⋯ 126

44. 觀放白鷹（李白）Letting the White Eagle Fly Away (Li Bai)
    棉花嶼之歌（林明理）The Song of Mianhua Island
    (Lin Ming-Li) ·· 128
45. 別董大二首（其一）（高適）Farewell to a Bosom Friend
    (No. 1) (Gao Shi)
    我將獨行（林明理）I Will Walk Alone (Lin Ming-Li) ······· 130
46. 塞上聽吹笛（高適）Fluting at the Frontier (Gao Shi)
    山問（林明理）Questions in the Mountain (Lin Ming-Li) ··· 132
47. 題汾橋邊柳（岑參）To Riverside Willows (Cen Shen)
    和平的使者—To Prof. Ernesto Kahan（林明理）
    A Peacemaker: To Prof. Ernesto Kahan (Lin Ming-Li) ······ 133
48. 春思二首（其一）（賈至）Spring Thoughts (No. 1) (Jia Zhi)
    春信（林明理）Message of Spring (Lin Ming-Li) ············ 135
49. 送李侍郎赴常州（賈至）Seeing a Friend Off (Jia Zhi)
    給我最好的朋友一個聖誕祝福（林明理）A Christmas
    Greeting to Cheer You, My Good Friend (Lin Ming-Li) ······ 136
50. 巴陵夜別王八員外（賈至）Bidding Farewell to a Friend in
    the Night of Baling (Jia Zhi)
    在寂靜蔭綠的雪道中（林明理）Along the Snowy Path of
    Quiet Green Shade (Lin Ming-Li)·················· 138
51. 絕句二首（其二）（杜甫）Two Quatrains (No. 2) (Du Fu)
    五分車的記憶（林明理）Memory of the Five-Pointer
    (Lin Ming-Li) ·· 140
52. 江畔獨步尋花七首（其五）（杜甫）Strolling along the
    River in Search of Flowers (No. 5) (Du Fu)
    花蓮觀光漁港風情（林明理）The Customs of Hualien
    Sightseeing Fishing Harbor (Lin Ming-Li) ··············· 142
53. 江畔獨步尋花七首（其七）（杜甫）Strolling along the
    River in Search of Flowers (No. 7) (Du Fu)
    天鵝湖（林明理）The Swan Lake (Lin Ming-Li) ··············· 144
54. 贈花卿（杜甫）To Hua Qing (Du Fu)
    科爾寺前一隅（林明理）A Corner in Front of the
    Kol Temple (Lin Ming-Li) ·································· 145

唐詩明理接千載
古今抒情詩三百首 漢英對照

55. 漫興九首（其一）（杜甫）Nine Random Quatrains (No. 1) (Du Fu)
    在黑暗的平野上（林明理）On a Dark Plain (Lin Ming-Li)‥147

56. 漫成一首（杜甫）A Random Poem (Du Fu)
    在邊城（林明理）In the Border Town (Lin Ming-Li) ……… 148

57. 歸雁（杜甫）Returning Geese (Du Fu)
    回鄉（林明理）Return Home (Lin Ming-Li) …………… 150

58. 逢雪宿芙蓉山主人（劉長卿）A Night Arrival to the Cottage (Liu Changqing)
    詠高密（林明理）Ode to Gaomi (Lin Ming-Li)………… 152

59. 聽彈琴（劉長卿）Lute Playing (Liu Changqing)
    如果你立在冬雪裡（林明理）If You Stand in the Winter Snow (Lin Ming-Li)……………………………………… 156

60. 尋張逸人山居（劉長卿）Looking for the Residence of a Recluse (Liu Changqing)
    黃陽隘即景（林明理）The Sight of Huangyang Pass (Lin Ming-Li) ……………………………………………… 158

61. 江中對月（劉長卿）Facing the Moon in the River (Liu Changqing)
    曲冰橋上的吶喊（林明理）The Cry on the Qubing Bridge (Lin Ming-Li) ………………………………………… 159

62. 送上人（劉長卿）Seeing a Monk Off (Liu Changqing)
    DON'T BE SAD（林明理）Don't Be Sad: For the March 26, 2016 Belgium Victims (Lin Ming-Li) ………… 162

63. 春行寄興（李華）Spring Notes (Li Hua)
    山桐花開時（林明理）When the Tree Blossoms (Lin Ming-Li) ……………………………………………… 164

64. 銜魚翠鳥（錢起）Kingfisher Catching Fish (Qian Qi)
    紅尾伯勞（林明理）The Brown Shrike (Lin Ming-Li) ……… 166

65. 江行無題一百首（其六十九）（錢起）At the Riverside (No. 69) (Qian Qi)
    風雨之後（林明理）After the Storm (Lin Ming-Li)………167

目錄

66. 歸雁（錢起）Returning Geese (Qian Qi)
    凜冬將至（林明理）Severe Winter Is Around the Corner
    (Lin Ming-Li) ··· 169
67. 夜泊鸚鵡洲（錢起）Night Mooring on Parrot Islet (Qian Qi)
    寫給成都之歌（林明理）A Song for Chengdu (Lin Ming-Li) ·· 171
68. 聽鄰家吹笙（郎士元）Hearing the Neighbor Playing *Sheng*
    (Lang Shiyuan)
    暮來的小溪（林明理）The Stream of Twilight (Lin Ming-Li) ·· 174
69. 夜泊湘江（郎士元）Night Mooring in Xiang River
    (Lang Shiyuan)
    寫給蘭嶼之歌（林明理）Ode to Orchid Island (Lin Ming-Li) ·· 176
70. 滁州西澗（韋應物）The West Creek at Chuzhou (Wei Yingwu)
    與詩人有約（林明理）A Date with the Poet (Lin Ming-Li) ·· 178
71. 詠聲（韋應物）On the Voice (Wei Yingwu)
    燈下憶師（林明理）In Memory of My Tutor Under the
    Lamp (Lin Ming-Li) ··· 180
72. 秋夜寄邱二十二員外（韋應物）To a Friend on an Autumn
    Night (Wei Yingwu)
    長巷（林明理）The Long Lane (Lin Ming-Li) ······················ 181
73. 秋齋獨宿（韋應物）Sleeping Alone in an Autumn Studio
    (Wei Yingwu)
    吉貝耍‧孝海祭（Kabua Sua‧Maw-isal）（林明理）Kabua
    Sua‧Maw-isal (Lin Ming-Li) ·· 183
74. 聞雁（韋應物）Hearing the Geese (Wei Yingwu)
    母親（林明理）Mother (Lin Ming-Li) ·································· 186
75. 寒食（韓翃）Cold Food Day (Han Hong)
    木框上的盆花（林明理）Potted Flowers on a Wooden Frame
    (Lin Ming-Li) ··· 187
76. 楓橋夜泊（張繼）Night Mooring at Maple Bridge (Zhang Ji)
    我曾在漁人碼頭中競逐（林明理）I Used to Race in
    Fisherman's Wharf (Lin Ming-Li) ······································ 189
77. 月夜（劉方平）Moonlit Night (Liu Fangping)
    雨後的夜晚（林明理）The Night After the Rain
    (Lin Ming-Li) ··· 191

78. 登樓望水（顧況）Gazing Afar on a Riverside Tower (Gu Kuang)
一棵開花的莿桐老樹（林明理）An Old Flowering Parasol Tree (Lin Ming-Li) ················193

79. 悲歌（顧況）A Dirge (Gu Kuang)
沒有第二個拾荒乞討婦（林明理）There Is No Second Scavenger and Beggar (Lin Ming-Li) ················195

80. 秋日（耿湋）The Autumn Sun (Geng Wei)
秋晨在鯉魚山公園（林明理）Autumn Morning in Lei Yue Mountain Park (Lin Ming-Li) ················198

81. 別離作（戎昱）On Separation (Rong Yu)
我握你的手（林明理）I Shake Your Hand (Lin Ming-Li) ···200

82. 與暢當夜泛秋潭（盧綸）Night Boating on Autumn Lake with a Friend (Lu Lun)
回到過去（林明理）Back to the Past (Lin Ming-Li) ·········202

83. 春夜聞笛（李益）Hearing Fluting in a Spring Night (Li Yi)
橄欖花（林明理）Olive Flowers (Lin Ming-Li) ················204

84. 登鸛雀樓（暢當）Climbing the Stork Tower (Chang Dang)
惦念（林明理）Solicitude (Lin Ming-Li) ················205

85. 望春詞（令狐楚）Song of Spring View (Linghu Chu)
趵突泉即景（林明理）Sight of Baotu Spring (Lin Ming-Li)··207

86. 早春呈水部張十八員外二首（其一）（韓愈）Early Spring (No. 1) (Han Yu)
晨露（林明理）The Morning Dew (Lin Ming-Li) ············209

87. 湘中（韓愈）By Miluo River (Han Yu)
晨光下的將軍漁港（林明理）The General Fishing Harbor in Morning Twilight (Lin Ming-Li) ················210

88. 春雪（韓愈）Spring Snow (Han Yu)
偶然的佇足（林明理）Occasional Stopping (Lin Ming-Li) ··212

89. 江雪（柳宗元）The Fisherman (Liu Zongyuan)
海祭（林明理）Sea Sacrifices (Lin Ming-Li) ················213

90. 秋風引（劉禹錫）Autumnal Wind (Liu Yuxi)
知本濕地的美麗和哀愁（林明理）The Beauty and Sorrow of Zhiben Wetland (Lin Ming-Li) ················216

目錄

91. 浪淘沙九首（其一）（劉禹錫）Waves Washing Sands (No. 1) (Liu Yuxi)
懷柔千佛山（林明理）Qianfo Mountain of Huairou (Lin Ming-Li)·················218
92. 烏衣巷（劉禹錫）Lane of Black Clothes (Liu Yuxi)
夢橋（林明理）The Dream Bridge (Lin Ming-Li)············220
93. 台城（劉禹錫）An Ancient Imperial City (Liu Yuxi)
詠車城（林明理）Ode to Checheng (Lin Ming-Li)··········222
94. 襄陽寒食寄宇文籍（竇鞏）To a Friend on the Cold Food Day (Dou Gong)
憂鬱（林明理）Melancholy (Lin Ming-Li)··············224
95. 秋夕（竇鞏）An Autumn Evening (Dou Gong)
池上風景一隅（林明理）View of Chishang (Lin Ming-Li)····226
96. 洛橋晚望（孟郊）Night View on Luoyang Bridge (Meng Jiao)
雖已遠去（林明理）Though Far Away (Lin Ming-Li)·······228
97. 秋思（張籍）Autumn Thoughts (Zhang Ji)
墨菊（林明理）Black Chrysanthemum (Lin Ming-Li)·······229
98. 成都曲（張籍）Ode to Chengdu (Zhang Ji)
寫給包公故里——肥東（林明理）To the Hometown of Bao Gong: Feidong (Lin Ming-Li)···················230
99. 湘江曲（張籍）Ditty of Xiang River (Zhang Ji)
歷下亭遠眺（林明理）Overlooking in the Distance at Lixia Pavilion (Lin Ming-Li)·······························233
100. 江陵使至汝州（王建）Arriving at Ruzhou from Jiangling (Wang Jian)
緬懷金瓜石老街（林明理）In Memory of Jinguashi Old Street (Lin Ming-Li)··························235
101. 菊花（元稹）Chrysanthemums (Yuan Zhen)
香蒲（林明理）The Bulrush (Lin Ming-Li)···············238
102. 離思五首（其四）（元稹）Five Poems About Parting Emotions (No. 4) (Yuan Zhen)
思念似穿過月光的鯨群之歌（林明理）Longing Is Like the Song of Whales Through the Moonlight (Lin Ming-Li)········239

39

103. 夜雪（白居易）Night Snow (Bai Juyi)
　　 如果我是塵沙（林明理）If I Were Dust (Lin Ming-Li)……240
104. 暮江吟（白居易）A River at Sunset (Bai Juyi)
　　 畜欄的空洞聲（林明理）The Hollow Sound of the Corral
　　 (Lin Ming-Li)………………………………………………242
105. 大林寺桃花（白居易）Peach Flowers in Dalin Temple
　　 (Bai Juyi)
　　 向開闢中橫公路的榮民及罹難者致敬（林明理）Salute to
　　 the Veterans and Victims of the Construction of the Central
　　 Cross Highway (Lin Ming-Li)……………………………243
106. 白雲泉（白居易）White Cloud Fountain (Bai Juyi)
　　 思念在藍色海洋慢慢氳開…（林明理）Yearning Is
　　 Slowly Spreading in the Blue Ocean… (Lin Ming-Li)……245
107. 村夜（白居易）The Village Night (Bai Juyi)
　　 在雕刻室裡（林明理）In the Carving Room (Lin Ming-Li)…247
108. 寒閨怨（白居易）Complaint of Cold Palace (Bai Juyi)
　　 暴風雨（林明理）The Rainstorm (Lin Ming-Li)…………248
109. 遺愛寺（白居易）Yi'ai Temple (Bai Juyi)
　　 詩河（林明理）The Poetic River (Lin Ming-Li)…………250
110. 春風（白居易）Spring Breeze (Bai Juyi)
　　 逗留（林明理）Sojourn (Lin Ming-Li)……………………251
111. 鶴（白居易）The Crane (Bai Juyi)
　　 來自珊瑚礁島的聲音（林明理）Sounds From the Coral
　　 Islands (Lin Ming-Li)………………………………………253
112. 望月懷江上舊遊（雍陶）Missing an Old Playmate in a
　　 Moonlit Night (Yong Tao)
　　 致杜甫（林明理）Tribute to Du Fu (Lin Ming-Li)………255
113. 晚春江晴寄友人（韓琮）To a Friend in Late Spring When
　　 It Shines on the River (Han Cong)
　　 致吾友──Prof. Ernesto Kahan（林明理）To My Friend
　　 Prof. Ernesto Kahan (Lin Ming-Li)………………………257
114. 洞靈觀流泉（李郢）Watching a Waterfall (Li Ying)
　　 巨石陣（林明理）Stonehenge (Lin Ming-Li)……………258

目錄

115. 泊秦淮（杜牧）Mooring by River Qinhuai (Du Mu)
    二二八紀念公園冥想（林明理）Meditation in the 228 Memorial Park (Lin Ming-Li) ………………… 260
116. 山行（杜牧）A Mountain Trip (Du Mu)
    風滾草（林明理）The Tumbleweed (Lin Ming-Li) ………… 261
117. 江南春絕句（杜牧）Spring in the Southern Shore (Du Mu)
    西漢高速（林明理）Xihan Highway (Lin Ming-Li) ………… 263
118. 歎花（杜牧）Lament for Flowers (Du Mu)
    重生的喜悅（林明理）The Joy of Rebirth (Lin Ming-Li) … 265
119. 江樓（杜牧）A Riverside Tower (Du Mu)
    月光、海灣和遠方（林明理）Moonlight, Bay and the Distance (Lin Ming-Li) ……………………………… 267
120. 赤壁（杜牧）The Red Cliff (Du Mu)
    挺進吧，海上的男兒（林明理）Advance, Man of the Sea (Lin Ming-Li) ……………………………………… 269
121. 長安秋望（杜牧）Gazing Afar in Autumn in the Capital (Du Mu)
    隆田文化資產教育園區觀展（林明理）The Exhibition of Longtian Culture Heritage Area (Lin Ming-Li) …………… 271
122. 贈別二首（其二）（杜牧）Two Parting Poems (No. 2) (Du Mu)
    愛情似深邃的星空（林明理）Love Is Like the Deep Starry Sky (Lin Ming-Li) ……………………………………… 272
123. 南陵道中（杜牧）On the Road of Nanling (Du Mu)
    最美的時刻（林明理）The Greatest Moment (Lin Ming-Li) ……………………………………………… 274
124. 憶梅（李商隱）Remembering Plum Blossoms (Li Shangyin)
    感謝有您——Athanase Vantchev de Thracy（林明理）Thanks to You: Athanase Vantchev de Thracy (Lin Ming-Li) … 276
125. 夜雨寄北（李商隱）Northward Missing in a Raining Night (Li Shangyin)
    時光的回眸：中山大學（林明理）Looking Back in Time: Sun Yat-sen University (Lin Ming-Li) ……………… 278

126. 嫦娥（李商隱）The Moon Goddess (Li Shangyin)
　　鐫痕（林明理）The Engraving Mark (Lin Ming-Li) ········· 280
127. 微雨（李商隱）A Drizzle (Li Shangyin)
　　流浪漢（林明理）The Vagrant (Lin Ming-Li) ················ 281
128. 夕陽樓（李商隱）The Tower Basking in Setting Sun
　　(Li Shangyin)
　　白河：蓮鄉之歌（林明理）White River: The Song of Lotus
　　Land (Lin Ming-Li) ·· 284
129. 天涯（李商隱）The Horizon (Li Shangyin)
　　為搶救童妓而歌（林明理）Child Prostitution (Lin Ming-Li) ·· 287
130. 靜夜相思（李群玉）Thoughts On a Silent Night (Li Qunyu)
　　短詩兩首（林明理）Two Short Poems (Lin Ming-Li) ········ 289
131. 引水行（李群玉）Conducting Water (Li Qunyu)
　　獻給勝興車站（林明理）Dedicated to Shengxing Station
　　(Lin Ming-Li) ··· 291
132. 過分水嶺（溫庭筠）Crossing the Watershed (Wen Tingyun)
　　致以色列拿撒勒（林明理）To Israel Nazareth
　　(Lin Ming-Li) ··· 293
133. 早春（儲嗣宗）Early Spring (Chu Sizong)
　　寫給未來的我（林明理）For My Future Self (Lin Ming-Li) ·· 294
134. 退居漫題七首（其一）（司空圖）Random Poems in
　　Retirement (No. 1) (Sikong Tu)
　　向建築大師貝聿銘致上最後的敬意（林明理）Paying Last
　　Respect to Renowned Architect Ieoh Ming Pei (Lin Ming-Li) ··· 296
135. 退居漫題七首（其三）（司空圖）Random Poems in
　　Retirement (No. 3) (Sikong Tu)
　　夢回大學時代（林明理）Dreaming Back to College
　　(Lin Ming-Li) ··· 298
136. 獨望（司空圖）Solitary Gazing (Sikong Tu)
　　走在彎曲的小徑（林明理）Walk Long the Winding Path
　　(Lin Ming-Li) ··· 300
137. 春草（唐彥謙）Spring Grass (Tang Yanqian)
　　想當年（林明理）Those Were the Days (Lin Ming-Li) ······ 301

138. 小院（唐彥謙）A Small Courtyard (Tang Yanqian)
    燈塔（林明理）The Lighthouse (Lin Ming-Li) ·················· 303
139. 田上（崔道融）In the Field (Cui Daorong)
    記憶中的麥芽糖（林明理）Maltose in Memory
    (Lin Ming-Li) ·· 305
140. 春日山中行（裴說）Walking in the Mountain in Spring
    (Pei Yue)
    閱讀布農部落（林明理）Reading the Bunon Tribe
    (Lin Ming-Li) ·· 306
141. 閩中秋思（杜荀鶴）Autumnal Thoughts in Fujian Province
    (Du Xunhe)
    墨竹（林明理）The Ink Bamboo (Lin Ming-Li) ·············· 310
142. 古離別（韋莊）At Parting (Wei Zhuang)
    寫給相湖的歌（林明理）A Song for Xianghu Lake
    (Lin Ming-Li) ·· 311
143. 江外思鄉（韋莊）Nostalgia Beyond the River (Wei Zhuang)
    自由廣場前冥想（林明理）Meditation in front of the
    Freedom Square (Lin Ming-Li) ······································· 314
144. 驚雪（陸暢）Snow of Pleasant Surprise (Lu Chang)
    在後山迴盪的禱告聲中（林明理）In the Echoing Prayers
    from the Back Hill (Lin Ming-Li) ·· 315
145. 農家（顏仁鬱）The Farmer (Yan Renyu)
    消失的湖泊（林明理）The Disappearing Lake
    (Lin Ming-Li) ·· 317
146. 感懷（李煜）Reminiscence (Li Yu)
    難忘邵族祖靈祭（林明理）Unforgettable Shao Ancestral
    Sacrifice (Lin Ming-Li) ··· 319
147. 春雪（東方虯）Spring Snow (Dongfang Qiu)
    蘆花飛白的時候（林明理）When the Reeds Are Flying
    White (Lin Ming-Li) ··· 321
148. 春日（宋雍）The Spring Day (Song Yong)
    在那雲霧之間（林明理）Between the Clouds (Lin Ming-Li) ·· 323

149. 金縷衣（杜秋娘）Golden Clothes (Du Qiuniang)
    流螢（林明理）The Flitting Firefly (Lin Ming-Li) ············325
150. 洛堤步月（上官儀）Strolling along the Dyke in Moonlight (Shangguan Yi)
    致以色列特拉維夫——白城（林明理）To Tel Aviv, Israel: the Big Orange (Lin Ming-Li) ·································326

唐詩明理 接千載
古今抒情詩三百首
漢英對照

唐詩明理 接千載
古今抒情詩三百首
漢英對照

1·

落葉 　　　　　　　　　　　孔紹安

早秋驚落葉，飄零似客心。
翻飛未肯下，猶言惜故林。

Falling Leaves 　　　　　　Kong Shao'an

Early fall is startled
at falling leaves,

which waft and tumble
like my homesick heart.

In the air they are
whirling and keeling:

from their twigs —
they hate to depart.

秋在汐止晴山[1] 　　　　　　林明理

恍如重溫一個夢
　剪剪秋風
不停地傳來潮水奔湧
一隻蝴蝶
　　飛上了
在瓜棚上的晴空裡

---

[1] 余與杭州作家葦子溶身臺北汐止山水之間，一路繞峰，秋陽杲杲。於「食養山房」入口，接有鐵鑄橋，越樹林，復得一水塘，錦鯉悠游眼底矣。美哉！窗外林木鬱深，鳳蝶翩飛，綴以美食相奉，三五席坐飲茗。歸返旅程，相對忘言，唯詩音與心靈共舞，特此以誌懷思。—2017.10.29 寫於台東小城

神話一般消隱
而我聽到輕微的梵音
在山鄉的遠處
　　慢慢流盪
從那鮮活記憶之底層
緊緊扣著我，——啊朋友
當群星靜寂，我只求為妳而歌

Autumn in Shixiqing Mountain[2]

Lin Ming-Li

As if reliving a dream
　　The clipping autumn wind
Keeps sending the sound of the surging tide
A butterfly
　　Flies into
The clear sky over the melon shed
To disappear like a myth
And I hear the gentle voice of Brahma
In the distance of the mountain country
　　Wandering slowly
From the bottom of the living memory
Holding me tight — O my friend
When the stars are silent, I only want to sing for you

---

[2] Hangzhou-based writer Wei Zi and I lost ourselves in the mountains and rivers of Xizhi, Taipei, where we are gazers of autumn sun. At the entrance of the "Food and Mountain House", there is an iron bridge, and beyond the forest, there is a pond where the koi fish are swimming. How beautiful! Outside the window, the trees are deep, the butterflies are flying, when food is served for three or five sitters while drinking tea. On the return journey, we face each other without words, the mind lingering and echoing with poetry. The poem is thus inspired. — October 29, 2017, written in the little town of Taitung.

唐詩明理接千載
古今抒牆詩三百首
漢英對照

✧✧✧

2.

晉安建陽題壁　　　　　　　　　王勃

江漢深無極，梁岷不可攀。
山川雲霧裡，遊子幾時還？

An Inscription on the Wall　　Wang Bo

The Yangtze River and
Han River are bottom-

less; Liangshan Mountain
and Minshan Mountain

defy scaling. Hills
and rills veiled in heavy

fog; when will the lost
wanderer come back?

兩岸青山連天碧——陪海基會走過二十年感時　　　　　　　　　林明理

多少次坐在歷史之岸尋舊夢
走過的風雨如昨日，月
凝神，遠山長滿相思
我把天際撥開，便覺香江不再遙遠
島嶼在頻頻傳遞，重續探親的
驚喜，落雪轉眼飄成白桐
多少人正開始寄盼

春從一笑後姍姍而來
我將希望之燈點燃，無視
時光悠遠，別後生命蒼涼之悲
每當四野的音樂吹響
Formosa 就以遼闊之藍，和雲朵競著唱和

多少回我似無家的風在林間低回
世間又有哪一朵雲，能歸後
再相逢？那淡漠的天空是否也
咀嚼著低吟的自由？
每當白鴿把
和平之鐘叩響時，山和水便合十了

啊，太平洋柔柔的海波
是否牽掛我第一次俯瞰母親
做大海之遊？
聽，那地母懷裡是否也有喜樂的心音？
那祖靈庇護的——
是否讓所有的言語都能融合你我

因為愛
能戰勝隔絕近半世紀的恐懼
如母親眼底的溫柔，今天我就要踏回故鄉
噢，親愛的，你是否
如滿天星斗早已守候：又或許
春神也執起牧鞭，整裝待發了

－於 2010.12.06，臺灣

Green Mountains and Blue Sky on Both Banks—Together with SEF Through the Past 20 Years Lin Ming-Li

How many times to sit on the bank of history to retrace the old dream
Through the wind and rain like yesterday, the moon
Is gazing, the distant mountains are filled with pining
When I brush the horizon away, I feel the Xiangjiang River is no longer distant
The islands are frequently delivering message, to continue the pleasant surprise
Of meeting relatives; in a blink the snow falls into white parasol trees

How many people are beginning to look forward
To spring which is approaching with a smile
I enkindle the light of hope, ignoring
The remote time, the bleak sorrow of life after separation
When the music of the four fields is aloud
Formosa, with the vast blue, competes in singing with the clouds

How many times I have been walking in the woods like the homeless wind
And what blossom of cloud in the world, can return
To meet again? Does the indifferent sky
Chew the freedom of crooning?
Whenever the white dove
Rings the bell of peace, the mountain and the water fold in a cross

Ah, do the soft waves of the Pacific
Care about my first sea trip
Overlooking my mother?
Listen, is there also a joyful heart in the bosom of the mother of the earth?

What the ancestral spirit shelters and protects —
Whether all words can merge you and me

Because love
Can overcome the fear of isolation for nearly half a century
Like the tenderness in Mother's eyes, today I will step back to my hometown
Oh, dear, are you
Already waiting for me like a skyful of stars: or perhaps
The spring deity has grasped the shepherd's whip, ready to go

       December 6, 2010, Taiwan

✧✧✧

3 ·

登城春望   王勃

物外山川近，晴初景靄新。
芳郊花柳遍，何處不宜春。

Spring View Atop the City Gate Wang Bo

Beyond the city gate hills
and rills are approachable;

a fine day freshens
the new-born clouds.

The suburbs are fair with
flowers and willows; spring

is here, spring is there
—spring is everywhere.

春日江中　　　　　　　　　　　林明理

我是在山中
櫓聲是妳傳動的笑容
那古老的藤蔓
斑駁粘附著翠壁
更有直入深潭
輕舞　漫歌

我是在雲中
在跳擲的浪頭
向晨光
逐漸接近——又
悵別在
岩面輪廓與靜謐的暝色

Spring Days on the River　　Lin Ming-Li

I am in the mountain
The scull is your turning smile
The age-old vines
Mottled to the green walls
And straight into the deep pool
To sing softly and dance gently

In the clouds
I am gradually approaching
The morning light on
The leaping waves — and
Melancholy parting with
The contours of the rock face and
the quiet and misty dusk

❖❖❖

4 ·

詠鵝   駱賓王

鵝，鵝，鵝，曲項向天歌。
白毛浮綠水，紅掌撥清波。

Geese   Luo Binwang

A goose, a goose,
another goose: in

a single file they
sing heavenward,

white feathers
swimming in green

water, red paws poking
waves clear and clean.

平魯古城的秋天[3]   林明理

我問老平魯的上蒼
我該如何隱蔽自我？
它緊貼著我的眼，
在漠漠中還以沉默。

我又問桌上的螢幕，
為何古城顫泛著一樣的
平靜與溫暖，
不曾改變過什麼？

---

[3] 山西省平魯古城，又名鳳凰城；當地人稱了「老平魯」。

噢，我可以遠離是非，
我也可以馱負寂寞——
可我怎能替代了天藍
只給了夜咯嗒敲響心中的歌。

Autumn in the Ancient City of Pinglu[4]

Lin Ming-Li

I ask the heaven obove the ancient city of Pinglu
How can I hide myself?
It clings to my eyes,
Still silent in detachedness.

I ask the screen on the table,
Why the ancient city is trembling with the same
Calm and warmth,
Nothing changed?

Oh, I can stay away from gossips,
I can also carry loneliness —
But how can I replace the sky blue
Only to rattle the night, aloud with the song in my heart.

✧✧✧

5 ·

送別　　　　　　　　　　　　　　　　駱賓王

寒更乘夜永，涼夕向秋澄。
離心何以贈，自有玉壺冰。

---

[4] The ancient city of Pinglu is in Shanxi Province, also known as Phoenix City. The locals are known as "Old Pinglu".

Farewell

Luo Binwang

Cold night appears
long; autumn evening

is cool and clear.
At separation: what

to make a gift? The heart
as clear as a pot of ice.

小象

林明理

牠看起來這麼憂傷
再也不會加入家族的歡笑
牠剛躲過洪水
卻等不到母親
　回
　　家
噢！可憐的伯格

The Little Elephant

Lin Ming-Li

He looks so sad
That he will never join the joyous family again
He has just escaped from a flood
And is still waiting for the
　Return of
　　His mother
Oh! Poor Berger

✧✧✧

唐詩明理接千載
古今抒情詩三百首
漢英對照

6.

渡漢江 宋之問

嶺外音書斷，經冬復歷春。
近鄉情更怯，不敢問來人。

Crossing River Han Song Zhiwen

News cut off from beyond
the mountain, all the year

round, from winter to spring
and onward. My growing

timidity gets the better of
me, as I approach my home:

I dare not inquire about
anything from anybody.

夜航 林明理

是秋的臘染
紫雲，浪潮拍岸
是繁星
旋轉，還有萬重山

當夜敲著故鄉的門
小樓的風鈴就傳開了

那海河的橄欖林
在銀色的石徑裡醒來
被風起的流光
點出滿身晶瑩的背影

只有我於天幕下
仰望高空
在雨濕來臨前
趁著黑夜
飛越玉壁金川……

Night Sailing　　　　　　　　　Lin Ming-Li

It is the wax dyeing of autumn
Purple clouds, waves beating the shore
The maze of stars
Rotating, and myriads of mountains

When the night knocks at the door of hometown
The wind chimes of the small building is spreading

The olive forest of the river and sea
Waking up in the silver stone path
And is illuminated into a glittering form
By the streamer of the wind

Under the curtain of the sky only I
Look up high in the sky
Before the rain
Under the cover of the night
To fly over the walls of jade and the rivers of gold…

✧✧✧

7.

邊詞　　　　　　　　　　　　張敬忠

五原春色歸來遲，二月垂楊未掛絲。
即今河畔冰開日，正是長安花落時。

A Frontier Song

Zhang Jingzhong

Frontier spring is late
to come as of old:

the branches in March
fail to put out buds.

When the ice in rivers
and lakes breaks, flowers

in the southern capital
are falling and fading.

岸畔

林明理

一隻松鼠
倒懸
不露生色的天空。

牠竄來跳去，無視
跌宕紅塵
唯有鳥影打破沉默。

我在岸畔行走
撈捕：風的腳履兒
深一步，淺一步
時光的蜻羽輕輕凝固。

偶抬眼，綠芭蕉升上
春之草垛
在裸石後　染亮了。

By the Shoreside

Lin Ming-Li

A squirrel
Hanging upside down
In the dim and distant sky.

He leaps about, ignoring
The tumbling world of red dust
Only the shadow of a bird breaks the silence.

I walk on the shore
Fishing: the footsteps of wind
A step leftward, and a step rightward
The dragonfly wings of time slightly solidify.

Occasionally I lift my eyes, the green plantain is arsing
The haystack of spring
After the bare stone   is dyed bright.

✧✧✧

8 ·

詠柳 賀知章

碧玉妝成一樹高，萬條垂下綠絲條。
不知細葉誰裁出？二月春風似剪刀。

Ode to Willows

He Zhizhang

Emerald jade is decorated
into the height of a tall tree;

thousands of twigs are drooping
with green silk braids.

Who has tailored so many
fair willow leaves? The spring

wind of March cuts sharper
than a pair of scissors.

一棵雨中行的蕨樹 　　　　　　　　林明理

一絲絲
　　細似蟲聲的雨
　　　　直下……
　　　　　　直下……
　　隱藏我於
炊煙淡起的霧邊

被風吹白的松林
都紛紛翹首，聽歸雀聲圓
　　而以擁抱的姿勢
　　　　印上我腮邊的吻
我已咀嚼到孤獨原是
　　難消的念

愛人啊
　　我撥開花謝
　　　　花亮的髮辮
　　　　　望落
守候千年不歇的
　　一江明月

A Fern Tree Walking in the Rain

　　　　　　　　　　Lin Ming-Li

A thin,
　Worm-like rain
　　Is falling…

       Falling...
    Hiding me from
    The fading mist

The windswept white pines
All turn their heads up, to listen to the finches
    And in an embrace
        To imprint a kiss on my cheek
I have chewed loneliness as
    An indispensable thought

Oh, my love
    I part the fading flowers
       The braid bright with flowers
       Look down
Waiting through thousands of years
       A riverful of bright moon

✧✧✧

9 ·

回鄉偶書二首（其一）   賀知章

少小離家老大回，鄉音無改鬢毛衰。
兒童相見不相識，笑問客從何處來。

Returning Home (No. 1)   He Zhizhang

I left home as a boy
and returned as an old

man, whose native accent
persists, though my hair

is heavily tinged with grey.
The children, gazing all over

me in candid wonder, ask:
"where are you from, sir?"

念故鄉 　　　　　　　　　　　　林明理

啊，你是哪裡來的風
多愁善感　猶如
空野中雛鷹　低低哀鳴

紫色小草望著你歎息
蜜棗樹為你深藏憂鬱
而茫茫天地
也無視你早已飛離的距離

生命之河啊
在此幽微的夜裡
我開始遺忘
你是怎樣蹙眉　嗟嘆　怎樣挺立

啊，你是哪裡來的風
又在哪兒甦醒
悠長的歌聲　撫綠了我故鄉的風景

Longing for Home 　　　　　Lin Ming-Li

Ah, wind, where do you come from
So sentimental　like
A young eagle in the wild air　lowly wailing

Purple grass looks at you sighing
The jujube tree hides deep melancholy for you
And the vast world

Also ignores the distance where you have already flown away

Oh the river of life
In this dark night
I begin to forget
How you frown   sigh   and stand

Ah, wind, where do you come from
And where to wake up
The long song   has caressed green the landscape of my hometown

✧✧✧

10 •

賦得自君之出矣　　　　　　張九齡

自君之出矣，不復理殘機。
思君如滿月，夜夜減清輝。

Since You Left Me, My Lord Zhang Jiuling

Since you left me,
my lord, I no longer

see to the fading loom.
A full moon, O, is my

heart, which wanes
from night to night.

給敬愛的人　　　　　　　　　　　　　　林明理

穿過雪林
你的影像或遠或近
落在水鏡上
與我心的回聲之間
在宇宙的隙縫中
我是小小的詩人
而你的歌
是繆斯的豎琴
穿越千年的時光之舞

To My Beloved　　　　　　　　　　　Lin Ming-Li

Through the snow forest
Your image is now far and then near
Falling on the water mirror
Between the echo of my heart
In the gap of the universe
I am a little poet
And your song
Is the harp of the Muse
The dance of time through thousands of years

✧✧✧

11．

照鏡見白髮　　　　　　　　　　　　　　張九齡

宿昔青雲志，蹉跎白髮年。
誰知明鏡裡，形影自相憐。

Gray Hair in the Mirror   Zhang Jiuling

High aspirations
of yore: gray hairs

see youth wasted.
In the bright mirror,

oh, pitiable form
and pitiable shadow.

夜思   林明理

與秋空連接的
在一縷行雲間
迴轉往復

縱使無法駕馭長風
卻也甘心化為一棵老松
聽雨在燈下
清音在心境
從流逝不定的靈感
黑暗中尋思光點

任白髮悄然延伸
多少年後
依然瀟灑自如

Night Thoughts   Lin Ming-Li

Connecting with the autumn sky
In a wisp of clouds
It repeats and rotates

Even if unable to ride the long wind
Yet willing to turn into an old pine
Listening to the rain under a lamp
Pure sound in the frame of mind
From the passing indefinite inspiration
In search of a dot of light in the dark

In spite of my hair quietly graying
Years later
Still free and unrestrained

✧✧✧

12 ·

南樓望　　　　　　　　　　　盧僎

去國三巴遠，登樓萬里春。
傷心江上客，不是故鄉人。

South-Gazing Tower　　　　Lu Zhuan

Away from home, Sanba
is remote; climbing atop

the tower, myriads of
miles of spring. A heart-

broken wanderer on the
river is no native dweller.

觀七股鹽田園區　　　　　　林明理

陳列在展示區的
鹽業史和昔日景物，
像電影般一幕幕映過。

而巨大白色風車
在冷風中
發出它的絮語。

我向著百年前的鹽場窺視,
看到黑面琵鷺長影,
沒有煩囂,只有曬鹽的人。[5]

Watching the Idyllic Area of Qigu Salt Mountain[6]

Lin Ming-Li

The history and past scenes of the salt industry
Displayed in the exhibition area
Are shown one after another like a movie.

And the great white windmill
In the cold wind
Is whispering by itself.

---

[5] 七股鹽山(Qigu Salt Mountain)曾是臺灣最大的曬鹽場,因時代變遷,已在 2002 年結束臺灣 338 年曬鹽歷史。臺鹽公司將其轉型為觀光園區,展示鹽屋、鹽業史、遊園小火車等,遂成為臺南知名的景點之一。2024 年 12 月 7 日上午,初次參觀後發現,園區內也有井仔腳鹽場環境解說、多幅精美的野鳥以及曬鹽場攝影作品等景物,有感而作。—2024.12.14

[6] Qigu Salt Mountain, once the largest salt production site in Taiwan, has finished in 2002 its salt production history of 338 years in Taiwan, and the Taiwan Salt Company has transformed it into a tourist attraction, exhibiting the salt houses, the history of salt industry, and the small trains in the area, thus becoming one of the well-known scenic spots in Tainan. On the morning of December 7, 2024, after my first visit, I find there are also environmental explanations for Jingzai Foot Salt Farm, a host of photography works of wild birds and salt fields in the area. The poem is thus inspired.— December 14, 2024

I peer into the salt farm of a hundred years ago,
To see the long shadow of a black-faced spoonbill,
Without any noise, only the salt man.

✧✧✧

13．

涼州詞二首（其一）　　　　　王翰

葡萄美酒夜光杯，欲飲琵琶馬上催。
醉臥沙場君莫笑，古來征戰幾人回。

The Border Song (No. 1)　　　Wang Han

The wine of grapes in night-
glowing cups; on the verge

of drinking, a bugle sounds
to mount the steeds. No

laughing, if we lie drunk
on the battlefield, please ─

how many fighters can
be back safe and sound?

別哭泣，敘利亞小孩[7]　　　　林明理

別哭泣，孩子。
　我用掌心觸碰你蒼白之臉，
　我以沉痛寫出戰爭無情的詩篇。

---

[7] 據統計，流亡難民的時間可能長達十七年。——寫於 2018.1.18

你說，流亡扼殺了我們，
你說，只能在睡夢中或
　　只能透過想像夢想著夢，
你說，敘利亞是永遠的故鄉，
　　但故鄉何其遠？
只有唯一真實的月光
才能無懼地說出心底的思念。
你說砲聲響過，坦克車來了！
　　為什麼要不停地殺害我們？
啊　你短短的問話，
　讓大地同悲，眾神也無言。

Don't Cry, Syrian Child[8]　　　Lin Ming-Li

Don't cry, my child.
　I touch your pale face with my palm,
　　With sorrow I write a poem about the cruel war.
You say, exile has strangled us,
You say, only in sleep or
　　In your dream can you dream,
You say Syria is your everlasting home,
　　　But how far away is your hometown?
Only the sole genuine moon
Can tell the longing in the heart without fear.
You say after roaring of guns, the tanks roll!
　　Why they keep killing us?
Ah... your brief question
　Makes the earth sad, and gods wordless.

✧✧✧

---

[8] According to statistics, the average time for refugees in exile may be as long as 17 years.—Written on January 18, 2018.

14.

鹿柴　　　　　　　　　　　　　　　王維

空山不見人，但聞人語響。
返景入深林，復照青苔上。

A Secluded Forest Scene　　　Wang Wei

Not a single soul is seen in the empty
mountain — save some whispering,

the echoing sound as of a human voice
— where a wandering shaft of light,

through lacing boughs of the forest,
is flickering and trickling down, broken

and subdued to soft light — before
falling full upon the green moss aground.

殘照　　　　　　　　　　　　　　林明理

牛車上
映著淡紫的煙霞
遲歸的老農合起疲憊的眼，拋下
被遺忘了的辛酸歲月
緩緩地從小路回家

天蓋的四周織起了輕羅
向趕路的牛兒催走
皺紋的臉
沉重的步履，不停地流著汗
乾草在堆疊的綑綁中哎哎作響

後山是比夕陽還娟秀的樹林
前面是幾隻歸鳥覓宿的悅音
而他，安詳的，對老牛輕柔的叮嚀
彷彿在微風中才有著寧靜……

The Evening Glow　　　　　　Lin Ming-Li

On the ox cart
Reflecting with the lilac mist
The late-returnining old farmer, with closed tired eyes, leaves beind
The bitter years which have been forgotten
To go home slowly along the path

Around the canopy is woven a thin gauze
Hurrying away the cattle on the way
The wrinkled faces
Heavy footsteps, constantly sweating
Dried hay rumbling in the bundling of the stacks

The back mountain is the woods more beautiful than the setting sunset
In the front is the pleasant voice of a few homing birds to find a shelter
And he, peaceful, gentle exhorting the old cattle
As if with quietude only in the breeze…

✧✧✧

15．

竹裡館　　　　　　　　　　　　王維

獨坐幽篁裡，彈琴復長嘯。
深林人不知，明月來相照。

A Retreat in Bamboos　　　　　Wang Wei

Alone I sit in a secluded
grove of shady bamboos:

I play my lute while whistling
along. In the depths of woods

no one knows I am here,
and I am privy to none

but the bright moon, who
is my boon companion.

在遠方的巴列姆山谷[9]　　　　　林明理

地表上的達尼人小孩
　　在野果中
　　在夜空下
　　　　甜甜地睡去
母親為他蓋上了被子。
狂野的河浪，山豬的蹤跡
　　都離得遠遠的……
美麗的花兒啊
　　在河邊綻放
勇士們把獵物牢牢放好。
他們汲水而歌，燧石而舞
　　遠離煩囂；
而我深信
百年以後這美妙的山谷
　　在紅薯梯田

---

[9] 巴列姆山谷（Baliem Valley）位於印尼巴布亞省的中央山脈裡，為海拔 1600 多米的天然山谷。–2018.2.5

與陡峭的山峰之間，
仍有部落歌舞著——恰似
　　時光在歌唱。

In the Remote Balmain Valley[10]

Lin Ming-Li

On the ground in the middle of wild fruits
　　A Dani child is having
　　A sweet dream
　　　　Under the night sky
His mother spreads a blanket over him
Wild river current, traces of mountain pigs
　　　　Are all far away⋯
Beautiful flowers
　　Are blooming by the river
Warriors put away their preys
They sing while drawing water, dance while chipping rocks
　　　　Far away from hustle and bustle
And I am convinced
A hundred years from now this wonderful valley
Between the sweet potato terraces
And the steep peaks
Still some tribal songs and dances — as if
　　　　Time is singing.

✧✧✧

---

[10] Baliem Valley is located in the central mountains of Papua Province, Indonesia, and it is a natural valley with an elevation of over 1600 meters.—February 5, 2018.

16．

辛夷塢　　　　　　　　　王維

木末芙蓉花，山中發紅萼。
澗戶寂無人，紛紛開且落。

The Magnolia Retreat　　　Wang Wei

Magnolia flowers
in a tree bloom red

in deep mountain.
Hills and rills are

deserted and still:
the tree comes into

blossoms, before it
loosens a drift of petals.

楊潔[11]　　　　　　　　　林明理

彷若山芙蓉，楊潔，
堅強而溫柔，——
　潔白如天使的歌聲
在谷中迴響……
　　結合晨光的世界。

山芙蓉　林明理攝

---

[11] 今天收到楊潔寄來耶誕節的祝福電郵，很開心，有感而作。——2024.12.19

Yang Jie[12]   Lin Ming-Li

Like a mountain hibiscus, Yang Jie,
   Strong and gentle, —
White like an angel's song
   Echoing in the valley...
In combination with the world of morning light.

✧✧✧

17 ·

鳥鳴澗   王維

人閒桂花落，夜靜春山空。
月出驚山鳥，時鳴春澗中。

The Deep Peace of Spring Dale   Wang Wei

The falling of osmanthus flowers,
witnessed by idlers, is the only

sound that breaks in upon the
uniform tranquility of the empty

spring mountain veiled in still night.
The occasional twittering of mountain

birds, startled by moonrise, breaks
the deep peace of the spring dale.

---

[12] Today, I am very happy to receive an email of Christmas blessing from Yang Jie, hence the poem.—December 19, 2024.

唐詩明理 接千載
古今 抒情詩三百首
漢英對照

青藤花 　　　　　　　　　　　　　　　林明理

將雨要來
一株青藤花
靜聽著雲端裡的低的
雷聲，忽而幾顆雨點
開始打在額上
悒鬱的
青藤花
無端地笑了

屋外很遼闊
你聽，蚯蚓聲如雨
如雷
你是否聞到泥土的香？
是否也曾細心咀嚼便玩味書中了！
在這初夏之夜，我便看見
一個凝定的容顏
浸透了轉動的世界

Sinomenia Flowers 　　　　　Lin Ming-Li

It threatens rain
A vine flower
Quietly listens to the low thunder
In the clouds; suddenly a few drops of rain
Begin to hit its forehead.
The melancholy
Vine flower
Smiles for no reason

Outside the house it is so vast
Listen, earthworms sound like rain
And like thunder

Do you smell the fragrance of earth?
Whether you have carefully chewed and savored the book!
On this early summer night, I see
A frozen face
Permeating the turning world

✧✧✧

18·

雜詩三首（其二） 　　　　　王維

君自故鄉來，應知故鄉事。
來日綺窗前，寒梅著花未？

Miscellaneous Poems (No. 2) Wang Wei

Coming from my home-
town, you must be familiar

with native things. In
front of my latticed

window, pray: are plum
blossoms abloom?

當白梅花開 　　　　　林明理

冬原的雪，襯得紫雲
如一海島的船
疏林外，星子沿著簷邊歸來
聽白梅 臨風輕舞

啊，是誰無聲的喚我
衝出雲端又帶怯悄默

唐詩明理接千載
古今抒情詩三百首
漢英對照

互視著傳遞春信
卻一點也聽不見什麼

When White Plum Blossoms Are Blossoming
          Lin Ming-Li

The snow of winter field sets off the purple clouds
Like the ship from an island
Beyond the sparse forest, the stars return along the eaves
Listen to white plum blossoms　gently dancing in the wind

Ah, who is calling me soundlessly
Breaking out of the clouds in silence with timidity
Looking at each other while expressing the message of spring
But can hear nothing

✧✧✧

19 •

雜詩三首（其三）   王維

已見寒梅發，復聞啼鳥聲。
心心視春草，畏向階前生。

Miscellaneous Poems (No. 3) Wang Wei

Cold plum blossoms are
seen to bloom; birds are

heard to twitter tuneful.
Green grass greets the eye,

with gloom; climb not
onto the steps, withal.

冬望　　　　　　　　　　　　　　林明理

梨花的容顏
是一朵青空的飛雲
水珠在臉上
破曉在一方

初醒後
那蘋果也似的雙頰
充滿天真清脆的笑聲
飄揚迴響
掠過山巔水色

我刻不出這圖騰
後有淺澗
前有石級
一幅冰綃
而開展的宮闕

將茶裡的醇香
吟味與枝頭的精靈

Winter Sight　　　　　　　Lin Ming-Li

The face of the pear flowers
Is a blossom of flying clouds in the blue sky
Water beads on the face
Breaking dawn in the horizon

Upon waking up
The apple-like cheeks
Are full of naïve and crisp laughter
Wafting and echoing
Through waters and across mountaintops

唐詩明理接千載
古今抒情詩三百首
漢英對照

I cannot carve the totem
Behind there is a shallow stream
In front there are stone steps
An ice gauze
And the palace which slowly opens

The mellow flavor of tea
The taste and the spirits atop the branches

✧✧✧

20・

白石灘　　　　　　　　　　　　王維

清淺白石灘，綠蒲向堪把。
家住水東西，浣紗明月下。

The White-Stone Beach　　　Wang Wei

Stones are white in
clear water which seems

shallow; green leaves
of cattail fill the palm

when plucking. Living
upstream and downstream,

the girls are washing
clothes in the moonlight.

流動中的靜謐　　　　　　　　　林明理

三月的傍晚，我撐著
顛簸的夕陽靠岸

浪峰悄然
但街道喧響

我牽著焦煤的夜
信步小山崗
群花叢草
向月亮投遞訊息

而后，我在燈前冥想：
粗糙的草稿
總賦予我堅定沉著
在顫動的夢弦上

Quiet in Motion   Lin Ming-Li

On a March evening, I hold
A bumpy sunset to come ashore
The waves are quiet
But the streets are noisy

I pull the night of coke coal
Strolling in the hills
Alive with flowers and grasses
To deliver messages to the moon

Then, I meditated before the lamp:
The rough draft
Always gives me calm and confidence
On the vibrating strings of dreams

✧ ✧ ✧

唐詩明理接千載
古今抒情詩三百首
漢英對照

21．

田園樂七首（其四）　　　　　　　王維

萋萋芳草春綠，落落長松夏寒。
牛羊自歸村巷，童稚不識衣冠。

Joy in Fields and Gardens (No. 4)
Wang Wei

Spring grass is lushly green;
tall pine trees offer a cold

shade in summer. Oxen
and sheep leisurely return

to their lanes; the children
know no official robes.

晨野　　　　　　　　　　　　　林明理

原野經過一夜的好眠，
決定，探出了頭，
迎接北來的鳴客，
再不容幾番秋雨。

捎起露珠兒採訪他鍾愛的花木，
凝聚片刻，
一泓清泉洗滌他的容顏。

風替他加冕了片片草葉的芬芳，
他跟著莊稼的呼喚，
游進靜謐中。

The Morning Field
Lin Ming-Li

After a nightlong sound sleep,
The field decides to poke out its head,
To welcome a guest from the north,
Not to tolerate a few autumn rains.

Backing dewdrops to interview his favorite flowers and trees,
To condense for a moment,
A clear spring to wash his face.

The wind crowns him with the fragrance from blades of grass,
With the call of crops,
He swims into silence.

✧✧✧

22 •

華子岡 裴迪

落日松風寒，還家草露晞。
雲光侵履跡，山翠拂人衣。

Huazi Mound
Pei Di

The setting sun sees
cold pine wind; I

return home, when
grassy dewdrops are

dried. Cloud light
invades my footsteps,

唐詩明理接千載
古今抒情詩三百首
漢英對照

when mountain green
is kissing my clothes.

山影 林明理

清波給了你明鏡，你柔綠如茵，
我撥開平窗，看不清日暮的蒼黃，
我的沉思，我的心，在風前張望。

當朵朵銀花在激石裡酥碎紛落，
那是從雲梯之下升起的縷縷飛煙，
而我仍懸掛著你頂上的一道彩虹。

The Shadow of Mountains Lin Ming-Li

The clear waves give you a mirror,
and you are soft green
I open the flat window,
but fail to see the dark yellow at dusk,
My meditation, my heart, looking in front of the wind.

When one after another silver flower crumbles
in the rock,
They are the wisps of smoke rising from the ladder,
And I still hang a rainbow above you.

✧✧✧

23 •

宮槐陌 裴迪

門前宮槐陌，是向欹湖道。
秋來山雨多，落葉無人掃。

The Path of Palace Pagoda Trees Pei Di

The path of palace
pagoda trees leads

lakeward. Autumn
witnesses plentiful rain-

fall; with fallen leaves
— without sweepers.

月光小棧之讚 林明理

三月的一個午後,到達月光小棧時,
我用雙臂擁抱大自然,閉目靜聽
圓柱狀的空間中水琴窟的妙音。
真想在都蘭山麓的鳥鳴蝶舞中歡呼,
翠綠叢林和太平洋的湛藍——
都交融成最美的景致。

你說:遠方的綠島
有著世界上最古老的活珊瑚群體,
正以極緩慢的速度移向福爾摩沙……
而我像大冠鷲留戀盤旋不去。
微風習習,天空澄靜,
那轉瞬淡去的暮色 覓得春神的蹤跡。[13]

Ode to a Moonlit Inn Lin Ming-Li

One afternoon in March,
when I arrive at the Moonlight Inn,

---

[13] 位於臺灣臺東縣都蘭山麓的月光小棧,前身是都蘭林場行政中心。懷舊的日式木造建築前可遠眺太平洋的湛藍及遠方的綠島,林木蔥綠,甚為美麗。—寫於 2019.3.11。

I embrace nature with my arms and close my eyes
to listen attentively
To the wonderful sounds of the water harp cave
in the cylindrical space.
I really want to cheer in the bird song and butterfly dance
of the foothills of Duran Mountain,
The green jungle and the blue of the Pacific Ocean —
All blend into the most beautiful scenery.

You say: the distant Green Island
Has the oldest living coral colony in the world,
Moving at a glacial pace towards Formosa…
And I hover like a crowned vulture.
The breeze is gentle, the sky is quiet
And the fading dusk finds the trace of the spring God.[14]

✧✧✧

24 •

宿建德江   孟浩然

移舟泊煙渚，日暮客愁新。
野曠天低樹，江清月近人。

Lodging by Jiande River   Meng Haoran

I pole my boat by a
misty islet: at dusk the

---

[14] Located in the foothills of Dulan Mountain, Taitung County, Taiwan, the Moonlight Inn was formerly the administrative center of Dulan Forest Farm. In front of the nostalgic Japanese wooden building, you can overlook the blue Pacific Ocean and the green island in the distance, which affords beautiful scenery. — Written on March 11, 2019.

wanderer is overcome
by a touch of sorrow.

The boundless field
lowers trees in the

horizon; the moon in
clear river is approachable.

枋寮漁港暮色　　　　　　　　　　　林明理

我想安靜地登上紅燈塔，
用金色波光來點綴討海人
　　奮勇的背影，
同海鷗和寒風一起嬉戲，
　　一起等待黑夜到來。

那時會有夜鷺在溼地的
　　木麻黃上哺育，
有魚兒在夢中發育生長，
而我只想繼續
　　在漁港的柔美中穿行。

—2024.12.16.

Dusk at Fan-Liau Fishing Harbor
Lin Ming-Li

I want to climb up the red light tower quietly,
To adorn the courageous back of the sea people
With golden waves,
To play with the seagulls and the cold wind,
While waiting for the black night.

There will be night herons feeding
On the casuarina in the wetlands,
There are fish growing in their dreams,

And I just want to
Continue to walk through the soft beauty of the fishing harbor.

December 16, 2024.

✧✧✧

25.

詠風 虞世南

逐舞飄輕袖，傳歌共繞梁。
動枝生亂影，吹花送遠香。

Ode to Wind Yu Shinan

Chasing and dancing, gentle
sleeves wafting; a song travels,

lingering about the beam.
Swaying branches produce

riotous shadows; flowers blown,
remote fragrance overflowing.

北風散步的小徑上 林明理

瑩白的夜，溜過原野
顫顫地在風中翩動
遠處是九梅樹橋
繡著一條碧澄的河階

在部落：一片青樹黃花
倒影於香馥的迴頭灣
但等著吧

等吧，這可是藍色的黎明
在迴唱？在久久站立的
曙光中北風散步的小徑上
四面的微茫，如海波
流轉著曠野盡頭的徬徨

當半邊隱滅的星劃過長空
垂落的雲氣，水波不興
我的愛在熙攘之外
遺落的足印，清冷不滅

On the Trail Where the North Wind Strolls
Lin Ming-Li

The white night, slipping across the field
Trembling and fluttering in the wind
In the distance is the Nine Plum Tree Bridge
Embroidered with the steps of a clear river

In the tribe: a stretch of green trees with yellow flowers
Reflected in the fragrant back bay of Huitouwan
But wait
Wait, this is the blue dawn
Singing back? In the long standing
Dawn, along the path of the strolling north wind
Dimness on all sides, like the sea waves
Flowing with the hesitation at the end of the wilderness

When the half disappearing star falls across the sky
The falling clouds, water waves do not stir
My love is beyond the crowd and noises
The lost footprints, cold and immortal

✦✦✦

26・

龍標野宴　　　　　　　　　　王昌齡

沅溪夏夜足涼風，春酒相攜就竹叢。
莫道弦歌愁遠謫，青山明月不曾空。

Picnic in Liaobiao County　Wang Changling

Summer wind blows cool along
Yuan River; in a bamboo grove

we drink wine to our heart's
content. Don't be emotional

at string music and feel sorry
for my being banished to such

a remote place; the bright moon
and green hills are my companions.

旗山老街的黃昏[15]　　　　　　林明理

一條閱盡滄桑但殘存溫暖的路
一幅古樸然而不曾消逝的掛圖
一座天后宮，千萬次的護持淨土
這裡，曾是香蕉王國
這裡，曾是製糖重鎮
未來，仍是否可尋？

---

[15] 旗山位居高雄市中央。此地係日本殖民統治臺灣時期的製糖重鎮，臺灣光復後是香蕉王國。旗山老街以近百年歷史的旗山火車站為起點，由於載客量驟減，旗尾線於 1978 年全面停駛。荒廢後的火車站曾歷經 4 次火災。老街上有指定為歷史建築與仿巴洛克式街屋，此外還有重建後的旗山車站維多利亞式的外貌及哥德式八角斜頂，與旗山區農會、天后宮等文化資產，為臺灣旅遊觀光景點之一。

呵,讓我也向著前人的足音
莫要驚擾我
在浴火重生的站前
讓我與祖靈悄悄對視
像這冬陽眼中沒有一絲貪婪
像那紅燈籠長長地等待著
也許撥動旅人的夢
也許又細訴
那殿前的脊頂
雙龍拜三仙的故事
莫要再喚我
我要淡然而行
輕拾那承雨牆上的淚珠

Dusk of Qishan Old Street[16]　Lin Ming-Li

A road that has witnessed all the vicissitudes of life
but remains warm
An antique wall map that has never disappeared
A Heavenly Queen Palace, protecting the pure land
for thousands of times
Here, it has been a banana kingdom

---

[16] Qishan is located in the center of Kaohsiung City. The area was a major sugar-producing town during the Japanese colonial rule of Taiwan, and after the restoration of Taiwan, it was a banana kingdom. The Qishan Old Street starts from the nearly century-old Qishan Railway Station, and due to a sharp decline in passenger capacity, the Qishan Tail Line was completely closed in 1978. The abandoned railway station has experienced four fires. The old street has designated historical buildings and imitation baroque street houses, in addition to the reconstructed Qishan Station Victorian appearance and Gothic octagonal tilt roof, and Qishan District farmers Association, Tianhou Palace and other cultural assets, one of the tourist attractions in Taiwan.

Here, it has been a sugar town
In the future, can it still be found?
Oh, let me follow the footsteps of predecessors
Do not disturb me
Before the station of rebirth through fire
Let me and the ancestral spirit quietly look at each other
Like the eyes of winter sun without a hint of greed
Like the red lantern which is waiting long
Perhaps moving the dream of the traveler
Perhaps gently telling
The story of the ridge top in front of the temple
Double dragons worshiping three fairies
Do not call me again
I want to go forward in a detached way
While gently picking up the tears on the rainy wall

✧✧✧

27 •

送郭司倉　　　　　　　　　　　王昌齡

映門淮水綠，留騎主人心。
明月隨良掾，春潮夜夜深。

Seeing Off My Friend Guo Sicang
Wang Changling

The green water of Huai River
is reflected upon the door,

where time and again I try
to stay the host without any

effect. The bright moon is his
follower and my heart, like

the spring tide, keeps missing
and yearning from night to night.

大明湖秋思[17]   林明理

連山躺在群泉當中
　　染上深淺不一的綠
你由北水門流過小清河，向東
就要注入渤海了
看哪，在垂柳的岸上
我想拍攝畫舫　徐徐
　　漂向純淨的藍與蔥蘢之間

誰用千萬根銀絲
　　織就這珍珠湖面
誰讓這樓台亭樹　映入你的軀懷
我想循著老殘的腳步
去聽一聽那大鼓曲子
在秋日馳向你的時候
心音是綠的

在歷山腳下，無論度過
幾度寒暑，你依然
霪雨不漲、久旱不涸
啊，大明湖，多美的景致

Autumn Thought at Daming Lake[18]
                                                 Lin Ming-Li

Hills are lying in a group of springs
    Tinctured with different shades of green

---

[17] 大明湖位於中國山東省濟南市的歷下區。
[18] Daming Lake is located in Lixia District, Jinan City, Shandong Province, China.

You run by the north water gate through the little clear river, eastward
To be injected into the Bohai Sea
Look, on the shore of weeping willows
I want to photograph the painted boat   slowly
    Drifting to the pure blue and verdant

With tens of millions of silver silks
    Who weaves the pearl-like lake
Who lets the pavilions to be reflected into your body
I want to follow the old footsteps
To listen to the drum tune
When the autumn sun is galloping to you
The heart sound is green

At the foot of Lishan Mountain, no matter how many
Summers and winters, still you
See rainy days without a flood, a long drought without shortage of water
Ah, Daming Lake, what beautiful scenery

✧✧✧

28 ·

出塞二首（其一） 　　　　　　　　王昌齡

秦時明月漢時關，萬里長征人未還。
但使龍城飛將在，不教胡馬度陰山。

Out of the Frontier (No.1) Wang Changling

The moon of Qin Dynasty and
the pass of Han Dynasty; warriors

who have trekked thousands of
miles to guard the frontiers have

not returned home yet. If the Winged
General of Dragon City is still alive

today, not a single Tartar horseman
dares to cross the Yin Mountain.

戰爭仍茫無盡頭　　　　　　　林明理

如同盲魚在無止境的
黑暗中，
戰爭仍茫無盡頭。
為何戰機轟擊了我的家？
為何連醫院也被摧毀？
為何敘利亞天空之雲
　　　飄浮得如此沉重？
我們的每一步都走在歷史上，
難民的嚴冬，風徹夜蕭瑟。

　　　　　　　　　　　　－2018.1.19

Still No End of the War　　Lin Ming-Li

Like a blind fish
In the endless darkness,
Still no end of the war.
Why the fighter jet has bombarded my home?
Why even the hospitals were destroyed?
Why the clouds in the Syrian sky
　　　Are floating so heavily?
Our every step becomes history,
In the winter of refugees, the wind is blowing through the night.

✧✧✧

29．

涼州詞　　　　　　　　　　　王之渙

黃河遠上白雲間，一片孤城萬仞山。
羌笛何須怨楊柳，春風不度玉門關。

A Border Song　　　　　　Wang Zhihuan

The Yellow River runs
afar into white clouds,

a lonely town amid soaring
peaks. Why should the

minority flute blame
the willows? Spring wind

never blows beyond
the Jade Gate Pass.

甘南，你寬慰地向我呼喚[19]　　　林明理

　　甘南，你寬慰地向我呼喚：「到這邊來吧，」你說。
　　於是，我遠從彼岸越過海洋，在雪域高原與你相遇。在聖湖前，匆匆留下一吻，好似輕落的灰雁，香巴拉的春天。
　　甘南，你寬慰地向我呼喚：「到這邊來吧，」你說。
　　我們已久候了五百年。是的。你永遠像僧侶般——沉靜而年輕。而我的眼眸不住地回想，永遠像雲般深情。
　　甘南，你寬慰地向我呼喚：「到這邊來吧，」你說。

---

[19] 甘南藏族自治州，簡稱甘南州，是中國甘肅省下轄的一個自治州。位於甘肅省的南部，青藏高原東北，黃河上游。

我們的草原茵茵，我們的清泉傾訴著愛情的話語，鮮鮮河水，群山依依，這就是我們溫暖的家居。
　　甘南，你寬慰地向我呼喚：「到這邊來吧，」你說。
　　那兒有黃河第一彎，再往東南，便到郎木寺前。我在一起一落間，像蝴蝶徜徉於大地，重新笑了……
　　甘南，你寬慰地向我呼喚：「到這邊來吧，」你說。
　　七仙女又採摘野花了，一朵朵——唱給聖湖聽，唱給陽光。唱給所有山山水水，唱給我。讓我輕輕靠近你的夢。
　　甘南，你寬慰地向我呼喚：「到這邊來吧，」你說。
　　六月，是最好的季節，牧場裡肉香奶甜，多麼欽羨！我再也不必嫉妒，因你永遠會妝扮這古老傳統的佳節。
　　甘南，你寬慰地向我呼喚：「到這邊來吧，」你說。
　　當熊熊柏火燃起，我們起舞、賽馬或摔跤，歌聲熱誠而俊美。你會聽到我的祈禱，恰似嘹亮的拉也，直到聽不見黎明的號笛。
　　甘南，你寬慰地向我呼喚：「到這邊來吧，」你說。
　　西梅朵合灘的花，在你的懷抱裡緩緩盛開了。我在飛，清風吹拂，眾鳥飛躍，瑪曲的純真，無法忘卻……
　　甘南，你寬慰地向我呼喚：「到這邊來吧，」你說。
　　這是你孕育的牧民，這是你熟悉的青稞酒，這是你飛翔過的佛塔與森林，在你嬉戲過的沼澤，每一處生物都記得你的容貌。
　　啊，甘南，在我們即將分別的時刻，我沒有哭泣……
　　因為每年春末夏初，成群的草原百靈想念我的時候，那是我的目光——它就像守望的星辰，直想你雄壯的歡樂。

Gannan, You Call to Me in Relief[20]

Lin Ming-Li

    Gannan, you call to me in relief:"Come here," you say.
    So, I cross the ocean from the other side to meet you in the snowy plateau. In front of the holy lake, hurriedly leaving a kiss, like a gently falling gray goose, the spring of Shambhala.
    Gannan, you call to me in relief: "Come here," you say.
    We've been waiting for 500 years. Yes, you are always like a monk — quiet and young. And my eyes keep recalling, forever as deep as clouds.
    Gannan, you call to me in relief: "Come here," you say.
    Our grassland is lush, and our spring pours out the words of love, fresh rivers, lovely mountains; this is our warm home.
    Gannan, you call to me in relief: "Come here," you say.
    There is the first bend of the Yellow River, and then to the southeast, you come to Langmu Temple. During the up and down, I, like a butterfly flying on the earth, am smiling again...
    Gannan, you call to me in relief: "Come here," you say.
    The seven fairies are picking wildflowers again, one after another — sing to the holy lake, and to the sun. Sing

---

[20] Gannan Tibetan Autonomous Prefecture, referred to as Gannan Prefecture, is an autonomous prefecture under the jurisdiction of Gansu Province, China. It is located in the southern part of Gansu province, northeast of the Qinghai-Tibet Plateau and upstream of the Yellow River.

to all the mountains; sing to me. Let me gently approach your dream.

Gannan, you call to me in relief: "Come here," you say.

June is the best season, the pasture is rich with milk and meat, how admirable it is! I need not be jealous any more, for you will always adorn the ancient tradition.

Gannan, you call to me in relief: "Come here," you say.

We dance, race, wrestle, sing cordially and beautifully when the fire is blazing. You will hear my prayer, like the sound of a siren, until you no longer hear the trumpet of the dawn.

Gannan, you call to me in relief: "Come here," you say.

The flowers of Ximeiduohe Beach are slowly blooming in your arms. I am flying, the wind blowing, the birds flying, the innocence of Maqu, unforgetable...

Gannan, you call to me in relief: "Come here," you say.

This is the herdsmen you give birth to, this is the barley wine you are familiar with, this is the stupa and forest over which you have ever flown; the swamp you play in, every living thing remembers your face.

O Gannan, when we are about to depart, I do not weep...

Because every year at the end of spring and the beginning of summer, when groups of grassland larks are missing me, it is my eyes — it is like the watchful stars, always thinking of your magnificent joy.

✧✧✧

30．

登鸛雀樓　　　　　　　　　王之渙

白日依山盡，黃河入海流。
欲窮千里目，更上一層樓。

Ascending the Stork Tower　Wang Zhihuan

The light is dimming as the
golden beams begin to disappear

from the mountain tops, which
are to swallow up the white

sun; the Yellow River is emptying
itself into the sea. To enjoy a

panoramic view, climb —
climb up to a greater height.

珠江，我怎能停止對你的嚮往[21]　　林明理

珠江，我怎能停止對你的嚮往
你有著最最美麗名字
孕育了多少個靈動的魂
青山點點錯落
銀波淼淼，江水絢爛
這白晝的序曲
像漂泊的詩行凝結在高塔傍
我怎能不投下一次次的驚嘆

---

[21] 珠江，又名奧江，是廣州的母親河；其下游的沖積平原是著名的珠江三角洲，具有南國水鄉的獨特風貌。

那無以數計的帆
雖然一概寂默
但無論置身何處
嶺南依舊在那兒
散發著豐富的意涵
河海交匯的影跡
我又怎能從記憶裡一筆抹去

啊我就像一尾飛魚
在闌珊燈火處
就這樣幾小時地
靜聽珠江在夜裡的呼吸
當月光照在大橋中
有一種思念
正緩緩划過天空,跨越兩岸

Pearl River, How Can I Stop Longing for You[22]

Lin Ming-Li

Pearl River, how can I stop longing for you
You have the most beautiful name
Gestation of how many clever souls
Blue mountains like scattered dots
Silver waves and brilliant rivers
The overture of the day
Like the wandering lines of poetry coagulated by the tower
How can I not cast a wonder after another wonder

The countless sails
Though silent

---

[22] The Pearl River, also known as Aojiang, is the mother river of Guangzhou. Its downstream alluvial plain is the famous Pearl River Delta, with the unique features of southern water towns.

唐詩明理接千載
古今抒情詩三百首
漢英對照

Wherever they are
The Southern Range is still there
With its rich meaning
The shadow of the meeting of the sea and river
How can I erase it from my memory

Ah, I am like a flying fish
In the place of dim light
Thus for several hours
Silently listen to the breathing of the Pearl River in the night
When the moonlight shines in the bridge
There is a kind of yearning
Which is slowly crossing the sky, over the two sides

✧✧✧

31 •

夜宿山寺　　　　　　　　　　　　李白

危樓高百尺，手可摘星辰。
不敢高聲語，恐驚天上人。

Spending Night in a Mountain Temple
Li Bai

The imposing temple towers
heavenward; the hard night

sky, throbbing with stars,
is within reach and the

twinkling stars are quite
close at hand. Not a breath

stirs the chill quiet, lest
people in heaven be startled.

靜寂的黃昏　　　　　　　　　　　　　　林明理

一隻秋鷺立著，它望著遠方。
萋萋的蘆葦上一葉扁舟。
對岸：羊咩聲，鼓噪四周的蛙鳴。
它輕輕地振翅飛走，
羽毛散落苗田，
彷彿幾絲村舍的炊煙。

The Silent Dusk　　　　　　　　Lin Ming-Li

An egret is standing, gazing far away.
Among luxuriant reeds there is a small leaf-like boat.
The other shore, the gentle baaing of sheep and the croaking
of frogs far and near.
Fluttering its wings, the egret flies away,
Its feathers scattering in the field,
Like the threads of smoke from the chimneys of cottage
kitchens.

✧✧✧

32 ·

玉階怨　　　　　　　　　　　　　　　　李白

玉階生白露，夜久侵羅襪。
卻下水晶簾，玲瓏望秋月。

Grievances of Jewel Stairs   Li Bai

White dew grows heavy
on jewel stairs, which

soaks silk stockings deep
into the night. Crystal

curtain is let down to
shut out the light, before

she casts a lingering
glance at the moon.

在交織與遺落之間   林明理

秋夜在交織與遺落之間徘徊，
與它暈染的霜葉相戀。
那是我曾在夢境中尋覓過的
世界在那裡是寂靜的
只要我想許願，它就近在咫尺
又何必捨近慕遠？

在那裡，一切都可顯現——
風語，胡楊，長河，月亮灣…
都歇息於喚你名字的輪迴。
然後在遠離牧道的地方，我醒來
時間卻已重複
像駝鈴般同樣孤零的音旋。

是光把冰冷的書頁轉變成
青鳥悠然遨翔於雲天，
讓我的思想越過了彩虹——
尋覓一處如你盯視的眼眸的重疊。

如果愛情也能時刻散佈
那麼，為何我仍停頓又走動於人間？

Between Interweaving and Oblivion
       Lin Ming-Li

The autumn night lingers between interweaving and oblivion,
In love with its frosty leaves.
It is what I have been in search in my dreams
The world there is silent
So long as I wish, it is close by me
Why adore something afar instead of near?

There, everything can be revealed —
The words of wind, the poplar, the river,
the Moon Bay…
All rest in the cycle of calling your name.
Then, far from the pasture, I wake up
Yet time is repeating itself
The solitary tune like a camel bell.

It is the light that turns the cold pages of the book
Into a blue bird that flies in the clouds
While sending my thoughts through the rainbow —
To seek an overlap of eyes like yours.
If love can be spread all the time
Then, why do I still stop and walk in the world?

✧✧✧

33．

  勞勞亭   李白

天下傷心處，勞勞送客亭。
春風知別苦，不遣柳條青。

The Parting Pavilion   Li Bai

The most heart-
breaking spot is

the Parting Pavilion.
Even the spring wind

knows the pain: willow
twigs are not greened.

思念似雪花緘默地飛翔   林明理

思念似雪花緘默地飛翔
從地球彼端
沿著一條直線
穿越長長的山巒和河水
來回走動
引我期盼
就這樣把它迎進了門窗

我是顆渺小的水滴
自我耽溺於
一片廣闊的天空
當我緩緩地搖晃
落在大雪漫天的夜晚
啊，我想要歡呼
有什麼比得上你強大的靈魂
和那神采奕奕的光芒

—2022.12.27.

Thoughts Fly Silently Like Snowflakes
Lin Ming-Li

Thoughts fly silently like snowflakes
From the other side of the earth
Along a straight line
Through meandering mountains and rivers
Back and forth
Leading me to look forward
And welcome them into my door and window

I am a tiny drop of water
Self-indulged
In the boundless sky
When I shake slowly
In the snowy night
Ah I want to cheer
There is nothing like your strong soul
And the resplendent light

✧✧✧

34 •

早發白帝城　　　　　　　　　　李白

朝辭白帝彩雲間，千里江陵一日還。
兩岸猿聲啼不住，輕舟已過萬重山。

Morning Departure from White King City
Li Bai

In the morning I leave White
King City, crowned with

唐詩明理接千載
古今抒情詩三百首
漢英對照

clouds; in the same day I reach
Jiangling, which is hundreds

of miles away. The monkeys
are crying along the banks,

when my boat has passed
through thousands of mountains.

奔騰的河流　　　　　　　　　　林明理

在你無羈的蛇行中
　　從源頭來到出海口
有許多部落棲息著。
我像匹馬
　　豎耳傾聽，
那昏暗的林冠層下
　　　是雨林和沼澤，
有鼓聲喧響
──族人歡舞；
　　分享古老的傳說。

哦，奔騰的河流
　　鹹水鱷的出沒
　　峽谷的濃霧
　　種子的呼吸
　　禽鳥展翼之中
我想跟著你奔跑
　　　跳躍；
未來的困難是不可避免的，
但沒有目標，
就不算是英雄。

The Torrential Stream Lin Ming-Li

Stretching like a snake
   From the source to the entrance of the sea
There are a great number of tribal inhabitants.
I, like a horse
   Listen to the drumbeats,
Under the dark canopy
The clans are dancing,
   Sharing an age-old legend.

Oh, torrential stream
   The appearance and disappearance
   Of salt water crocodiles
   Heavy fog in the canyon
   The breath of seeds
   The flapping wings of birds
I want to run with you
   And jump;
The future difficulties are inevitable,
But without a goal
There won't be any hero.

✧✧✧

35 ·

望廬山瀑布 李白

日照香爐生紫煙，遙看瀑布掛前川。
飛流直下三千尺，疑是銀河落九天。

Watching the Waterfall of Mount Lu

Li Bai

Incense Burner is curling with
purple smoke in the sunshine.

A waterfall pours into the river:
viewed from afar it is like a

piece of white cloth hanging
three thousand feet, which is

suggestive of the Silver River
tumbling down from Heaven.

南湖溪之歌[23]

林明理

是自由的風不停地
　　帶著我
來到中央山脈的最深之處。
白雲躺在水裡，
　　花間野鳥妝點了高灘地。
小小山屋，在圈谷的邊緣⋯
南湖溪，你漾蕩的影子
　　在樹群和青草上晃動著。
沿溪而下，芒草林瑟瑟縮縮。
當風吹過
　　環山部落的吊橋，
我聽見了更高、更遠

---

[23] 南湖溪是台灣高山河川，流域位於台中市和平區，為中央山脈第三高峰、在著名的台灣百岳之中，南湖大山與玉山、雪山、秀姑巒山、北大武山合稱「五岳」，為台灣最具代表性的五座高山。而保育的山椒魚已在地球存活了三億年，預計在未來十年，櫻花鉤吻鮭也會在此當作放流鮭魚的路線，實值得我們高度的期待。—寫於 2018.12.3.

更原始的山區,
有山椒魚和櫻花鉤吻鮭
　　在看不見的群峰裡的回聲。
我聽見了泰雅族耆老
　　在尋找兒時記憶的低語。
我聽見了水意和月光
　　向著碎石坡,循環往復。
我聽到了松林任由季節的更迭,
　　仍用深情的目光守望著⋯
　　這一片野色如夢。
我聽到了海拔森林的呼喚,
　　那胡麻花的幻影,
　　那雲霧嬝繞的巨木步道,
　　那北國印象的天然雪景,
　　那屋宇層疊相間的山谷部落,
有我無盡的思念⋯在暮色中,
　　　　在時光之外。

Song of South Lake Creek[24]　　Lin Ming-Li

It is the winds of freedom
　　That carry me
To the deepest parts of the Central Mountains.

---

[24] Nanhu River is a high mountain river in Taiwan, located in the Heping District of Taichung City. It is the third highest peak in the Central Mountains. Among the famous mountains in Taiwan, Nanhu Mountain is called the "Five Mountains" together with Yushan Mountain, Xueshan Mountain, Xiugushan Mountain and Peiwu Mountain, which are the five most representative mountains in Taiwan. The conservation of the mountain pepper fish has survived on the earth for 300 million years, and it is expected that in the next ten years, cherry hook salmon will also be used as a route for the release of salmon, which is worth our expectations.
— Written on December 3, 2018.

White clouds lie in the water,
　　And wild birds in flowers decorate the beach.
A little hill house, on the edge of the valley…
South Lake Stream, your rippling shadow
　　Is shaking on the trees and grass.
Down the stream, the miscanthus forest is shivering.
When the wind blows
　　Over the drawbridge around the Mountain tribe,
I could hear the echoes of higher, farther
　　And more pristine mountains,
The unseen peaks of the mountain
　　Pepper fish and the sakura salmon.
I hear the whispers of the Atayal elders
　　Searching for their childhood memories.
I heard the water and the moon
　　Moving time and again up the gravel slope.
I hear the pine forest which is free to seasonal changes,
　　Still I watch with loving eyes…
　　　　The wild color of this place is like a dream.
I hear the call of the altitude forest,
　　The illusion of the flumes,
　　The giant wooden walk curling in the clouds,
　　The natural snow scene of northern impression,
　　The valley tribes with overlapping house layers,
I have endless thoughts... in the twilight,
　　Beyond time.

✧✧✧

36．

黃鶴樓送孟浩然之廣陵　　　　　李白

故人西辭黃鶴樓，煙花三月下揚州。
孤帆遠影碧空盡，惟見長江天際流。

Seeing My Friend Off at Yellow Crane Tower
Li Bai

My friend Meng Haoran
leaves the Yellow Crane Tower

in the west to Yangzhou in
mist-veiled April. Your lonely

sail sails until it is a mere speck
against the boundless blue sky,

when Yangtze River is rolling
endlessly in the horizon.

在那恬靜的海灣
林明理

曙光下
平靜的海灘上
漂流木打成的一個愛心，──
鐫刻著平安的烙印…
　…正微笑著向我接近

它較不為人知
　卻藏著南國海岸的風情
綠島也躺在海平線的那端
就像靠在母親的臂膀，──
　靜靜地諦聽
山海的一些古老神話

而我低頭看見雨後水窪中
小小的漣漪，還有天光雲影
啊，那來自山嵐的樂音
　輕輕地撥動我…

恰如被一朵浪花擁抱，——
　　使我莫明感動。

In the Quiet Bay 　　　　　　　　Lin Ming-Li

Under the dawn
On the calm beach
A loving heart made of driftwood —
Engraved with the brand of peace…
　　…Is approaching me with a smile

It is less known
　　But hidden with the flavor of the southern coast
The green island is also lying on the horizon
Like lying in Mother's arms —
　　Quietly listening
To some of the ancient myths of the seas & mountains

And I look down to see the small ripples
In the puddles after the rain, and clouds in the sky
Ah, the music from the mountains
　　Gently touching me…
As if embraced by a blossom of spray —
　　And I am touched for no reason.

✧✧✧

37 ·

望天門山　　　　　　　　　　　　　　李白

天門中斷楚江開，碧水東流至此回。
兩岸青山相對出，孤帆一片日邊來。

Viewing Tianmen Mountain Li Bai

The Heavenly Gate Mountain
is cut into two halves by

Yangtze River; the green
water, charging eastward,

here turns northward. Two
green hills facing each other,

when a solitary sail sails
slowly from the horizon.

菜斯河向晚 林明理

在我心中有一座岸橋
橋上長廊,橫跨雪河的閃蕩
立在垛樓上
陽光如幻影
蝶般地被妝點成暮雲
棲息在山崗外,掠過星斗

當晚鐘輕輕喚醒
最深記憶底的
是每自回首的名字
我試圖將往事
藏在忍冬蔦蘿的
葉堆,隨舟子悠然自得

The Rio Tarcoles River Toward the Evening Lin Ming-Li

In my heart there is a shore bridge
On a long corridor, a flash across a snowy river

On the palletico
The sun is like a phantom
Like a butterfly to be painted into dusk clouds
Perching beyond the hills, skimming over the stars

When the evening clock gently awakens
From the bottom of the deepest memory
The name of each backward glance
I try to hide the past
In a pile of honeysuckle
Leaves, leisurely with the boat

✧✧✧

38 ·

春夜洛城聞笛　　　　　　　　李白

誰家玉笛暗飛聲，散入春風滿洛城。
此夜曲中聞折柳，何人不起故園情？

Fluting in Luoyang in a Spring Night
Li Bai

From which home comes
the stealthy fluting?

Wafting in spring wind,
it spreads to the whole

city of Luoyang. Hearing
the tune of *Breaking*

Willows, who can refrain
from missing his hometown?

致貓頭鷹的故鄉－水里[25]　　　　林明理

灼灼星光在彼處璀燦
　　霎時間
夢中的翅膀　飛入
貓頭鷹的故鄉

心關閉
是否再不會感到被土石淹沒了的痛
亦或
近在咫尺的你　就是沉定的力量

啊，多麼美麗的風中之花
　　舞蹈於部落的向晚
我在冰霧中等待
　　等待朝陽依然徐徐爬上山梁

To Shuili: the Home of Owls[26] Lin Ming-Li

The twinkling stars are shining in the distance
　　In an instant
The dreamy wings　fly into
The hometown of owls

The heart is closed
Or it will no longer feel the pain of being submerged by earth and stone
Or
In the close neighborhood you are the quiet power

Ah, what beautiful flowers in the wind

---

[25] 車埕位於臺灣南投縣水里鄉，傳說是鳥居的故鄉。
[26] Checheng is located in Shuili Township, Nantou County, Taiwan. It is said to be the hometown of birds.

Dancing in the tribe's evening
I am waiting in the mist and ice
Waiting for the morning sun to creep up the mountain beam

✧✧✧

39・

螢火　　　　　　　　　　　　　　李白

雨打燈難滅，風吹色更明；
若飛天上去，定做月邊星。

The Firefly　　　　　　　　　　Li Bai

The rain cannot smother
your fire; swept by

wind, you are brighter.
If you fly to the sky on

high, you'll be viewed
as a moon-side star.

咏撫順　　　　　　　　　　　　林明理

還記得嗎？
紅河谷的野花開了，
又謝。
一隻隻雀鳥
輕盈跳躍——
棲息在
壘石的樹梢。

看，城人怎歌著你的，
如果你側耳聽：
風依舊呼嘯，
一切過去的
無數悲喜與舊事。
讓我飛去吧，像雲那般，
鼓起豐羽的風帆，
鳥瞰溪谷和河道
鳥瞰花葉和獸鳥

當秋月懸掛枝頭，
而我想親近你的時候
那四季的足音，
就像遙遠的時光之機，
馱來你的訊息。
你讓每度春光都帶來幸福的圖彩，
你讓每一窗花都把輕浮關在城外。

還記得嗎？
紅河谷的野花開了，
又謝。
原來　那門前老樹
依舊傳來
生機昂然的歌謠⋯

Ode to Fushun　　　　　　　　Lin Ming-Li

Do you remember?
The wildflowers in the Red River Valley are blooming,
Before withering.
One after another bird
Are hopping lightly —
Perching on
The treetops of the rock.

唐詩明理接千載
古今抒懷詩三百首
漢英對照

See, how the city sings to you,
If you listen attentively:
The wind still whistles,
All the countless joys and sorrows
And the old things of the past.
Let me fly, like the clouds,
With their plumed sails,
With a bird's eye view of the valleys and rivers
And of the flowers and birds & beasts

When the autumn moon hangs over the branches,
And I want to be close to you,
The four seasons' footings,
Are like the time machines of the distant past,
Carrying your message.
You let every spring light bring happiness,
You let every window flower shut frivolity without the city.

Do you remember?
The wildflowers of the Red River Valley is blooming
Before withering
It turns out from the old tree
In front of the door still
Travels a vibrant song…

✧✧✧

40 ·

夜下征虜亭　　　　　　　　　　　李白

船下廣陵去，月明征虜亭。
山花如繡頰，江火似流螢。

120

Heading for Zhenglu Pavilion in the Moonlight
Li Bai

The boat heading for
Guangling, when Zhenglu

Pavilion is bathed in
moonlight. Mountain

flowers are fair like
girls' powdered faces;

lamps on fishing boats
are like flitting fireflies.

漫步在烏鎮的湖邊[27]
林明理

漫步在烏鎮的湖邊
你的古樸滄桑
總是真實,沒有虛妄
那可是白牆黛瓦
或是巷裡瀉出的月光

我聽到輕微的花鼓聲
或近或遠,牽引著我
那熟悉的藍染
一如往昔樸素靜致
你的笑容使月嬌羞
比三白酒更醇厚清純

漫步在烏鎮的湖邊
我心宛似歌雀
在黑暗之中歌頌

---

[27] 烏鎮位於中國浙江省銅鄉市,是江南著名古鎮之一。

你的古樸滄桑
不再憂愁，欣欣燃亮

Walk by the Lake in Wuzhen[28]

Lin Ming-Li

Walk by the lake of Wuzhen
Your simple vicissitudes of life
Are always real, no vanity,
But it is the white wall & blue tiles
Or the moonlight pouring out of the lane

I hear a slight flower drum sound
Near or far, pulling my
Familiar blue dye
As in the past simple and quiet
Your smile overshadows the moon
More pure and mellow than the liquor

Walk by the lake of Wuzhen,
My heart is like a sparrow
Singing in the dark
Your simple vicissitudes of life
No longer sad, joyfully lighting up

✧ ✧ ✧

41 ·

憶東山二首（其一）

李白

不向東山久，薔薇幾度花。
白雲還自散，明月落誰家。

---

[28] Wuzhen is located in Tongxiang City, Zhejiang Province, China. It is one of the famous ancient towns in south China.

Two Poems about the East Mountain (No. 1)
Li Bai

Long time not to the East Mountain, roses blossom

and wither time and again. White clouds disperse by

themselves; the bright moon, falling into which courtyard?

冬憶——泰雅族祖靈祭[29]
林明理

冬日,每一想起祖靈祭
風在流霞間悠悠地轉
在一片空曠而蒼茫的平疇上
我也向著歸巢的鷗兒
向著你的純淨　深邃張望

神啊,你是否也步履微醺
聆聽那部落長老們對吟

---

[29] 泰雅族的族名〈Atayal〉,原意為「勇敢的人」。傳說中,其祖先的起源,首先是於雪山山脈大霸尖山。其傳統舉行 Buling nutx〈靈祭祖〉的季節是小米收割後,將新穀貢獻祖靈的祭祀。祖靈祭舉行的時間,由頭目或長老開會商議後;晚上,要先做好蒸糯米飯(Sumul)、糯米年糕(Tnapaq-rhkil),以及糯米酒(Quaw-Tayal)等祭物。族人在天未亮、雞啼三聲時,幾乎同時抵達離部落不遠的祭場。他們手持竹棒,串刺上糕肉、水果、玉米,或用蕉葉包裹等祭物與酒,為獻給祖靈之供品,定位後就開始召喚祖靈。祭典結束的祭品向來是不帶回家的,直到天色逐漸明亮時,才開始送客。他們送客時,是用大聲的叫喊,叫著:「Usa la-usa la-」(回去吧!回去吧!)。歸途前族人須跨越火堆,以示與祖靈分隔,或象徵著汙穢的潔淨,才陸續踏回部落。

唐詩明理接千載
古今抒情詩三百首
漢英對照

當熊熊的營火升起
頭目開始獻祭
溫暖了多少遊子的心

我知道你遙指發祥村而不語
而我卻只能跪下雙膝
我知道你閉上眼，在暗空
在浩漫宇宙裡為勇士舞而舒坦
直到黎明，你的雙手，像山之臂，
再次迎接苦痛的陽光……

而我知道，那浮雲將沿著你的影子
繼續為沒有盡頭的明天
用清澈的眼睛，寂寞地迴轉。

Winter Memory: Tai Ya Ancestral Sacrifice
            Lin Ming-Li

In winter, at the thought of the ancestral spirit festival
The wind is flowing leisurely in the clouds
In an empty and vast field
Towards the nest-ward gulls
Towards your purity a profound look

Oh deity, do you also walk tipsy
And listen to the singing of tribal elders
When the raging campfire is roaring
The leaders begin to offer sacrifices
How many wandering hearts are warmed

I know that you point to the village in silence
While I kneel down on my knees
I know that you close your eyes in the dark sky
Dancing comfortably for the warriors in the vast universe
Until dawn, your hands, like the arms of the mountain,
Again welcome the painful sun....

And I know, the clouds will continue along
Your shadow to turn lonely
With clear eyes, for the endless tomorrow. [30]

✧✧✧

42 ·

宣城見杜鵑花　　　　　　　　　李白

蜀國曾聞子規鳥，宣城還見杜鵑花。
一叫一回腸一斷，三春三月憶三巴。

Azalea Flowers in Xuancheng　Li Bai

In the state of Shu cuckoo
is heard; in the town of

---

[30] The Ayal's clan name, "Atayal" means "brave people". According to legend, the origin of its ancestors is first in the snow mountain range Daba Jian Mountain. The traditional season for Buling nutx is when millet is harvested and the new grain is sacrificed to the ancestors. The time for holding the ancestral rites shall be discussed by the leaders or elders at a meeting. In the evening, sacrifices such as steamed glutinous rice (Sumul), tnapak-rhkil (glutinous rice cake), and Quaw-Tayal (glutinous rice wine) are made. The people arrived at the sacrifice ground not far from the tribe almost at the same time, before dawn and with the crow of the chickens. They hold bamboo sticks, skewer cake meat, fruit, corn, or wrapping banana leaves and other sacrifices and wine, as offerings to the ancestral spirit, after positioning, begin to summon the ancestral spirit. The sacrificial offerings at the end of the festival are never taken home until the day begins to brighten. When they see them off, they shout loudly, "usa la-usa la-" (Go back!Go back!) . Before returning home, the people must cross the fire to show their separation from the ancestral spirit, or symbolizing the cleanliness of the unclean, before stepping back into the tribe.

Xuancheng azalea flowers
are seen. The first cry

of cuckoo renders me
heartbroken; the fourth

moon of spring alas,
arouses my homesickness.

蓮　　　　　　　　　　　　　　　　林明理

霜化後那片緋紅，你像
滿園的綠，臨風微顫
湖光歷歷使人愁……

The Lotus　　　　　　　　　Lin Ming-Li

After the frost the crimson, you like
A gardenful of green, trembling in the wind
The vivid lake light saddens people…

✧✧✧

43 •

送陸判官往琵琶峽　　　　　　　　李白

水國秋風夜，殊非遠別時。
長安如夢裡，何日是歸期？

Seeing a Judge Off to the Lute Gorge
　　　　　　　　　　　　　　　　　Li Bai

The night of the land of
water where autumn wind

is blowing is unsuitable
for parting. The capital

appears to be in a dream;
when is the date of return?

北風 　　　　　　　　　　　　　　　　林明理

經了萬年雪
再遠的路
也會奮起攀過
彼岸遙望

輕雲在山口等待
故鄉的面孔愈來愈清
在無止盡的漂泊裡
眼睛偶爾也會隱隱作痛

一顆孤星仍在亭臺
在茱萸依然盈手的階下
閃著如朝露般的未來

The North Wind 　　　　　　Lin Ming-Li

Through ten thousand years of snow
No matter how far the road
Will appear for climbing
Looking from the other shore

The light clouds are waiting in the mountain pass
The face of hometown is more and more clear
In the endless wandering
There is occasional dull pain in the eyes

唐詩明理接千載
古今抒情詩三百首
漢英對照

A lone star is still standing in the pavilion
Under the steps of a handful of dogwood
Brilliant is the future like morning dew

❖❖❖

44 •

觀放白鷹 　　　　　　　　　　　　李白

八月邊風高，胡鷹白錦毛。
孤飛一片雪，百里見秋毫。

Letting the White Eagle Fly Away
Li Bai

August witnesses high
wind on the border;

the eagle here is white-
plumed. A solitary flight

makes a single flake
of snow; discernible

are its fine feathers
hundreds of miles away.

棉花嶼之歌 　　　　　　　　　　　林明理

在浪潮的夾縫間，
　　眾鳥疾行；
海芙蓉，似棉花般綻放。
我凝望，
　　那矗立不搖的燈塔，

心中揣測濤聲的奧妙。
若是春天
大水薙的巢洞裡，──
　　　幼鳥已茁壯吧。
牠會在風頭浪尖上
　開始低空飛翔或
　　　　水上漂浮著？
而我也想　藉著月光，
輕輕繞過岩石和斷崖……
　　　越過山峰的最遠處，
看清北方三島的容貌。[31]

The Song of Mianhua Island　Lin Ming-Li

In the crevices of the tide,
　　　Birds speed;
Sea hibiscus bloom like cotton.
I stare
　　　At the lighthouse standing firm,
Wondering in the heart the mystery of the waves.
If it is spring
In the nest hole of water —
　　　The young bird has grown strong.
Atop the waves he
　　　Will start flying low
　　　　　Or floating on the water？
And I want to by the moonlight
Gently glide around rocks and cliffs....

---

[31] 棉花嶼 Mianhua，位於臺灣基隆的外海。其名稱取自海鳥眾多，宛如棉絮飛揚而名之。與花瓶嶼 Huaping Islet、彭佳嶼 Pengjia Islet 合稱北方三島；島上有珍貴的保育類鳥種玄燕鷗 Brown Noddy、白眉燕鷗 Bridled Tern、遊隼 Peregrine 和稀珍大水薙鳥 Streaked Shearwater，生態很豐富。

Across the furthest distance of the peak,
To see the visage of the three islands in the north.[32]

✧✧✧

45 ·

別董大二首（其一）　　　　　　　　高適

千里黃雲白日曛，北風吹雁雪紛紛。
莫愁前路無知己，天下誰人不識君？

Farewell to a Bosom Friend　　Gao Shi

Yellow clouds extending thousands
of miles dim the white sun,

the wild geese against snow
whirling in the blowing of

north wind. No worry: on your
way ahead there will be new

friends, since your fame as a
musician spreads far and wide.

我將獨行　　　　　　　　　　　　林明理

多少次
我們走過這小徑，

---

[32] Mianhua Island is located in the open sea of Keelung, Taiwan. Its name comes from the numerous seabirds, like flying cotton wool. Together with Huaping Islet and Pengjia Islet, it is called the three northern Islands. The island is rich in ecology with rare conservation bird species such as Brown Noddy, Bridled Tern, Peregrine and rare Streaked Shearwater.

月寂寂。山脈諦聽著海音
夜鷺緩踱

大海看似平靜
肥沃的田野睡在星輝中
總是相視、無語
細碎的足聲踏響整個天際

今日，我將獨行――
依然走在這條舊路
你已遠去，而我心悠悠
重逢是未來歲月的憂愁

I Will Walk Alone   Lin Ming-Li

How many times
We have walked through the trail,
The moon is silent. The mountains are listening to the sound of the sea,
A night heron is pacing slowly.

The sea seems calm,
The fertile field sleeps soundly in the starlight.
Always looking at each other, wordless,
The sound of our footsteps echoes across the sky.

Today, I will walk alone —
Still along the old trail,
You are gone, and lingering is my heart
Reunion is the worries of the future years.

✧✧✧

唐詩明理接千載
古今抒情詩三百首
漢英對照

46·

塞上聽吹笛 　　　　　　　　　　　高適

雪淨胡天牧馬還，月明羌笛戍樓間。
借問梅花何處落，風吹一夜滿關山。

Fluting at the Frontier 　　　Gao Shi

At the frontier where ice and
snow melt, pasture horses

return; in bright moonlight
sentry post is overflowing

with fluting. Whence plum
blossoms drop and fall?

Throughout the night the wind
is blowing them from hill to hill.

山問 　　　　　　　　　　　　　林明理

穿越千年孤寂
擇取唯一希望
棲息於島嶼

雨，滴在塔樓
串成妳的名字
古堡將所有祕密
折疊成我的詞曲

然後慢慢地
藏進滿天星與隔著的
海灣，對望。

Questions in the Mountain   Lin Ming-Li

Through a thousand years of solitude
To choose the only hope
To perch on an island

Raindrops drop on towers
To string your name
The ancient castle folds
All secrets into my songs

Then slowly
To hide into a skyful of stars and
Across the bay, mutual gazing.

✧✧✧

47 ·

題汾橋邊柳   岑參

此地曾居住，今來宛似歸。
可憐汾上柳，相見也依依。

To Riverside Willows   Cen Shen

Once a dweller
here, now like

home return.
The riverside

willows linger
at sight of me.

和平的使者—To Prof. Ernesto Kahan
林明理

你的眼睛深邃如海
閃著一種天藍的自由
當世界的、戰地鐘聲又起
你穿過風雨前來
感嘆唱著歌曲
那白袍下的熱血
深入最需要的世界各角落
如同現代史懷哲

—2016.3.13

A Peacemaker: to Prof. Ernesto Kahan[33]

Lin Ming-Li

Your eyes are deep like the blue sea
Shining with some sky-blue freedom
When the world and battle-field bell tolls again
You come through the storm
Sighing and singing
Blood boiling under the white robe
To enter each and every corner of the world
Like contemporary Schweitzer

✧✧✧

---

[33] On March 12, 2016 I receive professor Ernesto Kahan's email, telling me that in his Spanish speech, he has made into slides the SUGGESTION, my book comment for him which is published in the United States (*Atlanta News*) on March 4, 2016. I open his speech file folders, to discover a total of 26 slides, among which the 20th and 21st are the book review I wrote for him. A great honor for me!

48．

春思二首（其一） 賈至

草色青青柳色黃，桃花歷亂李花香。
東風不為吹愁去，春日偏能惹恨長。

Spring Thoughts (No. 1) Jia Zhi

Green is the grass and
yellow is the willow.

Peach flowers run riot,
apricot blossoms fragrant.

My sorrow, the east wind
fails to blow it away:

spring days only lengthen
and deepen my sorrow.

春信 林明理

年初一，爆竹重臨這南鄉
清風如岸柳兀自呢喃
而故鄉的殘雪
猶存幾許白光於我底心上

我聽梅樹伸展嫩葉聲
蒲公英綿綿細話
啊，那春間小雨
又漫天漫落
小溪也一派輕鬆地歌咏

只有長巷門口
半開半掩，雲雀穿梭如蝶

唐詩明理接千載
古今抒懷詩三百首
漢英對照

戲舞在牆隅花叢
不識人間輕愁

Message of Spring   Lin Ming-Li

On the first day of the New Year,
firecrackers come again to the south
The breeze such as the coast of the willow murmurs
And the hometown remnant snow
Still a few dots of white light linger in my heart

I listen to the plum trees stretching the leaves
Of the dandelions which are whispering
Ah, the spring rain
Is falling slowly
The stream is also singing easily

Only the door of the long lane
Is half open, the larks shuttling like butterflies
Dancing in the wall of flowers
As strangers to human sorrow

✧✧✧

49 •

送李侍郎赴常州   賈至

雪晴雲散北風寒，楚水吳山道路難。
今日送君須盡醉，明朝相憶路漫漫。

Seeing a Friend Off   Jia Zhi

The snow clears up as cold north
winds disperse clouds amain;

mountains and rivers make
the southward way hard to go.

Today we must drink till
drunk since we'll part;

tomorrow a long way is between
us: fond memories remain.

給我最好的朋友一個聖誕祝福　　　林明理

在這繽紛的佳節
無論你身處之處下雪
　　或者不會下雪
當月光輕灑在藍海上
啊朋友
你聽見了嗎
我將祈願變成千隻雪鳥
　　飛向你——
恰午夜時分的耶誕神曲
　　滿耳都是祝福

A Christmas Greeting to Cheer You, My Good Friend
Lin Ming-Li

In this colorful festival
No matter it snows in your place
　　Or it does not snow
When the moonlight sprinkles on the blue sea
Ah dear friend
Do you hear
I wish to become a thousand snowbirds
　　To fly to you —
Just as the midnight Christmas song
　　The ears are filled with blessings

唐詩明理接千載
古今抒情詩三百首
漢英對照

✧✧✧

50.

巴陵夜別王八員外　　　賈至

柳絮飛時別洛陽，梅花發後到三湘。
世情已逐浮雲散，離恨空隨江水長。

Bidding Farewell to a Friend in the Night of Baling
Jia Zhi

In the season of flying catkins
I bid farewell to Luoyang;

after plum flowers blossom
I arrive at Shanxiang.

The vicissitudes of life
disperse with floating clouds;

the parting emotion is endless
like the Yangtze River.

在寂靜蔭綠的雪道中　　　林明理

在寂靜蔭綠的雪道中
風偷走了我的夢
它像小冠花對晶瑩的樹
把我心弦拋向雲層

這是怎樣的命運？無論
何處，都無法當成一首歌

在我褪去所有光輝的一刻
生命已無所求

啊⋯孤寂的十月
彷彿能看到你詩思篇篇
你是我懵懂歲月的樂聲
夜裡的海洋、聖壇的明燭

爾後,我將忘卻我的驕傲
在你轉身時綻出一絲焦灼
溶入花傘下
驟然聚凝的蒼穹

Along the Snowy Path of Quiet Green Shade
Lin Ming-Li

Along the snowy path of quiet green shade
The wind has stolen my dream
It is like little coronas to glittering trees
To cast my heartstrings into the clouds

What fate is this? Nowhere
Can it be a song
When all my glory is gone
Life wants nothing more

Ah... lonely October
Seems to be able to see your poems
You are the music of my ignorant years
The sea at night, the altar of the candle

Then, I will forget my pride
When you turn away there is a wisp of burning
Melted under the flower umbrella
The sky suddenly threatens with clouds

❖❖❖

51.

絕句二首（其二）   杜甫

江碧鳥逾白，山青花欲燃。
今春看又過，何日是歸年？

Two Quatrains (No. 2)   Du Fu

The birds are white
over a blue river; the

flowers burn in green
mountains. This spring

is fleet and gone: O,
when can I return?

五分車的記憶   林明理

我愛糖廠[34]的五分車，
    自由快樂地奔馳——
在田野，在山林。
我聽著鳴笛
    由遠而近……

啊，好一個黃昏
平交道的柵欄緩緩落下
    鐵道守衛在吹著哨子……

---

[34] 高雄橋頭糖廠興建於 1901 年，是臺灣第一座現代化機械式製糖工廠，園區內保有多處的古蹟、日式木屋、五分車修理室、糖業歷史館等，是休憩的好去處。

兒時的舊事——依然清晰，
我仍奔跑著，做著夢。

夢見馳過無邊無際的白雲，
　　馳過我燦亮的眼睛。
哦，我知道——故鄉依舊
　　　在風裡，在雨中
　　　反覆推挪呼應。

夕陽躺在我臂彎，
　　五分車的背影，無限延伸。
那裡我曾坐在大樹下，
　　眼前是一大片甘蔗田……
啊，回憶　也是一種幸福。

Memory of the Five-Pointer　Lin Ming-Li

I love the five-pointer operated
by the Taiwan Sugar Company[35].
　　Running freely and happily —
In the fields, in the mountains.
I listen to the whistle
　　Approaching from afar…

Oh, what a wonderful evening
The railroad gate comes down slowly
　　The guard is blowing a whistle....
Memories from my childhood remain vivid,
I am still running and dreaming.

---

[35] The Kaohsiung Ciaotou Sugar Refinery is Taiwan's first modern mechanical sugar factory which was built in 1901. It now consists of many historical sites, including Japanese-style wooden houses, the five-pointer cars repair shop, and sugar historical museums, etc. It is also an ideal touring and resting place.

Dreaming of the white clouds,
   Continuously passing before my bright eyes.
Oh, I know — my hometown is still
      Being pushed and pulled endlessly
      By the wind and rain.

The setting sun lies in my arms,
   As the five-pointer pulls away further and further.
As usual, I sit under a big tree.
   Before me is a large sugarcane field...
Ah, what happy memory!

✧✧✧

52 •

江畔獨步尋花七首（其五） 杜甫

黃師塔前江水東，春光懶困倚微風。
桃花一簇開無主，可愛深紅愛淺紅？

Strolling along the River in Search of Flowers (No. 5)
Du Fu

Before Huangshi Pagoda
the river pours eastward;

languid spring leans in the
gentle breeze. A cluster

of peach blossoms are
fair and ownerless; which

are more lovely: crimson
petals or pink blossoms?

142

花蓮觀光漁港風情   林明理

那個歡樂麗日的晨光裡
　賞鯨碼頭變得璀璨
微風吹拂
向日廣場前閃耀的海
　水靜無波
不管是船筏或遊艇
　都開始夢想出海

天空如是遼闊
驀然回頭，遠山疊雲
看見一隻海鳥掠過
牽引我詩想，雀躍欲動

The Customs of Hualien Sightseeing Fishing Harbor
                              Lin Ming-Li

In the morning light of that happy day,
　The whale watching dock becomes brilliant
The breeze is blowing
The shining sea in front of the Sunny Square
　Still water without waves
Whether boats or yachts
　All begin to dream of going out to sea

The sky is so vast
Suddenly turn back, remote mountains heavy with clouds
To see a seabird skimming
Stirring my poetic thought, on the capering

❖❖❖

53 •

江畔獨步尋花七首（其七）   杜甫

不是愛花即欲死，只恐花盡老相催。
繁枝容易紛紛落，嫩蕊商量細細開。

Strolling Along the River in Search of Flowers (No. 7)   Du Fu

Not that I love flowers
to death, but I dread old

age threatens when flowers
fall. Full-blown flowers

tend to flutter and fade;
tender petals, O, please

be slow of opening
and blossoming.

天鵝湖   林明理

拉起裙擺，行個禮
而你低頭凝視
把天地轉得飄然入夢

The Swan Lake   Lin Ming-Li

Pull up the hemline, to salute
While you stare down
And the world spins into a dream

◇◇◇

54·

贈花卿   杜甫

錦城絲管日紛紛,半入江風半入雲。
此曲只應天上有,人間能得幾回聞?

To Hua Qing   Du Fu

The Silk Town is noisy
with music from strings and

flutes; half of it wafts in river
wind and half of it flies into

clouds. Such melodious music
can only be heard in Heaven;

in mortal world, how many
times can you appreciate it?

科爾寺前一隅[36]   林明理

啊,但願此刻在這裡,趁這深夜
我從夢中甦醒,猶記得:
落羽松上的歌雀和三五村寨
炊煙前　已落霞滿天
聽,那雪花紛飛
在石牆,在月的眉睫

隆冬一過,三月翩至
綠芽鑽出頭兒,蜜蜂前來寺前
我倚向窗台

---

[36] 科爾寺位於中國四川省甘孜州理塘縣。

簷前的冰柱和蜘蛛
映照著枝條下的紅草地
一群藏族小妹妹奔跑著,把牛場都踏遍

究竟是為了什麼?
難道想重新捕捉一個印跡
我猜了又猜,直到露水浸滿白塔
一切又回到原點
啊,原來那片刻邂逅
已讓世界在閃爍,唯星兒入眠

A Corner in Front of the Kol Temple[37]

Lin Ming-Li

Oh, I wish now here, in the depth of night
I wake up from my dream and still remember:
The songbirds on the pines and the smoke of three or five villages
Before kitchen smoke   the sky is filled with falling clouds
Listen, snowflakes are flying
On the stone walls, on the brows of the moon

After the severe winter, March arrives
The green buds shoot out, bees come to the temple
I lean on the windowsill
The eaves icicles and the spiders
Reflecting the red lawn under the branches
A group of Tibetan little sisters running all over the cattle field

For what, exactly?
Want to recapture a mark

---

[37] the Kol Temple is located in Litang County, Ganzi Prefecture, Sichuan Province, China.

I guess and guess, until the dew soaks the white tower
Everything goes back to the beginning
Ah, the original moment of encounter
Has made the world twinkle, only the stars are sleeping

✧✧✧

55 ·

漫興九首（其一） 杜甫

眼見客愁愁不醒，無賴春色到江亭。
即遣花開深造次，便覺鶯語太丁寧。

Nine Random Quatrains (No. 1) Du Fu

The guest is steeped
in sorrow which refuses

to awaken, and devilish
spring invades river-

side pavilion. It blooms
flowers high and low,

and orioles twitter here
and there: too noisy.

在黑暗的平野上 林明理

即使這秋風也在顫嗦。
木輪停下來。一只野鳥
投入樹林
雲氣也就
更明淨了，不知何處莊稼地
淒淒地吹響牧笛

在平野中間，有許多記憶升起：

那是夜蟬的歌聲。
清晰 持續
輕喚著
此處或彼處
我的繆思，合起了眼瞼

而靈魂從冰草叢中探出。

On a Dark Plain   Lin Ming-Li

Even the autumn wind is trembling.
The wooden wheel stops. A wild bird
Flies into the woods
And the clouds
Are clearer, and somewhere in the crop field
A mournful flute is being played
In the field, how many memories are arising:

That is the song of night cicada.
Clear and persistent
Gently calling
Here or there
My Muse, eyelids closed

And the soul peeks out of the icy grass.

✧✧✧

56．

漫成一首   杜甫

江月去人只數尺，風燈照夜欲三更。
沙頭宿鷺聯拳靜，船尾跳魚撥刺鳴。

A Random Poem   Du Fu

The river moon is only
several feet away from

people; the lamp in the
wind shines in the night

of wee hours. Egrets
sleep quietly in the sand;

the fishes at the boat tail
produce noise of jumping.

在邊城   林明理

我像一隻磨菇斜躺著，把臉
伸進春野的星宿
突然我睜開昏眼
讓月亮進來

我像綠光的蝴蝶
在開滿花樹的溪谷
比喜鵲更快地加入了悠揚的合唱
直到黑夜從邊陲降臨
閃著夏日山徑的殷紅
隱遁，馬車已到達另一個邊緣

In the Border Town   Lin Ming-Li

I lie reclining like a mushroom, thrusting
My face into the springfield stars
Suddenly I open my dark eyes
For the moon to come in

唐詩明理接千載
古今抒情詩三百首
漢英對照

Like a green butterfly
In the valley of blooming trees
Faster than the magpie I join the melodic chorus
Until night falls from the border
The crimson shining with summer mountain trail
Retreats, the carriage has reached the other edge

✧✧✧

57 •

歸雁 　　　　　　　　　　　　　　　　杜甫

東來萬里客，亂定幾年歸？
腸斷江城雁，高高向北飛。

Returning Geese 　　　　　　　　　Du Fu

Roamers: thousands
of miles from the east,

when can war chaos
stop for us to return?

Heartbreaking: the
geese over riverside

town are soaring and
flying freely northward.

回鄉 　　　　　　　　　　　　　　　　林明理

我，流浪者，來這裡租地耕作
可是這裡卻不見故鄉的煙霧與泥土
也看不到故鄉的鷹

那些被毀壞的橋,經歷多次風災的路
那些頹垣茶村[38],啊,哪裡有我立身之處?

你看那雲豹故鄉,有祖先的足印
過去我種小米和香蕉
也種茶葉和樹豆
如今只剩下回憶
那些祭祀慶典和吃過的山餚

回鄉,是我唯一的出路
回鄉,是我唯一的渴求
只有湖神依然為我祝福
將我的歌,藏進
他深而悲傷的眼眸

Return Home   Lin Ming-Li

I, a wanderer, come here to rent land for farming,
But here I cannot see the smoke and soil of
my hometown
Nor can I see the eagles of my hometown
Those destroyed bridges, the roads that
have experienced many storms
Those tea villages[39], ah, where can I find a shelter?

---

[38] 在臺灣的部落論壇中,多位專家提及,好茶村、瑪家村、長治鄉、霧台鄉等族人,都希望政府重視讓他們回鄉耕種的意願,避免重建政策淪為族民心中的痛。

[39] In the tribal forum in Taiwan, many experts mention that the Good Tea Village, Ma Jia Village, Changzhi Township, Wutai Township and other ethnic groups hope that the government pays attention to their willingness to return to their hometown for farming, and avoid the reconstruction policy becoming a pain in the hearts of the people.

Look at the clouded leopard's hometown, with the
footprints of my ancestors
I used to grow millet and bananas
I also grow tea and tree beans
Now only with memory
Those sacrificial ceremonies and the mountain dishes I eat

Going home is my only way
Going home is my only wish
Only the lake deity still blesses me
To hide my song
Into his deep, sad eyes

❖❖❖

58 •

逢雪宿芙蓉山主人　　　　　　劉長卿

日暮蒼山遠，天寒白屋貧。
柴門聞犬吠，風雪夜歸人。

A Night Arrival to the Cottage
Liu Changqing

Sundown, bleak hills remote;
a white cottage, wretched,

forlorn, is sheltered under
cold heavens. I am slowly

and steadily approaching the
door through dragging my weary

body, when I hear the barking,
in soothing accents, of a dog.

詠高密

林明理

當高粱沃野映紅而大豆花莢飄香
我就要沒入膠河[40]的胸膛——
東眺,沉睡的青島
西望,風箏的故鄉
十月的秋風在街頭遊蕩
山雀也追逐著溪流

當葡萄化成酒紅而種籽脫殼萌芽
我就要畫出濰坊的倒影——
從葉兒滴翠到斑鳩成雙
從泥塑頑童到剪紙窗花
正月的冬雪,在草尖兒上泣別
呵,吾友,可仍記得綿鄉水長

當大地春風不再可憐的飄泊而
像英雄一樣忠實地吹著
我就要沒入這多彩的年畫之鄉——
用欣喜來相識
名相晏嬰、鄭玄和劉墉

誰不願意飛去瞻仰 像雲那樣
啊,大雁
你可把我的希望帶得更遠更廣
讓這裡的江水永遠清秀
讓小曲兒也跟著哼唱
呵,吾友,可還記得這夜的釉綠如海洋

我願是隻黑鳥停泊在幸福的海上
在夢醒時分

---

[40] 膠河,位於中國山東省東部。

唐詩明理接千載
古今抒情詩三百首
漢英對照

在牛馬的草坡、朝氣的海疆
還有高粱穗在心中猛烈地激盪
但我不想拂拭什麼
除了那浸透孤獨的月光

聽，那北國松濤還在呼嚎
飛鴻也不曾停腳
我想我認得這夜裡的歌
那肯定是勞動者吃力孕育大地的聲響
呵，吾友，你可知今年高密糧食豐收
百姓也歡笑展顏了

Ode to Gaomi   Lin Ming-Li

When the sorghum field is red and the soybean flower pod is fragrant
I will fall into the chest of the Jiaohe River[41] —
Looking east, sleeping Qingdao
Looking west, the hometown of kites
The October autumn wind is wandering in the street
The chickadees are chasing the stream

When the grapes turn into wine red and the seed shucking sprout
I will draw the reflection of Weifang —
From the leaf dripping with green to the pairing turtles
From the clay sculpture urchins to paper-cut window flowers
The winter snow of the first month, is parting in tears on grass
Oh, my friend do you still remember the water of Mianxiang

When the spring breeze of the earth is no longer pitifully drifting

---

[41] the Jiaohe River is located in eastern Shandong Province, China.

Blowing faithfully like a hero
I will not enter the colorful hometown of New Year pictures —
With joys to meet
Famous governors of Yan Ying, Zheng Xuan and Liu Yong

Who is not willing to fly to have a look like the clouds
Ah, wild goose
You can take my hope farther and wider
For the river here to remain beautiful
For the song to be hummed
Oh, my friend, do you still remember the night's glaze green like an ocean

I would like to be a black bird perching at the sea of happiness
In the moment of waking up from a dream
On the grassy slopes of cattle and horses, the vigor of the sea
And the ears of sorghum are violently stirring in the heart
But I do not want to wipe anything
Except the moonlight soaked in loneliness

Listen, the northern pines are still howling
The flying geese never stop for a rest
I think I know the song of the night
It must be the sound of the laboring worker who nurse the earth
Oh, my friend, do you know that this year's harvest is plentiful in Gaomi
And the people are beaming with smiles

✧✧✧

59·

聽彈琴　　　　　　　　　　　　　　　　　劉長卿

泠泠七弦上，靜聽松風寒。
古調雖自愛，今人多不彈。

Lute Playing　　　　　　　　　　　Liu Changqing

From the seven strings:
cool, clear, far-reaching,

cold wind is heard
to be blowing through

pines. Though I
love this old ditty,

people nowadays
refuse to play it.

如果你立在冬雪裡　　　　　　　　　　　林明理

如果你立在冬雪裡
用沾濕的眼眸
向我端視
猶如抖落羽葉的風
等待
春日的小小呵欠

啊吾友，我的永念
為什麼歸程屢屢橫阻
為什麼冷雨頻頻滴淚
難道你聽不見
我的默喚似小舟
緩緩地盪著　　漾著

如果我立在交錯晃影的地鐵裡
或癡望原野上
只要有你，只要有你的展顏
哪怕星光不語
哪怕月兒隱遁
你就是篇溫和的詩章，如菖蒲般綠

If You Stand in the Winter Snow

Lin Ming-Li

If you stand in the winter snow
To look at me
With moist eyes
Like the wind that shakes off the leaves
Waiting for
The little yawn of spring

Oh my friend, forever I miss you
Why is my return time and again obstructed
Why does the cold rain frequently drop tears
Can't you hear
My silent call like a boat
Slowly swinging   rippling

If I stand in the subway of crisscross shadows
Or gaze into the field of delusion
With you, with your beaming face
Even if the stars are silent
Even if the moon is hidden
You are a gentle poem, green as calamus

✦✦✦

60 ·

尋張逸人山居 　　　　　　　　　劉長卿

危石才通鳥道，空山更有人家。
桃源定在深處，澗水浮來落花。

Looking for the Residence of a Recluse
Liu Changqing

The birds' passage among
perilous crags, human traces in

deserted mountains. A fictitious
land of peace must be in the

recesses: fallen flowers on
creek water are floating hither.

黃陽隘即景[42] 　　　　　　　　　林明理

楓紅泣古隘，怎不憐曉天。
苔綠穿老樹，又眺石階前。

The Sight of Huangyang Pass[43]
Lin Ming-Li

The red maples are
weeping at the ancient

pass; loveable is the
morning sky. Green

---

[42] 黃陽隘位於福建省寧德，是明代到清代的古建築。
[43] Huangyang Pass is located in Ningde, Fujian Province, and it is an ancient building from Ming dynasty to Qing dynasty.

moss rambles through
the old trees, before

looking afar on
the stone steps.

✧✧✧

61 ·

江中對月 　　　　　　　　　　劉長卿

空洲夕煙斂，望月秋江裡。
歷歷沙上人，月下孤渡水。

Facing the Moon in the River
　　　　　　　　　　　　　Liu Changqing

Over an empty isle
evening fog is gathered;

the moon is seen in
autumn river. On the

sand people are clear
and distinct, who is

wading cool, lonely
water in moonlight.

曲冰橋上的吶喊 　　　　　　　林明理

一個古老的遺址
橋上住著樸實的布農族

他們受制於水壩
卻沒有任何良策可尋
他們用聲音表達心中的痛
他們忍住淚水,如這幅畫:

彷彿冬日將凝的銀霜
我看到溪底曲折波動的流水
以及消坡塊的一岸
還有一大片農地消失在河床
每當惡水流竄
水田就被沖刷得悲鳴

聽,他們在吶喊
怎有人忍心推說是天災
任憑他們
年年
在曲冰橋上
受盡淒涼

再次走進雨中
我感覺祖靈依然沉重地
注視著這片家園
他們穿越時空
只是單純地希望
再度繁榮香糯米故鄉[44]

---

[44] 此詩提到的 TISAU「曲冰」部落是南投縣仁愛鄉萬豐村的舊名,是臺灣布農族分布最北的一支,全村數百居民。曲冰之名始於 1981 年挖掘到的史前聚落遺址「曲冰遺址」;1988 年間,曲冰遺址被列為三級古蹟。部落位居於濁水溪上游,沿岸一度農田密集,居民多以務農為生。除了曲冰橋,部落後糯米椒田叉路上山,有聖母亭、十字山。此外,還有多條生態步道、原始林、精靈瀑布、天使瀑布群、曲冰峽谷等,是香糯米故鄉。

The Cry on the Qubing Bridge[45]

Lin Ming-Li

An age-old historical site
On the bridge live the simple Bunun people
Who are trapped by the dam
But have no good solution
They express their pain in their voices
They hold back their tears, as in this painting:

Like frozen silver frost in winter
I see the meandering water at the bottom of the stream
And the bank of the slope
And a large area of agricultural land disappearing into the bed of the river
When evil water is running
The paddy field is washed to be crying

Listen, they are shouting
How can anyone have the heart to say that it is a natural disaster
In spite of their suffering

---

[45] The TISAU "Qubing" tribe mentioned in this poem is the old name of Wanfeng Village, Renai Township, Nantou County, and is the northernmost branch of Bunong ethnic group in Taiwan, with hundreds of residents in the village. The name of Qubing originates from the prehistoric settlement site "Qubing Site" excavated in 1981. In 1988, the Qubing site was listed as a third-level historic site. The tribe is located in the upper reaches of Zhuoshui River, and the farmland along the coast was once dense, and the residents mostly made a living by farming. In addition to Qubing Bridge, behind the glutinous rice pepper field of the ethnic group, along the fork road, there are the Pavilion of the Virgin Mary and the Cross mountain. Besides, there are a number of ecological trails, original forest, soul waterfall, angel waterfall group, and ice canyon, etc. It is the hometown of sweet glutinous rice.

From year to year
From desolation
On the Qubing Bridge

Walking again into the rain
I feel the ancestral spirit is still seriously
Watching the home
They travel through time and space
With a simple hope
To make the land of sweet glutinous rice prosperous

✧✧✧

62·

送上人　　　　　　　　　　　　　　　劉長卿

孤雲將野鶴，豈向人間住。
莫買沃洲山，時人已知處。

Seeing a Monk Off　　　　　Liu Changqing

Like a wild crane riding
a lonely cloud, he is not

a mortal dweller. Buy
not the house in Mount

Wozhou: it is approachable
now by mortal beings.

DON'T BE SAD　　　　　　　　　　林明理

Don't be sad, my friend
你注視著世界以及苦難的人們
彷彿自己也在那兒感傷落淚

了解
和平真諦的你
得灌滅
仇恨的火焰
喚醒對地球未來懵懵懂懂的人
總得有人不怕失去生命
才能拯救沉淪的靈魂
你凝視未來
站在宇宙的屋脊
發出沉重之聲
大氣之中融合著你的祈願與深情[46]

Don't Be Sad: For the March 26, 2016 Belgium Victims   Lin Ming-Li

Don't be sad, my friend
You watch the world and the suffering people
As if you are among them in tears
Since you understand the true meaning of peace
You must quench the flame of hatred
And awaken the ignorant earthlings
There must be some people unafraid of losing their own lives
To save the sinking souls
You look into the future
Standing on the roof of the universe
Heaving a heavy sound
The air is with your affection and fond wishes[47]

✧✧✧

---

[46] 為比利時 2016 年 3 月 22 日受難者致哀。—2016.3.27
[47] Belgium March 27, 2016; respects paid to the victims.

63・

春行寄興　　　　　　　　　　　　　李華

宜陽城下草萋萋，澗水東流復向西。
芳樹無人花自落，春山一路鳥空啼。

Spring Notes　　　　　　　　　　Li Hua

Grass grows green and
lush beneath the city

walls; creek water flows
now east and then west.

Petals fall unadmired from
fragrant trees; the mountain

is overflowing with
birds' twitters, all in vain.

山桐花開時　　　　　　　　　　　林明理

窯在燈下，柴燒昨夜
相思落灰，遲遲；
縱橫撲滿衣袖
我在風中打旋，繼續流轉你的
清澈眼眸，背倚昆蟲
聆聽通氣室裡煙囪爆燃的聲音
紛紛翹首，一隻隻彩蝶與白鷺
也跟著顧盼，低語不休
落花在水天之間，但見
暮春西落
返影遁入石橋，五色鳥
在隱現中翩然回返
悄然佇立，油桐枝上

靜凝如蓮
急驟的雨,總來得不是時候
幾度敲醒,漾著盼望
漾著心情,點點滴滴──
交錯的足音
穿梭如魚
啊,那慌亂中的
容顏,在這一季叢山中閃爍著
靈光,彷若捲起千層白浪
唯一的半帆……

When the Tree Blossoms　　Lin Ming-Li

The kiln under a lamp, wood burns last night
Yearning dropping with ash, lingeringly;
Crisscross into the sleeves
I swirl in the wind, keep rolling your
Clear eyes, leaning against the insects
Listening to the chimneys in the aeration chamber
One after another head up, butterflies and egrets
Are looking while whispering
Falling flowers between water and sky, only to see
The late spring fading in the west
The reflected shadow retreats into the stone bridge, the five-color bird
Returns in dim appearance
Standing quietly, on the tree branches
Static like lotus
The sudden rain, always untimely
Several times to wake up, rippling with hopes
Rippling with a mood, bit by bit —
The staggered foot sound
Shuttling like fish
Ah, in panic,
The face, flashing in the seasonal mountain

Ethereal light, as if rolling up a thousand layers of white waves
The only half sail…

✧✧✧

64 •

銜魚翠鳥 錢起

有意蓮葉間，瞥然下高樹。
擘波得潛魚，一點翠光去。

Kingfisher Catching Fish Qian Qi

Fixing its stare at the
fish among lotus leaves,

suddenly the kingfisher
swoops down from a

high tree: parting waves,
it catches the swimming

fish, and a dot of light,
emerald, flies away.

紅尾伯勞 林明理

儘管是聒噪，
還朝著南方急進。
遙遠的未來，已幻成
秋野的樂音。

The Brown Shrike   Lin Ming-Li

In spite of the great noises,
Still moving speedily southward.
The distant future has become
The music of autumn field.

✧ ✧ ✧

65 ·

江行無題一百首（其六十九）   錢起

咫尺愁風雨，匡廬不可登。
只疑雲霧窟，猶有六朝僧。

At the Riverside (No. 69)   Qian Qi

A rainstorm brings a
great distance: the Lushan

Mountain, eight inches
away, is unapproachable.

In the cloudy cave,
who knows, there may

still be recluse-monks
of the six dynasties.

風雨之後   林明理

在一大片樹林前
在桃源山間
溢滿著植物氣味和光

唐詩明理接千載
古今抒情詩三百首
漢英對照

把東方慢慢映紅
光喚醒河灘的眼睛
我游向那一隅村莊
卻再也找不著昔日的歡樂

我拂拭著秋風
秋風總是堅定沉默
當鹹澀澀的雨溜過對岸

喧騰且濁重
可憐那變色的山崗——浸透
沉落

你聽
那沒有遮攔的星子
離去前的回應：
能不能把太陽撕成片片閃光
溫暖了族民的苦痛
看，那些無辜的小臉蛋
一臉蒼白又驚恐[48]

After the Storm   Lin Ming-Li

Before a large stretch of woods
The mountain of peach blossoms
Is filled with the scents of plants and light
The east is slowly reddening
The light wakes up the eyes of the river beach
I swim to the corner of village
But fail to find the past joys

I wipe the autumn wind
And the autumn wind is always firm and silent

---

[48] 為「八八水災」，罹難的臺灣同胞哀悼。

When the salty rain slips across the other shore

Noisy and cloudy
The discolored hills — soaked through
On the sinking

Listen
The unveiled stars
The response before leaving:
Can you tear the sun into flashing pieces
To warm the pain of the people
Look, those innocent little faces
Pale and frightened[49]

✧✧✧

66 ·

歸雁　　　　　　　　　　　　　錢起

瀟湘何事等閒回？水碧沙明兩岸苔。
二十五弦彈夜月，不勝清怨卻飛來。

Returning Geese　　　　　　Qian Qi

Rivers Xiao and Xiang are an
ideal place: green water and

clear sand and moss along two
banks. But why do you fly

northward？ Because the musical
notes from twenty-five strings

---

[49] We mourn for the victims of the "August 8 flood" in Taiwan.

in moonlit night are too
melancholy for me to bear.

凜冬將至　　　　　　　　　　林明理

一片片葉
落成
一幅幅水景
在星宿之間
此起
　　彼伏

離鄉太遙遠
魚兒馱我
咀嚼著
歷史的煙雲
啊，正月

一隻蝙蝠
就要飛起來
把我矇住眼
像霧中羊
直扎向
穗谷的天邊

Severe Winter Is Around the Corner
　　　　　　　　　　　　　　Lin Ming-Li

One after another leaf
Falling into
One after another waterscape
Among the stars
Rising and
Falling

170

Far away from home
The fish carries me
Chewing
The smoke of history
Ah, January

A bat
Is to fly up
To blindfold me
Like a sheep in the mist
Heading straight to
The horizon of grain

✧✧✧

67 ·

夜泊鸚鵡洲   錢起

月照溪邊一罩篷，夜聞清唱有微風。
小樓深巷聞方響，水國人家在處同。

Night Mooring on Parrot Islet   Qian Qi

On moonlit creek a
boat with awning; night

hears singing in the
breeze. Small mansions

& deep alleys are noisy
with percussion music;

leisurely are the homes
in the land of waters.

寫給成都之歌

林明理

1.
誰都會想起你
一座最偉大的堅霸
啊，都江堰
當夕陽輝耀著你的身影
橫跨千年之歌
也越發甜美清亮

文殊院鐘響了
武侯祠醒了
錦里古街點亮了
天府廣場沸騰了
啊，我的城
到處傳遍了悠揚的樂聲

而古老的皇城
在黑夜之外
回光照了千佛的塔
在光明裡
歌是靜肅的……

2.
誰都會想起你
一個最沉默的詩人
啊，杜甫
當陽光輝耀著你的身影
橫跨千年之後
你把故里引向文明

啊，我的城
再生的鳳凰

你的羽翅是那樣舒展
如雪的詩句響徹雲霄

而我
在彼岸的土地上
觸摸你歷史的斑痕
當太陽冉冉昇起
昔日勇士影子如巨人
唱響天際，光耀神鳥之都

A Song for Chengdu   Lin Ming-Li

1.
All people will think of you
A great strongman
Ah, Dujiangyan Dam
When the sunset shines on your figure
Across thousands of years
The song is more limpid and sweet

Wenshu temple bell is ringing
Wuhou Temple wakes up
Jinli Street is lit up
Tianfu Square is boiling with animation
Ah, my city
Is aloud with melodious music

And the ancient imperial city
Beyond darkness
The reflected light shines on the tower of a thousand Buddhas
In the light
The song is quiet....

2.
All people will remember you
A most silent poet
Ah, Du Fu

When the sun shines on your figure
Through thousands of years
You lead the homeland to civilization

Oh, my city
The reborn phoenix
Your wings thus spread
Like the lines of snow to ring through the clouds

And I
On the other side of the earth
Touch the traces of your history
When the sun rises slowly
The shadows of old warriors are like giants
Singing in the sky, shining over the city of divine birds

✧✧✧

68 •

聽鄰家吹笙　　　　　　　　　郎士元

鳳吹聲如隔彩霞，不知牆外是誰家。
重門深鎖無尋處，疑有碧桃千樹花。

Hearing the Neighbor Playing *Sheng*

Lang Shiyuan

Musical notes are produced,
as if through clouds from

heaven; not knowing who is
the neighbor beyond the wall?

A door after another door is
locked, nowhere to find it;

there must be thousands of
trees laden with peach flowers.

暮來的小溪 林明理

起初我只看到了火金姑
這兒和那兒的
飛在石徑旁
在林子裡
在我掌心
綴成仲夏雨
後來我看到了蝸牛
在花叢中找尋牠的
往日足跡。
薄霧在歸鳥身後
被溪圍繞
只有風在月岩上
乾著急。

The Stream of Twilight Lin Ming-Li

At first I see nothing but fire nuns
Here and there
Flying beside the stone paths
In the woods
In my palm
Drop into midsummer rain
Then I see snails
Tracing their former
Footsteps among the flowers.
The mist is surrounded by
the stream behind the bird
Only the wind is vainly worried
On the moon rock.

✧✧✧

唐詩明理接千載
古今抒情詩三百首
漢英對照

69·

夜泊湘江

郎士元

湘山木落洞庭波,湘水連雲秋雁多。
寂寞舟中誰借問?月明只自聽漁歌。

Night Mooring in Xiang River

Lang Shiyuan

Trees in Xiang Mountain shed
their leaves and Dongting Lake

is rippling with waves; the water
of Xiang River reaches clouds

where autumn geese abound.
In the lonely boat who is asking

questions? The bright moon is
listening to the fisherman's song.

寫給蘭嶼之歌

林明理

土地是帶有記憶的
　恰如浪花的弦律
歲歲年年
　歌咏著億萬種詩句
當清晨或暮靄時分
達悟人上山
　或出海返航時
它就發出歷史的回聲

那震人心魄的
　是大海在狂呼
還有海浪上閃耀流逝的身影

在他們望海的歲月裡
在他們想再次穿破浪頭的時候
這些渴望，如雲漂浮太空

但土地是帶有記憶的
它不會忘記
族人身上留有土地被破壞的痛
　留有勇士們在潮水中的吶喊
每當黎明到來
它便重複著　重複著
　　我們的歌

Ode to Orchid Island   Lin Ming-Li

The land has memory
　Like the rhythm of waves
From year to year
　Singing myriads of songs
In the morning or at dusk
Dawu people climb the mountain
　Or return from the sea
It echoes with history

What is soul-stirring
　Is the howling sea
And the figures flashing in the waves

In the years when they watch the sea
And when they want to go against the waves again
The yearnings are like clouds floating in the sky

But the land has memory
It will never forget
The pain of clansmen when the land is destroyed
　And the cries of warriors in tidal waves
When the dawn breaks

It is repeating our song
Time and again

✧✧✧

70.

滁州西澗 韋應物

獨憐幽草澗邊生，上有黃鸝深樹鳴。
春潮帶雨晚來急，野渡無人舟自橫。

The West Creek at Chuzhou Wei Yingwu

Lush green grass grows by a secluded
creek, above which orioles are twittering

in the thick foliage of trees. Spring tide
is running in strong sudden rushes of

water when the ferry, deserted, is
animated by a small boat nosing round

by itself against the current ineffectually,
amid an eddy of torrential water.

與詩人有約[50] 林明理

朋友，你是否看得見
　　福爾摩沙殷切的目光

---

[50] 當日，我們與多位笠詩人在日本料理餐廳用餐，相談甚歡。而後，也在高雄文學館合影，由鄭醫師主持暨安排旅美詩人非馬（馬為義博士）在館內演講，並約定下次非馬回台灣再聚，留下難忘的回憶。—2019.6.6

搜索著兒時的記憶
眷戀故鄉是多麼的美
朋友，你是否聽得見
這蟬鳴，這西子灣
這悄聲的落葉
月兒在故鄉　一度一度地圓
或許　你已然忘懷
但我重覆的詩句——
是不變的關懷，永不忘卻

A Date with the Poet[51]   Lin Ming-Li

My friend, do you see
   Formosa's eager eyes
      Still in search of childhood memories?
   How beautiful to be love with one's hometown
My friend, do you hear
The singing of cicadas, the Xizi Bay
The murmuring leaves?
The moon of hometown has been full time and again
Maybe you have forgotten
   Yet my repeated poetic lines —
Are the constant concern, never to forget

✧✧✧

---

[51] On that day, Dr. William Marr and I, as well as several local poets have had a good time chatting with each other in the Japanese restaurant. Later, Dr. William Marr gave a lecture on poetry at the Kaohsiung Literature Museum and promised to meet us again next time when he returns to Taiwan. The scene is memorable. —June 6, 2019.

71.

詠聲　　　　　　　　　　　　　　　韋應物

萬物自聲聽，太空恒寂寥。
還從靜中起，卻向靜中消。

On the Voice　　　　　　　　　　Wei Yingwu

All things on earth
are heard by the voice;

silent and still is
the outer space.

The voice from
silence up arises,

and into silence
it vanishes.

燈下憶師　　　　　　　　　　　　林明理

這時黃昏已近
不知何處投來的鳥兒
跳過這枝上藏著
連歌聲都變得婉轉了

窗台外
一朵茉莉花黯然低頭
離我遠遠地天籟
正鼓盪我的耳膜

面對這雨住雲散的天空
燈下的我
只能追憶着——

思念似微弱的風
飄向每一寂靜的角落……

In Memory of My Tutor Under the Lamp
          Lin Ming-Li

Now the evening is approaching
The birds from nowhere
Leaping and hopping on the branches
Even their songs become graceful

Without the windowsill
A jasmine flower bows its head
Away from me the sounds of heaven
Are aloud in my eardrum

Facing the sky free from rain and clouds
Under the lamp
I can only recall —
Yearning like gentle wind
Drifting to every silent corner…

✧✧✧

72 ·

秋夜寄邱二十二員外   韋應物

懷君屬秋夜，散步詠涼天。
山空松子落，幽人應未眠。

To a Friend on an Autumn Night
          Wei Yingwu

In such an autumn
night I miss you;

strolling, I enjoy
the cool frosty air.

The mountain empty,
pine fruits drop; my

recluse-friend must
be still awake.

長巷

林明理

這是一條古老久遠的長巷
從來不曾遙視過天際
以及被比手劃腳地解說
我在細雨中漫步，穿過梔子花叢
穿過木櫺花窗
又毫無抗拒地步上梯塔鐘樓
許多青石斑駁的砌牆
而今，在捕捉光線的坑道裡歎息

當我躑足盡頭
轉身望去，陽光自流雲中露面
斜入了鏤空磚孔
零星漁火
亮起在山巒的背後
這裡沒有人潮煩囂，也沒有
奇突的念頭
歸路的街燈
正似探訪的螢火蟲
等待逸出……

The Long Lane

Lin Ming-Li

It is an ancient, long lane
Which has never gazed afar into the sky

And has never been explained with hands and feet
I walk in the drizzle, through gardenia bushes
Past wooden mullion windows
Without resistance to the bell tower
A lot of bluestone walls
Now, sighing in the tunnel that catches the light

When I come to the end
Turning to look, the sun appears in the flowing clouds
Slanting into the hollowed brick hole
Scattered fishing fires
Lit up behind the mountain
Where there are no human noises, no
Strange ideas
The street lights
Are like visiting fireflies
Waiting to escape…

✧✧✧

73 ·

秋齋獨宿　　　　　　　　　　　　　　韋應物

山月皎如燭，風霜時動竹。
夜半鳥驚棲，窗間人獨宿。

Sleeping Alone in an Autumn Studio
Wei Yingwu

The cliff moon is bright
like a candle; wind &

frost wave bamboos
now and then. In mid-

night birds are startled
from their rest; within

the window a person
is sleeping alone.

吉貝耍・孝海祭（Kabua Sua・Maw-isal）[52]

林明理

每年農曆九月初五
牽曲後，在風中
我們沿著農路
佇立在黃昏盡頭
時間悄悄地過去
草蟲鳴鳴
黑夜之手正縫補著歷史的傷口

但是這夜祭的時刻，是什麼讓你煩憂著
什麼在給那苦難的地土吹奏？
也許
每當澤蘭放進祀壺而木棉開滿部落
我們又回到西拉雅〈Siraya〉
看陽光逐漸黯淡
看族民如何努力生活
畫出了東河村一片富足
看這雨後的寧靜
把耆老的夢拋向更遠的夜的懷抱……

遠遠地
我聽見了古老的叮嚀
那發自周遭的合鳴
使我不再感到淒苦

---

[52] 吉貝耍・孝海祭是臺灣台南縣東山鄉東河村平埔族的重要祭典。

啊……吉貝耍
──這名字
也從未消失過

Kabua Sua · Maw-isal[53] Lin Ming-Li

Annually, the fifth day of the ninth lunar month
After that, in the wind
Along the farm road
We stand at the end of dusk
Time quietly slips by
The grassy insects are chirping
The hands of night are sewing the wound of history

But at this hour of the night's sacrifice, what worries you
What plays to the land of suffering?
Perhaps
Each time Zelan is put into the sacrifice pot and the tribe is full of kapokay
We return to Siraya
To see the sun gradually dimming
To see how the people work hard to live
To paint a rich Donghe village
To enjoy the peace after the rain
Throwing the dreams of the old people into the arms of the farther night…

In the distance
I hear the ancient exhortation
The chorus from all sides
I no longer feel sad
Oh…Gibejoon
—The name
Has never disappeared

---

[53] Kabua Sua · Maw-isal is an important festival of Pingpu people in Donghe Village, Dongshan Township, Tainan County, Taiwan.

74·

聞雁 　　　　　　　　　　　　　　　　　　　韋應物

故園渺何處，歸思方悠哉！
淮南秋雨夜，高齋聞雁來。

Hearing the Geese　　　　　　Wei Yingwu

My native place is dim
and distant; my mind

is thronged with nostalgia.
South of the river sees

a night wet with
autumn rain, when

the flying geese are
heard in the high tower.

母親 　　　　　　　　　　　　　　　　　　　林明理

那雙長繭的手
與揮不盡的汗水
還有那聲音
有時像花蝶飛出牆前
在心中閃爍
有時像雨絲飄忽
如期而至。

多少次？在風中閃現
彷彿月落星移……

然而她專注而笨拙地
抄寫經書，來自寧靜
那熟悉的眼眸
在夢底深處
我慌亂地將她喊出。

Mother   Lin Ming-Li

The calloused hands
And the endless sweat
And the voice
Sometimes fly without the wall like a butterfly
Flickering in my heart
Sometimes ethereal like rain
Which falls at the appointed time

How many times? Twinkling in the wind
Like the moon setting and the stars moving...
Yet intently and awkwardly
She transcribes the scriptures, from quiet
The familiar eye
In the depths of my dream
I call her out in a panic

❖❖❖

75 ·

寒食   韓翃

春城無處不飛花，寒食東風禦柳斜。
日暮漢宮傳蠟燭，輕煙散入五侯家。

唐詩明理接千載
古今抒情詩三百首
漢英對照

Cold Food Day   Han Hong

Spring catkins fly here
and there in the capital;

in Cold Food Day the east
wind slants imperial

willows. At dusk candles
are passed on in imperial

palace; bright and smoky
are five mansions of nobility.

木框上的盆花   林明理

你坐在石牆裡
用幾分之一秒的快門
捕捉日輪的俯臉
這或許是
你生命中僅有的一瞥。

山城之夜已緊緊收攏
裹住金絲雀顧憐倦藏的彩羽。
你在落雪裡
輕搖，無羈的空間
好似我未曾在你身旁——
是光融化了冰冷的書頁。

Potted Flowers on a Wooden Frame
                                         Lin Ming-Li

You sit inside a stone wall
For a fraction of a second
You capture the sun's face

This may be
The only glimpse in your life

The night of the mountain city has tightly closed in
To gather the colorful feathers that bind the canary's pity
You rock gently
In the snow, in the unbound space
As if I were never by your side —
It is the light that has melted the cold pages

✧✧✧

76 ·

楓橋夜泊　　　　　　　　　　　張繼

月落烏啼霜滿天，江楓漁火對愁眠。
姑蘇城外寒山寺，夜半鐘聲到客船。

Night Mooring at Maple Bridge
　　　　　　　　　　　　　Zhang Ji

The moon setting, crows crying,
frost filling the sky; maple leaves

along river banks, lanterns on
fishing boats, sorrowful sleep.

Outside Suzhou City, from Cold
Mountain Temple, the sound of

its bell travels to a traveler's
boat in the great depth of night.

唐詩明理 接千載
古今抒情詩三百首
漢英對照

我曾在漁人碼頭中競逐

林明理

我曾在漁人碼頭中競逐
那是飄雪的蠟梅氣味
啊北國！我用這裡海風傾訴
對你有多麼摯愛

到底是過去了，那閃爍的寒冷
我再不離開你視野
心中對你的想像
殷切如細絃

在你的滿林中，沒有人知道如何
或何時才能擁有泥土般堅實的愛
我癡愛的人啊 搖著小風船
划過山頭又渡滄江

你聽那不斷的猿聲，與那
映著夜幕的高塔一樣孤單
啊我的愛，那最後一瞥望見的
恰是你暖響的呼喚

I Used to Race in Fisherman's Wharf

Lin Ming-Li

I used to race in Fisherman's Wharf
It is the scent of wax plums falling snow
Oh, northland! I use the sea breeze to tell you
How much I love you

Finally it is past, the twinkling cold
I will not leave your vision
In my heart my imagination of you
As strong as a fine string

In your full forest, nobody knows how
Or when to have the solid love like earth
Oh my crazy love   rocking the boat in gentle wind
Across the mountain and the Cangjiang River

Listen to the constant howling of apes, as lonely
As the tower against the night curtain
Oh my love, the last glance
Is nothing but your warm call

✧✧✧

77.

月夜 劉方平

更深月色半人家，北斗闌幹南斗斜。
今夜偏知春氣暖，蟲聲新透綠窗紗。

Moonlit Night Liu Fangping

Deep into the night half the house
is lit by the moon; the North Star

is aslant and the South Star
is setting. Only tonight knows

the approach of warm spring,
since the chirping of the insects

for the first time travels into the
window shaded by green leaves.

雨後的夜晚 林明理

雪松寂寂
風裏我

聲音在輕喚著沉睡的星群
梧桐也悄然若思

路盡處，燈火迷茫
霧中
一個孤獨的身影
靜聽蟲鳴

雕像上的歌雀
狡黠又溫煦地環伺著
突然，一陣樂音
隨夜幕飛來⋯拉長了小徑

The Night After the Rain Lin Ming-Li

The cedar trees are silent
The wind is wrapping me
The voice is gently calling the sleeping stars
The parasol trees are quietly thinking

At the end of the road, dim lamplight
In the fog
A lonely figure
Quietly listens to the insects

The songbirds on the statue
Sly and gentle in waiting upon
Suddenly, a gush of musical sound
Comes with the night... to elongate the path

✧✧✧

78．

登樓望水 顧況

鳥啼花發柳含煙，擲卻風光憶少年。
更上高樓望江水，故鄉何處一歸船？

Gazing Afar on a Riverside Tower

Gu Kuang

Birds twitter, flowers
blossom, willows are

misty; so many years
spent, only childhood

is remembered. Climbing
up the riverside tower

to gaze afar: a leaf of
boat is bound homeward…

一棵開花的莿桐老樹[54] 林明理

我知道，這棵樹爺爺多稀珍，
——專家已全力搶救多次，
但並不是所有的百年老樹
都能再度開花長出新葉。

---

[54] 臺東縣鹿野鄉瑞和村土地公廟旁有棵一百一十歲以上的莿桐老樹，過去曾遭到釉小蜂危害，經台大植物系等單位治療十年後，老樹又逐漸健康。今年四月中旬，當我初見到這棵珍貴老樹，內心激動不已。我的故鄉在雲林縣莿桐鄉，莿桐國小校園內，每年夏初，莿桐花開，鮮艷火紅，樹冠高大，花朵成簇，也是我童年最愛的鄉花。—寫於 2019.4.14.

今天，我邊思念著故鄉的樹
　　邊在土地公廟旁漫步。
心卻像小鳥般
在您再生的枝葉間上下跳動。

若不是馨香的風
　　吹落一地似雞冠的花瓣，
我便不會乘著一朵雲
滑過綠野，飛回故鄉的懷抱。

若不是樹葉沙沙……
　　在我耳邊低語……
我便不會幸運地親近了，
眼眸裡流轉著一脈深情的您。

An Old Flowering Parasol Tree[55]

Lin Ming-Li

I know how rare this tree is for Grandfather,
—The experts have tried to save it for many times,
But not all century-old trees
Can bloom again and grow new leaves.

Today, I am walking by the temple of the land
　　While missing the trees of my hometown.

---

[55] There is an old parasol tree over 110 years near the Temple in Ruihe Village, Luye Township, Taitung County. It was damaged by a swarm of bees in the past. After ten years of treatment by the Department of Botany of Taiwan University, the old tree has gradually thrived again. In the middle of April this year, when I first see this precious old tree, my heart is filled with excitement. My hometown is in Citong Township, Yunlin County; in Citong Primary School, each early summer Citong flowers, bright and red, with a tall crown and massive flower clusters. It is also my favorite childhood rural flowers. — Written on April 14, 2019.

But my heart beats like a bird
In your renewed branches and leaves.

If it were not for the scented wind
   To blow petals like a comb on the ground,
I would not be riding a cloud
To glide across green fields, and fly back to my hometown.

If it were not for the rustling of leaves....
   Whispering in my ears....
I will not be lucky enough to be close,
With a deep feeling of you flowing in my eyes.

✧✧✧

79 •

悲歌 顧況

我欲升天隔霄漢，我欲渡水水無橋。
我欲上山山路險，我欲汲水水泉遙。

A Dirge   Gu Kuang

I want to fly heavenward,
but the clouds check me;

I want to cross the river,
but there is no bridge over it.

I want to go up the hill, but
the mountain path is perilous.

I want to fetch water, but the
fountain is too remote from me.

沒有第二個拾荒乞討婦[56]　　　　　　　林明理

沒有第二個拾荒乞討婦
像她養十二個棄嬰
過得如此辛苦，當年因無生育力
被夫家趕出門只能睡在豬圈裡
或者
漫山遍野的瘋跑準備結束脆弱的靈魂之際
如果不是村民救起
如果不是純真的幼兒給予生存的勇氣
太陽啊，你是否也毫不在意
是什麼樣的愛使這苦命女平靜下來，而她的雙手
由於要飯哺育而變得如此蒼白
而她把吃剩的地瓜絲和洋蘿蔔曬乾收好
時時提醒自己以免生病不時之需

啊，她肯定是上帝不慎遺忘的孤女
她站在那兒，瘦弱而貧疾
世界啊，快來丈量她的軀體
難道這樣的故事還不夠
讓我們一起去想想
等在社會邊緣的那些身影
難道天使之窗吝於拉開帷幕
直到那冷漠之啄敲開

---

[56] 在 2011 年 9 月 23 日，中國新聞網有一則新聞，一位六旬老太太，19 年來共收養 12 個棄嬰，僅靠乞討、拾荒度日，但只養活了 4 個。她手上牽著大妹，背上背著二妹，筐裏挑著三妹和小妹，每天走街、串巷地乞討，便是黃老太給村裡人的印象。在她 21 歲時，因無法生育，被夫家趕出家門，連娘家也不願意接納她。她終日渾渾噩噩地過著，一直到撿破爛時收養了棄嬰，她才有了努力活下去的希望。他們一家日子雖苦，但其樂融融，有感而作。此詩被刊在臺灣的「人間福報 Merit Times」副刊，2012.10.01。

夜幕從我流轉的眼神中逃離
她是否獲得了她的救贖,她的驚喜

There Is No Second Scavenger and Beggar[57]

Lin Ming-Li

There is no second scavenger and beggar
Who, like her, raises 12 abandoned babies
Such a hard time, inability of birth in her youth
She was driven out of her husband's family into a pigsty
Or
To run crazy across the mountains, ready to end her weak soul
If not for the villagers' rescue
If not for the innocent children to give her the courage to survive
Oh the sun, do you care or not
What kind of love has calmed the miserable woman, while her hands
Are so pale from the feeding
And she collects the leftover sweet potatoes and radishes
To remind herself of the need in illness

---

[57] On September 23, 2011, China News Network carries a piece of news: an old lady of 60 years, through 19 years has adopted a total of 12 abandoned babies, to make living by begging and scavenging, but only 4 babies survive. She holds the elder sister in her hand, carries the second sister on her back, puts the third sister and the little sister in the basket, walking the streets to beg day after day, which is the village's impression of the old lady Huang. At the age of 21, because she could not bear children, she was driven out of her husband's family, and even her mother's family was not willing to accept her. She lived in a messy life until she adopted the abandoned babies when she was collecting rubbish, and she had the hope of trying to live on. Although the life of their family is hard, they are happy to enjoy it. This poem was published in the supplement of *Merit Times* in Taiwan. October 1, 2012.

Oh, she must be God's forgotten orphan
She stands there, thin and poor
Oh the world, please measure her body.
Is it not enough for us to think of these stories
Let us think together
Those figures on the margins of society
The windows of angels are reluctant to draw open the curtain
Until the cold pecks open
The night curtain escapes from my wandering eyes
Whether she has attained her salvation, her surprise

✧✧✧

80.

秋日　　　　　　　　　　　　　　　　耿湋

反照入閭巷，憂來與誰語？
古道無人行，秋風動禾黍。

The Autumn Sun　　　　　　　　Geng Wei

Reflected into the lane
is the sunlight; O,

whom to share my
worries so strong?

Not a soul is seen
on the ancient road:

maize and millet
waving in autumn wind.

秋晨在鯉魚山公園[58]　　　　　　林明理

秋風早臨
晨間運動的人不談颱風
　　或天氣的好壞
百年老榕下
許多老人家在跳舞唱歌
讓人羨慕
可愛的
樹鵲、綠繡眼及烏頭翁
在忠烈祠坡道上來回穿梭……
走在碑前的寧靜中
呼吸著茄冬樹的氣息
聽蟬聲唧唧——在古木的樹梢
而我用一首讚歌
同它們道別——
如逆光飛翔的瓢蟲

Autumn Morning in Lei Yue Mountain Park[59]　　Lin Ming-Li

Autumn wind is early
The morning sports people do not talk about the typhoon
　　Or the weather is good or bad
Under the banyan of hundreds of years
Many old people are dancing and singing
So enviable
The lovely

---

[58] 從空中俯瞰如魚形的鯉魚山是臺東市區最大的綠地,其公園連結著舊臺東火車站,園內有胡鐵花等紀念碑。
[59] Viewed from the air, the fish-shaped Lei Yue Mountain is the largest green space in downtown Taitung, with a park connecting the old Taitung Railway Station and monuments such as Hu Tiehua.

Tree magpies, green eyes and aconite
Shuttling back and forth on the ramps of Loyalty Temple...
Walking in the silence before the monument
Breathing the smell of the nightshade trees
Listening to the chirps of the cicadas — atop the ancient tree
With a hymn I
Say goodbye to them —
With the ladybugs flying against the light

✧✧✧

81 •

別離作　　　　　　　　　　　　　　　　　戎昱

手把杏花枝，未曾經別離。
黃昏掩門後，寂寞自心知。

On Separation　　　　　　　　　　　　Rong Yu

A handful of apricot
flowers; separation has

not been experienced.
When the door is closed

after dusk, the lonely
heart, O, who knows?

我握你的手　　　　　　　　　　　　　　林明理

是否你也感到
我片刻的溫柔？——當我們
在此楓紅的十月午後

同步在白樺木橋，
在微風習習的彎道？

不。我讀你的唇
然後捕捉你想像的騰越
我採擷一枯葉，愛它
如我原始的樸真
高雲卻如此地寧靜；

而我呢？我觸及了一縷懸念，
起初它氣若遊絲
橫在樹蔭光縫裏穿梭
不久，它像柔網花叢般的
霧，轉瞬已遛逝

I Shake Your Hand   Lin Ming-Li

Do you also feel
My moment of tenderness? — when we
Are in the maple-red October afternoon
Synchronizing on the birch bridge
On the breezy bend?

No. I read your lips
And catch the flight of your imagination
I pick a dead leaf, and love it
Like my primordial simplicity
The high clouds are so quiet;

And me? I touch a wisp of suspense,
At first its breath is like a gossamer
Crisscross and shuttling in the shadow light and cracks
Soon, it is like a soft net of flowers
Like fog, to disappear in a moment

唐詩明理 接千載
古今抒情 唐詩三百首
漢英對照

✧✧✧

82・

與暢當夜泛秋潭　　　　　　　　　盧綸

螢火揚蓮叢，水涼多夜風。
離人將落葉，俱在一船中。

Night Boating on Autumn Lake with a Friend
Lu Lun

Among lotus leaves
fireflies fly, when

night wind blows
cool water high.

A leaf and two
persons to part,

O, are in the same
lonely boat.

回到過去　　　　　　　　　　　　林明理

我依稀聽到
古老
荒涼的
珊瑚群
在沿海盡端
發出呼喊
那裡是哭泣的

海百合[60]和三葉蟲
各種小生物的故鄉

一瞬間
這世界
彷彿變了樣
在空中
在我不經意的回眸裡
那浮游的
食物鏈
因饑餓而倒下
就像失神的骨牌
對人類的嘩啦提醒

Back to the Past　　　　　　Lin Ming-Li

I can hear faintly
The cry of
Ancient, desolate
Coral colonies
At the far end
Of the coast
Which is home to
Weeping crinoids[61] and
Trilobites of all sorts

For a moment
The world
Seems to have changed
In the air

---

[60] 海百合是一種始見於石炭紀的棘皮動物，生活於海裡，具多條腕足，身體呈花狀，表面有石灰質的殼。

[61] Crinoids are sea-dwelling echinoderms from the Carboniferous period, which have multiple arms, flower-shaped bodies and calcareous shells.

In my casual backward glance
The floating
Food chain
Collapsed from hunger
Like a lost domino's
Clattering reminder to mankind

✧✧✧

83 •

春夜聞笛 　　　　　　　　　　李益

寒山吹笛喚春歸，遷客相看淚滿衣。
洞庭一夜無窮雁，不待天明盡北飛。

Hearing Fluting in a Spring Night

Li Yi

Fluting in a cold mountain
to summon spring; when

exiled wanderers look at
each other, tears wet their

clothes. Countless geese
resting by Dongting Lake

in the night, all fly northward before the day breaks.

橄欖花 　　　　　　　　　　林明理

人群散了，放眼四方──
按捺不住的焦慮，
被夕陽的衣裳披滿。

那地中海的徘徊,
是無法停止的腳步;
相遇的古月,又朗誦
即將消隱的淡傷。

但我不能打烊,
當秋風來的時候,請記得
我的容顏已然
凝聚成純潔的曙光……

Olive Flowers   Lin Ming-Li

The crowd disperse, looking everywhere —
Irrepressible anxiety,
Covered with the sunset clothes.

The wandering of the Mediterranean Sea
Is the unstoppable steps;
To meet the ancient moon, and to recite
The light injury about to disappear.

But I can't close the shop,
When the autumn wind comes, please remember
That my face has
Condensed into the pure dawn...

✧✧✧

84 ·

登鸛雀樓   暢當

迴臨飛鳥上,高出世塵間。
天勢圍平野,河流入斷山。

Climbing the Stork Tower   Chang Dang

It towers above the
flying bird; detached

from the mortal world.
The field is enclosed

by heaven; rivers run
into broken mountains.

惦念   林明理

雨落在山丘上
帶著野茴香充滿驚奇的味道

漁村中
那些穿著雨靴的老人
在上帝的祝福裡　勞動著
案前有封泛黃的信箋
像深鎖著歷史的紀念碑
一直被擱在某一角落
霧，很輕柔
寂靜中的回音，已然足夠

雨，繼續無聲息地落著
帶著如此甜蜜又苦澀的味道

Solicitude   Lin Ming-Li

The rain falls on the hills
With wild fennel filled with wonder

In the fishing village
The old men in their rain boots

In the blessing of God   laboring
With yellow letterhead on the desk
Like a monument of history locked deep
Always in a corner
The fog, very soft and gentle
Echo in silence, quite adequate

The rain continues to fall silently
With such a sweet and bitter taste

✧✧✧

85 •

望春詞   令狐楚

高樓曉見一花開,便覺春光四面來。
暖日晴雲知次第,東風不用更相催。

Song of Spring View   Linghu Chu

A high tower in the
morning sees a flower

blossoming, and the
view of spring is

suffusing everywhere.
In warm days fine clouds

know the order: no need
for the east wind to urge.

趵突泉即景[62]

林明理

雨落在泉池中,如同
　　一只只白玉壺。它們
仰望著天空和彩雲
它們緊密相連
　　齊聲迸發,聲勢浩蕩
向濟南的土地展開自己
在舊城的西南角形成一個奇觀

它們是地理上典型的自流井
　　在岩石裂縫間上升
　　在水壓下噴出
這泉中的玉珠
　　夜夜歡唱。在早晨
炫目的陽光下,洗濯了塵土
　　奔放不羈,勇往直前
它們的低訴
　　有時像李清照的詩
在夢中,或醒著
　　　都一樣迷人

Sight of Baotu Spring[63]

Lin Ming-Li

The rain falls on the spring pool, like
One after another white jade pot. They
Look up at the sky and colorful clouds
Which are closely linked
　　Bursting out in unison, with a great force
Spreading themselves out in the land of Jinan

---

[62] 趵突泉位於中國山東省濟南市歷下區。
[63] Baotu Spring is located in Lixia District, Jinan City, Shandong Province, China.

Forming a spectacle in the southwest corner of the old city

Geographically they are typical artesian wells
   Rising between rock fissures
   And squirting out under water pressure
The jade beads from the spring
   Singing from night to night. In the morning
Under the dazzling sunshine, washing the dust
   Unrestrained, charging forward
Their whispers
   Are sometimes like the poems of Li Qingzhao
In the dream, or awake
     Always charming

✧✧✧

86 ·

早春呈水部張十八員外二首（其一） 韓愈

天街小雨潤如酥，草色遙看近卻無。
最是一年春好處，絕勝煙柳滿皇都。

Early Spring (No. 1)   Han Yu

The heavenly street sparkles
in a soft creamy drizzle, when

the field is peppered with bits
of green: showing from afar

but disappearing on the approach.
It is the fairest view in spring,

when the imperial capital is misty
with willows here and there.

晨露 　　　　　　　　　　　　　林明理

那凝，那明眸，我已淺醉……
滿山的星星，妳數著。妳是
聰穎、靜寂，妳是晶瑩的碧翠。

The Morning Dew 　　　　Lin Ming-Li

The condensation, the bright eyes, I am slightly tipsy...
A mountainful of stars, you count them. You are
Smart, quiet, you are crystal green.

✧✧✧

87．

湘中 　　　　　　　　　　　　韓愈

猿愁魚踴水翻波，自古流傳是汨羅。
蘋藻滿盤無處奠，空聞漁父扣舷歌。

By Miluo River 　　　　　　Han Yu

Sorrowful apes cry and fishes
leap in churning water: it is

Miluo River where Qu Yuan[64]
drowned himself. Clover fern

and algae fill the brim of
the river, nowhere to offer

---

[64] Qu Yuan is the first influential and patriotic Chinese poet who drowned himself in Miluo River when disappointed with the ruler of his country, hence the Dragon Boat Festival in memory of him.

sacrifices; the fisherman is
singing the boat song in vain.

晨光下的將軍漁港[65]   林明理

數不盡的日夜
這捕魚的門戶
再次與新的裝置藝術
成為最亮眼的風景

船隻穿越於黑面琵鷺
偶現的水流之處
雖是在夢中,卻教我
滿懷幸福

The General Fishing Harbor in Morning Twilight[66]   Lin Ming-Li

Countless days and nights
The fishing homestead
Once again becomes the most eye-catching scenery
With the new installation art

The boats are shuttling among black-faced spoonbills
In the occasional running water
Although in a dream, yet it teaches me
To be filled with happiness

✧ ✧ ✧

---

[65] 將軍漁港為臺灣台南沿海最大的漁港。—2024.12.21.

[66] The general fishing port is the largest fishing port along the Tainan coast of Taiwan. —December 21, 2024.

88.

春雪　　　　　　　　　　　　　　　　　　　韓愈

新年都未有芳華，二月初驚見草芽。
白雪卻嫌春色晚，故穿庭樹作飛花。

Spring Snow　　　　　　　　　　　　　Han Yu

The advent of the New Year
fails to exhibit any beauty of

green things; the third moon
is startled to see young grass

stem pushing, budding, sprouting…
Snowflakes hate the late coming

of spring: they fall and fly, as
blossoms, through courtyard trees.

偶然的佇足　　　　　　　　　　　　　　　林明理

若是在雪路
我底歷史，你底眼神
便開始重疊……

呵，那冰島罌粟的落日
沉溺於春霞的花田，
早已遺忘了峰頭的月。

電車緩緩地接近，就離開
夢未曾覆蓋的夜，
櫻花的枝葉撫摸着
片片落進憐憫的雪；

如果再有什麼悲,看
春天是不會向誰告別
它是柔如密林的清晨一泓帶露花的泉。

Occasional Stopping　　　　　Lin Ming-Li

In case of a snowy road
My history, your eyes
Will begin to overlap…

Oh, the Icelandic poppy sunset
Drowned in the flower field of spring rosy clouds,
Forgotten for long is the moon above the peak.

When the tram approaches slowly, it leaves
The night which the dream has not covered,
The cherry trees and leaves are caressing
A flake after another flake dropping into compassion;

If there is any sorrow, look
Spring is not to say goodbye to anybody
It is a spring with dew flowers in the morning soft like a forest.

✧✧✧

89 ·

江雪　　　　　　　　　　　　　　柳宗元

千山鳥飛絕,萬徑人蹤滅。
孤舟蓑笠翁,獨釣寒江雪。

The Fisherman　　　　　Liu Zongyuan

Hundreds of hills cut off
flight of birds; thousands

of paths witness no human
trace. A lonely boat carries

an old fisherman wearing
a straw rain hat: quietly

he sits, no thought of time,
solitarily angling cold river snow.

海祭　　　　　　　　　　　　　　　　林明理

第一次俯瞰母親
做大海之遊
用遼闊之藍
和雲朵　競著唱和
啊，真切的 Formosa
　向山脊的鹿群問候
　向嬉戲的清溪召喚
那淡漠的天空
也咀嚼著低吟的自由

當冬月升起時
聽，
那地母懷裡
有喜樂的心音
將――喚醒每一束
沉睡的靈魂
那祖靈庇護的――
是讓所有的言語和歌聲
能融和你我

看哪，
　我們的沃土
　我們的方舟
那星子的深婉

如母親眼底的溫柔
總賦予我堅定沉著
每當妳輕輕…喚我一聲
就刻劃下又一個
無晴的蒼穹

Sea Sacrifices   Lin Ming-Li

The first time I look down at Mother
For a journey at the sea
With the vast blue
And clouds   vying in singing
Oh true Formosa
   Greeting the deer on the mountain ridge
   Calling to the frolicking clear stream
The indifferent sky
Is also chewing the crooning freedom

When the winter moon rises
Listen,
In the bosom of Mother Earth
There is joyful music of heart
To awaken each beam of
Sleeping soul
Sheltered by the ancestral spirit —
For all the words and songs
To merge you with me

Behold,
   Our fertile land
   Our ark,
The depth of the stars
Gentle like the eyes of Mother
Always giving me firmness and composure
Whenever you gently... call me
To mark another
Sky without sunshine

90 ·

秋風引　　　　　　　　　　　　　　　　劉禹錫

何處秋風至？蕭蕭送雁群。
朝來入庭樹，孤客最先聞。

Autumnal Wind　　　　　　　　　　　Liu Yuxi

Where arises the autumnal
wind? Rustling and moaning,

it carries the wild geese.
The morning sees it entering

the courtyard trees: its first
hearer is a lonely wanderer.

知本濕地的美麗和哀愁[67]　　　　　　　林明理

曾經
在一片河口濕地上
　雨一住，眾鳥齊飛
陽光依舊　映在湖之心
　有環頸雉啼叫著

多麼安靜的草澤
多麼安靜的綠野
　還有牛羊和諸多生物群

---

[67] 知本濕地曾是臺灣東岸唯一擁有濕地與草原共構的自然濕地，位於知本溪北側出海口附近。2014 年 11 月，知本濕地首度觀察到全球僅存約兩千多隻的東方白鸛蹤跡。

甚至那些沒有消波塊的
　海岸，漾在我心中

留鳥不停地飛翔
　穿過溪流和部落
　　穿過高山和島嶼
　　閃入大海的一瞬⋯⋯
貼近的風　是輕柔的

The Beauty and Sorrow of Zhiben Wetland[68]

Lin Ming-Li

Once upon a time
In a river mouth wetland
When it stops raining, the birds would fly together
The sun still shines   in the heart of the lake
The pheasants are crowing

How quiet is the grassy wetland
How quiet is the green field
And the cattle, sheep and many living things
Even the coast without the waving
　Blocks, rippling in my heart

The resident birds fly ceaselessly
　Through streams and tribes
　　Through mountains and islands
　　Flashing into the sea......
The approaching wind is gentle

---

[68] The Zhiben Wetland has been the only natural wetland mixed with grassland in the east coast of Taiwan, which is located near the north outlet of Zhibenxi River. In November 2014, only about 2,000 Oriental white storks were observed in the Zhiben Wetland for the first time.

91．

浪淘沙九首（其一） 　　　　　　　　劉禹錫

九曲黃河萬里沙，浪淘風簸自天涯。
如今直上銀河去，同到牽牛織女家。

Waves Washing Sands (No. 1) 　Liu Yuxi

The circuitous Yellow River
rolls with sands of thousands

of miles; washed by waves
and tumbled by winds, it

comes from the horizon. Now
it runs toward the Silver River,

where the Cowboy and Weaving
Girl live their happy life.

懷柔千佛山[69] 　　　　　　　　　　林明理

你，靜坐在巍巍泰山的腳下
　　聽滔滔黃河的風
滿谷是梵宇僧樓和松柏
　　遠處有公園，遼闊而古老

我從海岸奔來
　　像是初次飛臨的雀鳥

---

[69] 千佛山位於中國山東省濟南市南郊。

拙笨地飛舞
　　進入密林的迷宮

你憂，你思
　　你垂下頭
你歌，你笑
　　用雙臂迎向了我

於是，我飛得很慢很慢
用茫茫雲海遮面
　　讓愛穿透時空
讓盈盈之淚，落在
　　馳向千佛山的手

Qianfo Mountain of Huairou[70]

Lin Ming-Li

You, sitting at the foot of the mighty Mount Tai
　　Listening to the wind of the billowing Yellow River
The valley is filled with monks and pines & cypress
　　In the distance there is a park, vast and ancient

I come running from the shore
　　Like a bird flitting for the first time
Awkwardly flying into
　　The maze of dense forests

You worry, you think
　　You bend your head
You sing, you smile
　　With arms to meet me

---

[70] Qianfo Mountain is located in the southern suburb of Jinan, Shandong Province, China.

So, I fly very slowly
With the vast sea of clouds to cover the face
   For love to go through time and space
For copious tears, to drop
   Into the hand of Qianfo Mountain

✧✧✧

92・

烏衣巷 　　　　　　　　　　　　　　　劉禹錫

朱雀橋邊野草花，烏衣巷口夕陽斜。
舊時王謝堂前燕，飛入尋常百姓家。

Lane of Black Clothes 　　　　　Liu Yuxi

Wild grass grows beside
the Bridge of Birds;

the setting sun slants
over Lane of Black Clothes.

Swallows wheeling by
painted eves of yore

now fly into the homes
of common people.

夢橋 　　　　　　　　　　　　　　　　林明理

我從西螺橋[71]下走過，
向最後的殘陽揮手。

---

[71] 「西螺大橋」Hsilo Bridge 位於臺灣雲林縣。

橋上只有奔程，只有回歸，
沒有風和雨的旋飛。

我回首望著暗澹天，
想起了那走盡田隴的老爹。
在溪灘沙田的耕作裡，
承受那汗珠滴落的白眉。

老爹說，
他擔心著暴雨，
又怕颱風來威脅——
他溫柔地種了西瓜，
不怕孤零的疏星和曉月。

今夜，
他把我的童年悄然掀起，
像一只古老的笛琴，
向那紅塵十丈處輕吹⋯⋯

The Dream Bridge Lin Ming-Li

I pass under Hsilo Bridge[72],
Waving to the last setting sun.
There is only running on the bridge, only returning,
Without swirling wind and rain.

I look back at the dark sky,
To think of my father who has gone through all the fields.
In the cultivation of Shatin,
To bear the white eyebrows dripping with sweat.

---

[72] Hsilo Bridge is located in Yunlin County, Taiwan.

Father says,
He is worried about the rainstorm,
And afraid of the threatening typhoon —
He gently plants watermelons,
Unafraid of lonely sparse stars and the morning moon.

Tonight,
He lifts up my childhood quietly,
Like an ancient flute,
Gently blowing to the red dust of the ten feet…

✧✧✧

93 ·

台城　　　　　　　　　　　　　　　　　劉禹錫

台城六代競豪華，結綺臨春事最奢。
萬戶千門成野草，只緣一曲後庭花。

An Ancient Imperial City　　　Liu Yuxi

The ancient imperial city
has witnessed six dynasties;

the pavilions built by Monarch
Chen are the most sumptuous.

Myriads of doors and gates
are now choked with weeds,

owing to his favorite pleasurable
song *Backyard Flowers*.

詠車城[73] 　　　　　　　　　　　林明理

將一路上迎面而過的防風林留在身後
我遠離大都會
以無數個形象把你幻想
在尋找飛鷹的孤途中
我獨坐黃昏
那落山風
又在隱隱作痛
箏曲般
揚一縷忠貞的清昂

Ode to Checheng[74] 　　　　　　Lin Ming-Li

The windbreaks that pass along the way will stay behind
I am far away from the metropolis
With countless images to fantasize you
In the search for a flying eagle
I sit alone in the evening
The wind falling from the mountain
Is again faintly painful
Like the music of zither
Curling with a ray of loyalty

---

[73] 車城 Checheng 位於臺灣屏東縣。1874 年 5 月 22 日，日軍進抵石門，當地原住民據險以抗。在此役中，牡丹社酋長阿祿古父子身亡，6 月 1 日起日軍分三路掃蕩原住民部落，佔領後焚燒村屋並撤回射寮營地；7 月 1 日，牡丹社、高士佛社、女仍社終於投降，是為牡丹社事件。

[74] The city of Checheng is located in Pingtung County, Taiwan. On May 22, 1874, the Japanese army reached Shimen, and the local aborigines fought against it. During this battle, Aluku and his son, the chief of Mudan Society, were killed. On June 1, the Japanese army swept up the indigenous tribes in three ways, occupied the village houses, and withdrew to the Sheiliao camp. On July 1, the Peony Society, the Gaoshifo Society, and the Nüreng Society finally surrendered, which was called the Peony Society incident.

唐詩明理 接千載
古今抒情詩三百首
漢英對照

✧✧✧

94·

襄陽寒食寄宇文籍 竇鞏

煙水初銷見萬家，東風吹柳萬條斜。
大堤欲上誰相伴，馬踏春泥半是花。

To a Friend on the Cold Food Day

Dou Gong

Over water mist is dispersed:
a host of homes are seen along

the bank; blown in the east wind,
myriads of willows dance aslant.

Riding a horse and trotting on
the bank, nobody to greet me;

beneath horse hooves, half the
spring mud is mixed with flowers.

憂鬱[75] 林明理

憂鬱，憂鬱何以如此淒美
讓佈滿蝶豆的山丘凝固
在我因妳而心痛
絕望的呼喚中
天空是那麼荒蕪
大地是那麼沉寂
在一小青墳的邊緣

---

[75] 讀山東大學詩人高蘭的《哭亡女蘇菲》有感而作。

224

噢,那童真的笑容
和海上的殘雪
在夜的顫動裡升起,牽著
渾無忌憚的風
將我層層包裹
無視於我的心在到處摸索
直到被銳利的月牙劃破

憂鬱,憂鬱何以如此神秘
讓嬌嫩的花菱草黯然
在被淚雨淋濕的記憶中
黎明是多麼緩慢
生與死彷若無間
只有愛
耀眼的光輝……

Melancholy[76]   Lin Ming-Li

Melancholy, why is melancholy so beautiful
For the hills covered with butterfly beans to freeze
I feel heartbroken for you
In the desperate cry
The sky is so barren
The earth is so silent
At the edge of a small green grave

Oh, the childlike smile
And the remnant snow on the sea
Rising in the quiver of the night, leading
The unafraid wind
To wrap me in layers
To gnore my heart groping everywhere
Until it is cut by the sharp crescent moon

---

[76] Inspired upon reading *Crying My Deceased Daughter Sophie* by Gao Lan, a poet of Shandong University.

Melancholy, why is melancholy so mysterious
For the delicate flowers and grasses to be dispirited
In the wet memory of the rain of tears
How slow is the dawn
As if there is no one distance between life and death
Only love
The brilliant light of love…

◇◇◇

95·

秋夕 　　　　　　　　　　　　　　　　　　　　竇鞏

護霜雲映月朦朧，烏鵲爭飛井上桐。
夜半酒醒人不覺，滿池荷葉動秋風。

An Autumn Evening　　　　　　　　　　Dou Gong

Protective frost, clouds
mirror, the moon hazy; crows

and magpies vie to fly atop
the parasol tree by the well.

Awake from a drunken sleep
in midnight, nobody knows;

the pool, grown with lotus leaves,
is rustling in autumn wind.

池上風景一隅　　　　　　　　　　　　　　林明理

靜秋，稻穀結穗了，
在雨後的陽光下閃耀。
數十隻野鳥，

在電線桿上歌著，
被車聲干擾，——
箭一般地穿過半空，
一晃眼就消失了。
只有雲朵　泊在山凹，
　　像是在候著什麼？
水聲和溝壑縱橫
　　　　——湧流其中。
被山環繞的鄉村，
村落被稻田環繞。
當陽光微露
　　　直射大坡池，
一行白鷺從水面掠過……
欒樹開花了，
火把果也開得燦爛奪目。
我一邊諦聽風中微語，
一邊感受豐收的預兆。

View of Chishang   Lin Ming-Li

In quiet autumn, the corn has ears,
　　Shining in the sun after rain.
Dozens of wild birds,
　　Singing on the telephone pole,
Disturbed by the sound of cars —
　　Shooting through the air like arrows,
And disappear in the blink of an eye.
Only are clouds are wafting in the hollow,
　　As if waiting for something?
The sound of water and the ravines
　　　— Flowing in it.
Villages surrounded by mountains,
Villages are surrounded by paddy fields.
When the sun shines faintly
　　Directly on the slope pool,

唐詩明理 接千載
古今抒情詩三百首
漢英對照

A file of white egrets skimming over water...
The koelreuteria is blossoming,
The torch fruits are also blooming brilliantly.
As I listen to whispers in the wind,
I feel the signs of harvest.

✧✧✧

96 ·

洛橋晚望　　　　　　　　　　　　孟郊

天津橋下冰初結，洛陽陌上人行絕。
榆柳蕭疏樓閣閒，月明直見嵩山雪。

Night View on Luoyang Bridge　Meng Jiao

Beneath Luoyang Bridge
the ice begins to freeze, when

streets and lanes of Luoyang
are empty of walkers. About

quiet towers and terraces, elms
and willows are bare of branches;

in bright moon light, the snow
atop Mount Song is distinct.

雖已遠去　　　　　　　　　　　　林明理

在湖濱的秋聲
和萬葉的晚煙之間，
一行白鷺
飛起，如幻夢。

聽，夜蟲為誰而泣？大自然
又超乎尋常地將我包容，
可憐的風　繼續
擔任勇敢而坦蕩的角色。

Though Far Away   Lin Ming-Li

Between the autumn sound of the lakeside
And the evening smoke of ten thousand leaves,
A bevy of white egrets
Flying up, like a dream.

Listen, for whom are the night insects crying? Nature
Bear me most tolerantly
The pitiable wind continues
To play a brave and honest role.

✧✧✧

97 •

秋思   張籍

洛陽城裡見秋風，欲作家書意萬重。
復恐匆匆說不盡，行人臨發又開封。

Autumn Thoughts   Zhang Ji

In the capital autumnal
wind rises high, which

reminds me to write
a letter home. For fear

of something amiss
in the letter, I check

it again before
the postman departs.

墨菊 　　　　　　　　　　　　　　　　　林明理

你是多年前
從菊譜裡　飛出的
草龍
時間的長河中　笑容依是
如此嫻靜
而我
只是路過時　不慎回首的
行者　只想將你
匯入飄遊的夢中

Black Chrysanthemum 　　　　Lin Ming-Li

You are the grass dragon
Flying from the chrysanthemums
Many years ago
In the long river of time   smile is still
So quiet
When I am
Only a passersby, looking back
Occasionally   only to keep you
In my wandering dream

✧✧✧

成都曲 　　　　　　　　　　　　　　　　張籍

錦江近西煙水綠，新雨山頭荔枝熟。
萬里橋邊多酒家，遊人愛向誰家宿？

Ode to Chengdu   Zhang Ji

Running through Chengdu,
the Silk River is green and

misty; after a fresh shower,
litchi on the mountain slope

is ripe. Near Wanli Bridge south
of the city, there are many wine-

shops: which one do visitors
prefer to make their lodging in?

寫給包公故里——肥東   林明理

是怎樣的企盼，怎樣的憧憬？讓我飛越海洋的邊界，泊在巢湖之畔。
你說：「跟隨我吧！我是你的舵手。」
如果我往你身邊走，迎著的這股風，散發著彼處和遠方的芳菲——聽稻浪的柔音，還有那如海似的翠微。
頭頂參天老木，這裡只剩下美和真。
美在皖中腹地，真在耕者鋤禾裡。
輕快的白雲，群山和寧靜的沃土……都在我的血液中搏動。
溪流在岩邊跳著舞，古民也唱出心中的歌。它突破了語言的疆界，歌裡飽含著透徹的靈魂，使我聯想起自己久別的故里，沒有任何虛妄，但我驚訝於它如何歷經千年依然為世人所傳頌？
如果我閉目靜聽，就會聽到河湖的低語，如果我凝望著那藏在山谷外的藍霧，這對我來說，彷彿是豐富的饗宴。

啊，今夜，我依舊做著旅人的夢，夢裡用眼睛尾隨著飛逝的船隻，我感到莫名的幸福。當我目光與你對視，是你甜柔的歌聲，讓所有野花開放。

你屬於永恆，而我懷著這樣的深情，在我隱秘的心底，世上再沒有什麼樂音，讓我鼓舞地駛過萬頃波浪。

如果你看我，我就帶著江淮之間的夕陽和唇邊一朵微笑，邊哼著歡樂的小曲，邊駛向黑石咀的金色沙灘，在天宇間漫步，與你吟咏。

To the Hometown of Bao Gong: Feidong

Lin Ming-li

What kind of hope, what kind of longing? For me to fly across the boundary of the ocean, to moor on the side of Chaohu Lake.
You say, "Follow me, I am your helmsman."
If I go to your side, facing the wind, to exude sweet scent here and there — listen to the soft sound of paddy waves, and the ocean-like green. Overhead towering old trees, here only beauty and truth.
Beauty in the hinterland of central Anhui province, really in the cultivator' hoe.
Light white clouds, mountains and quiet fertile soil... All is beating in my blood.
The streams dance on the rocks, and the ancient people sing songs in their hearts. It breaks through the boundaries of language, the song is rich with a thorough soul, which reminds me of my hometown after a long absence, without any illusion, but I am surprised how it has been celebrated by the world for thousands of years. If I close my eyes to listen, I can hear the murmur of the lake and the river, and if I gaze at the blue mist hidden beyond the valley, it is like a feast to me.
Oh, tonight, I still have a traveler's dream, where with my eyes to follow the fleeting ship, I feel inexplicable

happiness. When I look at you, it is your sweet voice that makes all the wildflowers bloom.

You belong to eternity, and with such deep feeling in my secret heart, there is no music in the world to encourage me to sail through the boundless waves.

If you look at me, I will take the sunset between the Yangtze River and Huai River and a smile on my lips, while humming a song of joy and driving to the golden beach of Black Stone Tsui, walking in the sky, singing with you.

✧✧✧

99 •

湘江曲　　　　　　　　　　　　　　　張籍

湘水無潮秋水闊，湘中月落行人發。
送人發，送人歸，白蘋茫茫鷓鴣飛。

Ditty of Xiang River　　　　　Zhang Ji

No tide in Xiang River
and autumn water is wide;

the traveler starts off at
moonset in Xiangzhong.

Seeing people away,
seeing people back;

over boundless duckweed
partridges wheel and fly.

歷下亭遠眺[77]

林明理

秋夜
　溢香的荷花已經入睡了
當涼風徐吹
整個島上
所有的花木，還有盪漾的湖
　都不禁動容

你是大明湖中最美的一景
　久經滄桑
不變的是行吟詩人在夢中
　輕輕地唱著歌
每個音符都有一段故事
每個名士都讀懂你的心思

我聽見
　杜甫的歌流動著水鳥的聲音
當蔚藍的湖光沾上我的眼眸
我才知道
　　為了聚散兩依依
你可以給這客亭帶來四季春色

Overlooking in the Distance at Lixia Pavilion[78]

Lin Ming-Li

In an autumn night
　The fragrant lotus flowers have fallen asleep
When the cool wind blows

---

[77] 歷下亭（Lixia Pavilion），是濟南名亭之一。
[78] Lixia Pavilion is one of the famous pavilions in Jinan.

On the whole island
All the flowers and trees, and the rippling lake
   Cannot help but to be touched

You are the most beautiful scene in Daming Lake
   Through vicissitudes of life
Constant is the troubadour singing softly in the dream
   Singing gently
Each note has a story
Each famous man can read your mind

I hear
   Du Fu's songs flowing with the sound of waterfowls
When the blue light of the lake touches my eyes
I know that
   In order to gather and disperse leisurely
You can bring the four seasons of spring to this pavilion

✧✧✧

100·

江陵使至汝州 　　　　　　　　　王建

回看巴路在雲間，寒食離家麥熟還。
日暮數峰青似染，商人說是汝州山。

Arriving at Ruzhou from Jiangling
Wang Jian

Looking back: Sichuan road
meanders into clouds; I leave home

on Cold Food Day when the field
is tender green and return when

the field is golden with ripe wheat.
At dusk a few peaks loom blue

as if dyed; the businessman says
those are mountains of Ruzhou.

緬懷金瓜石[79]老街　　　　　　　　林明理

霧蒙住了遠方，老街靜滯黃昏裡。
　　天色暗下來，街燈便亮了。
如果山城中沒有昔日的歡笑，
　　沒有山脈的聲音在耳畔吟唱；
如果聚落不是那麼寧靜溫馨，
　　沒聽到你漸近的腳步聲……
我就不會在風中重覆呼喚你的名字，
　　在離你最近的地方等待著，
　　　　像等待時間老人一樣。

啊，我愛你乍雨初晴的容顏，
　　眼裡閃爍著熾熱的光芒；
愛你殘留的廣場和石造牆基，
　　芒草花開的悵然。
愛你和海洋相輝映和礦山聚落的味道。
愛你的巷道小橋，水碧山青和古厝。

即便是雨霧瀰漫，在我心中，
　　悅耳的山城小調響起來了。
啊，小河流啊，小河流，年年緩緩流過。
東海上　漁光點點，你的背影依然熟悉，
　　思念長長，我們的相會猶若夢中。

---

[79] 金瓜石 Jinguashi 在新北市瑞芳區，早期曾因開採金礦而為重要礦區，但隨著礦產枯竭而迅速沒落，如今朝向觀光休閒方向重新發展。

In Memory of Jinguashi[80] Old Street

Lin Ming-Li

Fog has covered the distance, and the old street is static in dusk.
    It is darkening, and the street lights come on.
If there is no laughter of yore in the mountain city,
    And no mountain voice singing in my ear;
If the settlement is not so peaceful and warm,
    Without hearing your approaching footsteps....
I would not have repeatedly called your name in the wind,
    Waiting in the place closest to you,
        Like waiting for the old time.

Oh, I love your sunny appearance from rain,
    With the blazing light in your eyes;
Love your residual square and stone wall base,
    Miscanthus flowers melancholy.
I love you and the ocean and the smell of my settlements.
I love your laneway bridge, water green mountains and ancient houses.

Even if the rain and fog fill the air, in my heart,
    The pleasant little tune of the mountain city is sounding.
Oh, little river, little river, year after year flowing slowly.
At the East China Sea dots of fishing light, your back is still familiar,
    The yearning is long, our meeting is like a dream.

✧✧✧

---

[80] Jinguashi is in Ruifang District, New Taipei City, and it has been an important mining area for gold mining in the early days, but it declines rapidly with the depletion of minerals, and now it is developing in the direction of tourism and entertainment.

101 ·

菊花　　　　　　　　　　　　　　　　　元稹

秋叢繞舍似陶家，遍繞籬邊日漸斜。
不是花中偏愛菊，此花開盡更無花。

Chrysanthemums　　　　　　　Yuan Zhen

Surrounded by clusters of
chrysanthemums, my house

is similar to that of Tao Yuanming
the flower-lover. Admiring golden

flowers along the hedge, the
sun is setting. Not that I favor

chrysanthemums, but no
other flowers to be admired.

香蒲　　　　　　　　　　　　　　　　林明理

用遠山淡青的晚煙
　　迎稀疏飛鳥的歸來
我似一柱香
　　點我默望的喜樂

The Bulrush　　　　　　　　　Lin Ming-Li

With the green evening smoke in the distant mountain
　　To welcome the return of sparse birds
Like a pillar of incense
　　To enkindle my joy of contemplation

✧✧✧

102．

離思五首（其四）   元稹

曾經滄海難為水，除卻巫山不是雲。
取次花叢懶回顧，半緣修道半緣君。

Five Poems About Parting Emotions (No. 4)
     Yuan Zhen

Having seen the vast sea,
no water is real water;

except for clouds over Wushan
Mountain, there are no clouds

in a real sense. Walking among
flowers, I do not deign to look

closely at them: partly out
of Taoism, partly out of you.

思念似穿過月光的鯨群之歌   林明理

思念似穿過月光的鯨群之歌
緩慢而綿長……

我傾聽，有時它驟然而降
每一個音符都清晰純淨
無法移動——

而那些沉溺其中的記憶
如我在讀你的時光

Longing Is Like the Song of Whales Through the Moonlight
Lin Ming-Li

Longing is like the song of whales through the moonlight
Which is slow and long...

I listen, and sometimes it falls so suddenly
That each note is clear and pure
And cannot be moved —

And the memories of those addicted to it
Are like the time I read you

✧✧✧

103 ·

夜雪　　　　　　　　　　　　　　白居易

已訝衾枕冷，復見窗戶明。
夜深知雪重，時聞折竹聲。

Night Snow
Bai Juyi

The quilt is surprisingly
cold, and I see my window

bright. Deep night knows
the heavy snow: occasionally

audible is the cracking
of bamboo branches.

如果我是塵沙　　　　　　　　　林明理

殘夜中
我將冉冉飛入
一片雪地
讓篤篤的馬蹄聲
不再恐懼於
被星掩蔽……

等黎明之光
喚醒我
曾是驚惶的
眼，它已邁出了
所有的
執著

If I Were Dust　　　　　　　Lin Ming-Li

In the remnant night
I will slowly fly
Into a snowy field
For the sound of horses' hooves
No longer to be afraid of
Being masked by the stars...

When the light of dawn
Awakens my
Eyes which have been terrified
It has stepped out of
All its
Attachments

✧✧✧

104·

暮江吟   白居易

一道殘陽鋪水中,半江瑟瑟半江紅。
可憐九月初三夜,露似真珠月似弓。

A River at Sunset   Bai Juyi

A beam of setting
sun paves the river:

half red and half
greenish. Loveable

is the third night
of the tenth moon:

dewdrops are pearls
and the moon is a bow.

畜欄的空洞聲   林明理

畜欄的空洞聲
在暮夏透亮的清晨
是這天際間
最最淡薄的顫動,——

那是泉石的重音
冷不提防地,敲醒我
在一瞬間
又依著小谷上推磨

水鏡的綠意
斟滿了我的思想,

紙莎草遠遠地宣示著
讓愛消瘦，長若雪河。

The Hollow Sound of the Corral

Lin Ming-Li

The hollow sound of the corral
In the bright morning of late summer
In the sky
Is the faintest quiver —

It is the accent of the spring stone
Unawares, to knock me awake
In an instant
To grind on the grain again

The green of the water mirror
Fills my thoughts,
The papyrus proclaims from afar
To make love thin and long as a river of snow.

❖❖❖

105 ·

大林寺桃花 白居易

人間四月芳菲盡，山寺桃花始盛開。
長恨春歸無覓處，不知轉入此中來。

Peach Flowers in Dalin Temple

Bai Juyi

When flowers fall
and fade in May, peach

flowers begin to blossom
in mountain temple.

For a long time I regret
the vanished spring,

without knowing that
it has retreated here.

向開闢中橫公路的榮民及罹難者致敬

林明理

若時光能倒回
　　　　便看得見
遠從千里外來的
　　　　一萬餘官兵
胼手胝足
　　無畏地勢險惡
　　用鐵鏟及炸藥
闢出一條中橫公路
冬去春來
　　這批開路榮民多已凋亡
遠去的年代
只留下經國先生多次視察
　　和築路者的身影
一部退輔會製作的黑白片
　　記錄了開山闢路的台灣心
這批榮民已盡了他們的責任
身後
　　應受到我們的懷念與尊榮

Salute to the Veterans and Victims of the Construction of the Central Cross Highway
Lin Ming-Li

If the light can go back
    It can be seen
Over ten thousand officers and soldiers
    From thousands of miles away
With callous hands and feet
    In spite of the evil terrain
    With shovels and explosives
To open a central cross highway
Winter out and spring in
  Most trail blazers in the group have withered away
In the years long past
Only Chiang Ching-kuo have inspected for many times
  And the figures of the road builders
A black & white film produced by the Retreat Society
  Has recorded the Taiwanese heart in blazing the trail
These veterans have done their duty
In the future years
  They should be remembered and honored by us

✧✧✧

106 ·

白雲泉 白居易

天平山上白雲泉，雲自無心水自閒。
何必奔沖山下去，更添波浪向人間。

White Cloud Fountain
Bai Juyi

White Cloud Fountain
is in Peaceful Mountain;

clouds are drifting
freely in the wind,

water running at ease.
Why should the water

run downhill to make
the noisy world noisier?

思念在藍色海洋慢慢氳開…　　　林明理

是誰發出低柔而清晰的聲音？
瞬間打破我心的寂寥。
天空已浮現黎明的前兆，
草海桐的花，引頸翹望。

在觸不到你，使我臉紅的
地方，只有在此一隅繼續歌唱。
思念在藍色海洋慢慢氳開…
足下的浪花也沉默不語。

　　　　　　　　　　　—2024.12.24

Yearning Is Slowly Spreading in the Blue Ocean...
Lin Ming-Li

Who makes the low, clear sound?
Suddenly to break the loneliness of my heart.
In the sky the precursor of dawn has emerged,
Sea lettuce flowers, looking forward.

Where I cannot touch you and it makes me
Blush, only in this corner to keep singing.
Yearning is slowly spreading in the blue ocean…
The waves beneath my feet are silent.

　　　　　　　　　　—December 24, 2024.

✧✧✧

107.

村夜　　　　　　　　　　　　　　　白居易

霜草蒼蒼蟲切切，村南村北行人絕。
獨出門前望野田，月明蕎麥花如雪。

The Village Night　　　　　　　Bai Juyi

In frost-bitten gray grass
insects are twittering;

from north to south of
the village not a soul is

seen. Solitarily I walk to
the village edge and gaze

toward the field: like snow
are flowers of buckwheat.

在雕刻室裡　　　　　　　　　　　林明理

天窗下的那雙手
　　全神貫注地
　　　　有如碼頭上的一盞燈
從孤寂海洋
　　　凝視記憶裡的小徑

沒人看到這個老人
　　燭光底下幾近透明的
臉及深碧的眼睛

啊，今晚且讓我的愛
也歪斜在空中敲響，叮叮噹噹……

In the Carving Room　　　　　Lin Ming-Li

The hands under the skylight
　　Are as engrossed as
　　　　A lamp on a pier
Gazing down a remembered path
　　　　From the lonely sea

Nobody sees the old man
　　　　Under candlelight nearly transparent
The deep blue eyes
　　　Ah, tonight for my love
To ring crooked in the air, on the tinkling...

✧✧✧

108 ·

寒閨怨　　　　　　　　　　　白居易

寒月沉沉洞房靜，真珠簾外梧桐影。
秋霜欲下手先知，燈底裁縫剪刀冷。

Complaint of Cold Palace　　　Bai Juyi

Low hangs the cold
moon and quiet is the

chamber; beyond bead
curtain parasol trees

are swaying. The hands
first know the descending

frost: needlework by the
candle, scissors are cold.

暴風雨 林明理

鬼哭神號
高舉著一盞不發光的燈
四處掠奪
是誰？
掩蓋著每一次戰慄
守望著黎明前的每一粒閃爍

當幽咽的流籠
回望古老的部落
一個啞默的小孩
緊緊拉住母親的手
記者追問：
你們需要什麼？

同是這樣的夜晚
卻是不一樣的天空
她，流著淚
用手指那湧向屋內的水
我們什麼也沒有了

風，正伏在外頭——

—寫於 2009.8.8 強颱莫拉克颱風夜

The Rainstorm Lin Ming-Li

Wailing like ghosts and howl like deities
Holding high a lamp that refuses to glow
To plunder here and there
Who is it?

Covering every shudder
Watching each grain of flicker before dawn

When the throbbed cage
Looks back to the ancient tribe
A mute child
Holds fast his mother's hand
The reporter asks:
What do you need?

The same night
Is a different sky
She, with tears
Pointing to the water pouring into the house
We have nothing

The wind is lurking outside —

          —Written on the night of Typhoon Morakot
                           on August 8, 2009

✧✧✧

109 ·

遺愛寺   白居易

弄石臨溪坐，尋花繞寺行。
時時聞鳥語，處處是泉聲。

Yi'ai Temple   Bai Juyi

Sitting by a creek,
fondling a stone,

in search of flowers,
I walk around temple.

From time to time
birds' twitters are heard;

from spot to spot
spring water is gurgling.

詩河   林明理

你來自八荒
　激勵我奇思冥想
那叮咚的回聲
時刻盤旋著，搖曳的銀波
　輕漾藍調的柔歌

The Poetic River   Lin Ming-Li

You are from extremely remote areas
　To motivate me into flights of thought
The ding-dong echo
Is on the rippling, silver waves
　Gently with a blue soft song

✧✧✧

春風   白居易

春風先發苑中梅，櫻杏桃李次第開。
薺花榆莢深村裡，亦道春風為我來。

Spring Breeze   Bai Juyi

first blows plum blossoms
in the capital garden,

those of cherry, apricot,
peach, plum in the wake.

Shepherd's purses and
elm seeds in the deep

village also claim spring
breeze as their blower.

逗留　　　　　　　　　　　　　　　　林明理

我知道誰是天空的小孩
儘管它的眼睛充滿了愛
它卻看不到我在此等待
那載滿甘蔗的小火車來

夕陽是我，我的寧靜海
看它每天想逗留
陪我嬉戲的時候
薄雲被風指使了
輕輕地披上粉紅嫁衣
只有落葉的微音
聽起來像是淡淡地歎息

但我必須迎向它的懷抱裡
迎向紫雲英的臉
迎向油菜花的手
迎向碗豆葉的鼻
讓田畝洋溢著笑語
讓凝視我的原野
不忍別離……

Sojourn
                                    Lin Ming-Li

I know who is the child of the sky
Whose eyes are full of love
But fail to see me waiting
For the little train loaded with sugar cane

The sunset is me, my quiet sea
To see it every day to stay
To accompany me to play
The thin clouds are ordered by the wind
Gently covered with pink wedding clothes
Only the faint voice of falling leaves
Sounding like a faint sigh

But I must welcome its embrace
To the face of Ziyunying
To the hands of rapeseed flowers
To the nose of the bowl bean leaves
For the field to be filled with laughter
For the field gazing at me
Can not bear to leave…

✧✧✧

111 ·

鶴   白居易

人各有所好，物固無常宜。
誰謂爾能舞，不如閒立時。

The Crane   Bai Juyi

Different people have
different preferences;

nothing is long-winded
and long-lasting.

Who says you are a
good dancer? Elegance

reigns when you are
standing leisurely.

來自珊瑚礁島的聲音[81]　　　　　　林明理

他浮游在呼嘯與沉默之間
猶如放牧的雲，
望眼欲穿的灰鷹；
時間與地平線傾斜
急疾地
飛過了呆立的容顏；
在揚起的貝殼沙上
顯得格外憔悴。
荒老的旋律也離得很遠……

今夜陸蟹正竊竊私語——
依稀聽到暴風雨的事：
層層海浪向我急急召喚
電光劈著熟悉的路徑
月兒掩面　星兒驚
存在與不存在，叫我忐忑不寧
到底天空之城
是否再也尋不回那美麗的椰景

---

[81] 因地球暖化，「消失的國界」與日漸增，有感而文。

Sounds From the Coral Islands[82]

Lin Ming-Li

He floats between whistling and silence
Like a grazing cloud,
The gray eagle with eager eyes;
Time and horizon tilt
Quickly
Flying over the stupid face;
On the raised shell sand
Looking very haggard.
The old melody is far away....

Tonight, the land crabs are whispering —
Faintly to the storm:
Layers of waves to me urgently call
The electric light is splitting the familiar path
The moon covers the face　the stars are startled
Existence and non-existence, making me uneasy
Finally the sky city
Whether or not to retrace the beautiful coconut scene

✧✧✧

112 ·

望月懷江上舊遊　　　　　　　　雍陶

往歲曾隨江客船，秋風明月洞庭邊。
為看今夜天如水，憶得當時水似天。

---

[82] Owing to global warming, there is more and more "disappearing of national borders", hence this poem.

Missing an Old Playmate in a Moonlit Night
Yong Tao

In years of yore I have ever
followed the guest ship;

at Dongting Lake, under
the bright moon, in autumn

wind. Tonight the sky is like
water, I still remember those

nights we enjoyed together
when water is like the sky.

致杜甫
林明理

我用天空寫下你的名字
你沿著足徑
　　　在地圖上飛行
數千年過去了
在千里沃野的天際之下
你的歌和濟世情懷
　　　仍影響著歷史
從老城的舊居
　　撼動著宇宙和神州

Tribute to Du Fu
Lin Ming-Li

I write your name in the sky
Along the footpath
　　You fly on the map
Thousands of years have slipped by
Beneath the sky of fertile field for thousands of miles
Your songs and the world-saving ambition
　　Still influence history

From the old obode of the ancient city
  Shaking the universe and the divine land

✧✧✧

113・

晚春江晴寄友人 韓琮

晚日低霞綺，青山遠畫眉。
春青河畔草，不是望鄉時。

To a Friend in Late Spring When It Shines on the River
Han Cong

The setting sun renders
rosy clouds low; a touch

of blue of the remote
mountain is like the brow

of a beauty. Spring wind
has greened the river-side

grass: it is not yet the
time to gaze homeward.

致吾友——Prof. Ernesto Kahan 林明理

巨大的冰河
也無法消融我的銘記。
你神奇地出現
激起所有思想的漣漪，
  如冰晶之中的幻影
  似原野樹梢的雪花；

257

唐詩明理接千載
古今抒情詩三百首
漢英對照

你對我說的每句輕聲細語，
　　讓我生命帶有
色彩、笑容和明燦的未來。

—2018.02.17

To My Friend Prof. Ernesto Kahan

Lin Ming-Li

Even great glaciers
Cannot melt my memory.
You magically appear
To stir the ripples of all thoughts,
　　Like visions in ice crystals
　　Like snowflakes on the tops of wild trees;
Each whisper you say to me
　　Brings color, smile and
Bight future to my life.

—February 17, 2018.

✧✧✧

114 ·

洞靈觀流泉

李郢

石上苔蕪水上煙，潺湲聲在觀門前。
千岩萬壑分流去，更引飛花入洞天。

Watching a Waterfall

Li Ying

Moss on the stone and fog
over water; the sound

of rippling water echoes
before the door. Thousands

of rocks and hundreds
of rills run separately,

which draw flying flowers
into the cave-sky.

巨石陣[83] 　　　　　　　　林明理

來自平原的風
混雜著巨人的歎息
　　幾千年過去了
他們仍手牽手圍成大圓圈
回應著星宿的召喚
在夏至月亮升起之光裡
　　歌詠著古老的舞曲

Stonehenge[84] 　　　　　　　　Lin Ming-Li

The wind from the plain
Is mixed with the sighs of the giants
　　Thousands of years have passed
They still form a big circle hand-in-hand
Responding to the call of the stars
In the rising moonlight of the summer solstice
　　They are singing the ancient dancing song

✧✧✧

---

[83] 巨石陣 Stonehenge，是世界文化遺產，英國威爾特郡馬平川平原上的史前建築遺跡。

[84] Stonehenge is the prehistoric monuments located in the plain of Horseflat, Wiltshire of Britain, and it is the world's cultural heritage.

115·

泊秦淮　　　　　　　　　　　　　　杜牧

煙籠寒水月籠沙，夜泊秦淮近酒家。
商女不知亡國恨，隔江猶唱後庭花。

Mooring by River Qinhuai　　　Du Mu

Cold water veiled in mist
and sand bathed in moonlight,

the ship brings me to a wineshop
by River Qinhuai, where

a singsong girl, unaware of
the sorrow of a conquered state,

is singing *Backyard Flowers*
on the river's other side.

二二八紀念公園冥想　　　　　　林明理

再讀一次碑文
天空如此寬廣
公園裡多麼安靜
流逝的光陰映出歷史的倒影
我願憧憬著未來
　　用愛來包容一切
我願在這個夏天
　　再次回到你身邊
像一株原野的魯冰花
臥看浮雲飄蕩
把話語鑲在千山萬壑間
再讀一次碑文

便熱血奔湧
高高的紀念碑⋯
⋯在陽光裡晶瑩閃亮

Meditation in the 228 Memorial Park

Lin Ming-Li

Once more to read the inscription
The sky is so wide
How quiet it is in the park
The bygone time mirros the reflection of history
I look forward to the future
　With love to bear everything
I would like to come back to you
　Again in this summer
Like a dull-ice flower in the field
Lying to see the floating clouds
To set words in the mountains and valleys
Once more to read the inscription
　Blood rushing and boiling
The tall monument....
　...shining brilliant in the sunlight

✧✧✧

116．

山行　　　　　　　　　　　　　　　杜牧

遠上寒山石徑斜，白雲生處有人家。
停車坐愛楓林晚，霜葉紅於二月花。

A Mountain Trip　　　　　　　Du Mu

A winding path leads heavenward — I clamber to the cold

mountaintop, to find a lofty
residence in the clouds of clouds.

I stop my coach to admire
eventide maple woods: frost-

bitten leaves are redder than
flowers of the third moon.

風滾草 　　　　　　　　　　　　　　　　林明理

在飄泊中
在大風裡
我看到一條寂寞的
河流
推醒流沙
穿過半折裂的樹

一叢風滾草
像朝聖者般
呼喊
聲音隱祕又低沉
閃光吐焰之處　不斷
傳來草原鳴啼的歌聲

The Tumbleweed 　　　　　　　　　Lin Ming-Li

Floating and wandering
In the great wind
I see a lonely
River
Pushing awake the running sand
Through half-broken trees

A cluster of tumbleweeds
Like a pilgrim

Calling
In a voice low and secret
Glowing flames   incessantly
The prairie songs keep coming

✧✧✧

117 ·

江南春絕句 　　　　　　　　　　杜牧

千里鶯啼綠映紅，水村山郭酒旗風。
南朝四百八十寺，多少樓臺煙雨中。

Spring in the Southern Shore　Du Mu

Orioles form a melodious concert,
from among the green foliage, which

is enlivened by red flowers blossoming
through thousands of miles, while tavern

banners are fluttering in riverside towns
and hillside villages. Hundreds of temples,

built in Southern Dynasties, are still
standing, enveloped in misty rain…

西漢高速 　　　　　　　　　　　　林明理

西漢高速把我帶進了
不可言喻的地方——
看那千山萬水
有無數個隧道

連接著橋樑
彷彿穿越了空中走廊
心中沒有其他雜想
嘴角洋溢著歡暢

那是秦嶺山脈的羚羊
還有金絲猴和熊貓
多美好的一天啊
新的鳥
在我心頭蕩漾
像是靜默地
指揮
縹緲的合唱

而我，怎麼也忘不了
這樣偉大的工程
是何等的榮耀
如何畫得出這美好的景象
難道這裡有
取之不盡的美
難道這裡是
繆斯建造的星國天堂

Xihan Highway　　　　　　　Lin Ming-Li

Xihan Highway takes me into
The indescribable place —
See thousands of mountains and rivers
With countless tunnels
Connecting bridges
As if crossing the air corridor
With no other thoughts in mind
The mouth brimming with joy

Those are antelopes of Qinling Mountain
As well as golden monkeys and pandas
What a beautiful day
The new birds
Hopping in my mind
As if to silently
To conduct an ethereal chorus

And I can never forget
The glory of such
A great project
How to paint such a beautiful scene
Is there an inexhaustible
Beauty here
Is this the kingdom of heaven built by Muse

✧✧✧

118 ·

歎花   杜牧

自是尋春去校遲，不須惆悵怨芳時。
狂風落盡深紅色，綠葉成陰子滿枝。

Lament for Flowers   Du Mu

I am late in search
of spring: no blame

— flowers blossom
early. After winds blow

off red colors, lush
green leaves greet fruits.

重生的喜悅[85]　　　　　　　　林明理

這清晨
這周遭和光的力
這窗外的寧靜
這初綻的花兒
我歡喜，我欲將重生。

啊，生命！啊，淚水！
彷若露珠泛著微光
心中洋溢希望
奔流著我斑斕詩想
我展翼，我想吟唱。

拿起筆———
只能寫出
感謝這場相會———
是你賜給我最慷慨的恩惠！
讓一切變得恬逸歡愉！

The Joy of Rebirth[86]　　　　　Lin Ming-Li

This morning
The force of the light around
The quietude outside the window
The budding flowers
I rejoice, I want to be reborn.

---

[85] 2013 年 6 月 17 日至 22 日住院，開刀大手術於四季台安醫院，特別向方俊能醫師及全體醫護人員致謝。—寫於 2013/6/22 出院日

[86] I was hospitalized from June 17 to 22, 2013, undergoing major surgery in Four Seasons Tai'an Hospital. Special thanks to Dr. Fang Junneng and all the medical staff. — Written on June 22, 2013, when I was discharged from the hospital.

Ah, life! Ah, tears!
Like shimmering dewdrops
The heart brimming with hope
Running through my beautiful poetic thought
I spread my wings, I want to sing.

I pick up a pen —
Can only write
Thanks for the meeting —
You give me the most generous favor!
For everything to become joyful!

✧✧✧

119 ·

江樓   杜牧

獨酌芳春酒，登樓已半嚑。
誰驚一行雁，沖斷過江雲。

A Riverside Tower   Du Mu

Alone, spring wine,
a drinker mounts

the tower, tipsy.
Who startles a

line of wild geese
which break clouds

floating at ease
over the river?

月光、海灣和遠方

林明理

月光、海灣和遠方，
還有從那暗暗的海床傳來的
一曲鯨魚之歌，
多麼難以言喻的情調。

當風中帶來你的回音，
從各個方向吹來…
而我，靈魂靜留在一塊礁岩上，
相思如雪，罩滿群山。

—2024.12.25

Moonlight, Bay and the Distance

Lin Ming-Li

Moonlight, bay and the distance,
And the song of a whale
From the dark sea floor,
What an indescribable sentiment.

When the wind brings your echoes,
Blowing from all directions....
And I, the soul remains on a reef rock,
Yearning like snow, filling to cover the mountains.

—December 25, 2024.

✧✧✧

120．

赤壁 　　　　　　　　　　　　　　　　杜牧

折戟沉沙鐵未銷，自將磨洗認前朝。
東風不與周郎便，銅雀春深鎖二喬。

The Red Cliff 　　　　　　　　　　Du Mu

Buried deep in sand for ages, the
halberd does not shed its iron; after

washing & polishing, it reveals
to be remains from the War of Red

Cliff. If the east wind fails to bring
Marshal Zhou a favor, the two beauties

of Qiao family would be imprisoned
in Bronze Bird Tower of his enemy.

挺進吧，海上的男兒[87] 　　　　　　林明理

去吧！海上的男兒
我們在你身後
看著你們無畏
波浪顛簸
無畏艦艇的驅逐
絕不在海中化作波臣
讓我感動

---

[87] 為 2012.09.25 臺灣出動史上最大的一次保釣漁船護主權行動，台日艦艇曾水柱對峙，有感而作。此詩畫刊在臺灣的「人間福報」副刊 2012 年 10 月 15 日。

挺進吧！海上的男兒
白鷗為你靜默
暴風不再跟著號啕
那釣魚台的風波依然盪漾──
啊，侵略者的劣徑
令我憂傷！
收復沼沼！

Advance, Man of the Sea[88]   Lin Ming-Li

Away! Man of the sea
We are behind you
Seeing you are fearless
Surging with waves
Fearless of the driving ships
Never to become a subject in the sea
Which touches me

March on! Man of the sea
The white seagull is silent for you
The storm no longer follows the wailing
The storm of Diaoyutai is still rippling —
Ah, the aggressor's evil deeds
Makes me sad!
To recover the distance!

✧✧✧

---

[88] On September 25, 2012, Taiwan dispatched the largest fishing boat in history to protect the sovereignty. Taiwan and Japan vessels have had water column confrontation, and this poem is inspired. The poem was published in Taiwan's *Human Happiness Newspaper* supplement on October 15, 2012.

121·

長安秋望 　　　　　　　　　　　杜牧

樓倚霜樹外，鏡天無一毫。
南山與秋色，氣勢兩相高。

Gazing Afar in Autumn in the Capital
　　　　　　　　　　　　　　　　　Du Mu

A tower stands above
a grove of frosty trees;

the sky is a mirror
which is spotless.

The southern mountain
and autumn air,

which one is higher?
It is hard to tell.

隆田文化資產教育園區[89]觀展　　　林明理

慢慢地，我在這裡
找到了許多產業的遺跡，
找到了初識官田的樂趣，
就像一隻水雉，
棲息在菱角田晨曦當中。

---

[89] 位於臺南官田區的隆田文化資產教育園區 Longtian Culture Heritage Area，保存了臺鹽「隆田儲運站」以及倉庫、嘉南大圳水文化、臺南考古遺址、水鐵、糖鐵、鹽鐵和台鐵的「四鐵共構」產業遺跡為主題，留有鐵軌、地磅室遺構，還有小朋友最愛的地景劇場，值得細細探究。—2024.12.14

The Exhibition of Longtian Culture Heritage Area[90]

Lin Ming-Li

Slowly, here I find
The ruins of a host of industries,
And the pleasure of getting to know the official field for the first time,
Just like a jacana,
Perching in the morning sun over the field of Diamond Horn.

✧✧✧

122 ·

贈別二首（其二）

杜牧

多情卻似總無情，唯覺樽前笑不成。
蠟燭有心還惜別，替人垂淚到天明。

Two Parting Poems (No. 2)

Du Mu

Affectionate, yet seemingly dispassionate; no smile

is coaxed before a wine cup. The candle hates

---

[90] The Longtian Cultural Heritage Area, located in Guantian District of Tainan, preserves the "Longtian Storage and Transportation Station" and the industrial relics of the "four railway structures" of Taiyan, the water Culture of Jianan Dazhin, Tainan archaeological sites, water iron, sugar iron, salt iron and Taitie. There are children's favorite landscape theater, which is worth careful exploring. — Written on December 14, 2024.

to say goodbye: it drops
tears throughout the night.

愛情似深邃的星空 　　　　　　　林明理

當愛情展翅翩翩，
誰都看得出它的快樂
就像孩童活潑的舞蹈！
在每一個重逢的瞬間，
魔法也在那兒。

但我更羨慕，
愛情似深邃的星空……
又像春天，滿身花朵！
它有隻奇異的眼睛，
永遠飽含著憂愁。

　　　　　　　　　　　—2023.10.01

Love Is Like the Deep Starry Sky

　　　　　　　　　　　Lin Ming-Li

When love spreads its wings,
All people can see its joy
Like the lively dance of children!
In each moment of reunion,
The magic is also there.

But I envy more,
Love is like the deep starry sky…
And like spring, full of flowers!
It has a strange eye,
Which is always filled with sorrow.

✧✧✧

123 ·

南陵道中 　　　　　　　　　　　　　　杜牧

南陵水面漫悠悠，風緊雲輕欲變秋。
正是客心孤迥處，誰家紅袖憑江樓？

On the Road of Nanling 　　　　　　Du Mu

The river water of Nanling is
running deep and slow; west wind

blowing light clouds, autumn
is around the corner. A lonely

traveler is melancholy in his heart,
when suddenly he sees a red-

sleeved girl standing against the
balustrade of a river-side tower.

最美的時刻 　　　　　　　　　　　　林明理

有人說
某些時刻會永存不滅
那就是愛
那就是最美的時刻

我聽到
海波輕柔地撫慰著
夜已深沉
星叢紛紛匯聚而來

沒有人能阻攔你們
以歌接近天宇蒼穹

沒有人能如此樸實
以歌激盪這島嶼的幸福

是什麼
能唱出我們的苦痛和沉默
是什麼
能揭示昔日的回憶和歡樂

四十年[91]過去了
你們仍以熱望擁抱未來
就像燃燒青春的火焰
共譜生命的讚歌

The Greatest Moment   Lin Ming-Li

Some say
There are moments that last forever
And that is love
That is the most beautiful moment

I hear
The sea waves are gently soothing
The night is deep
As the clustes of stars gather

Nobody can stop you
From approaching heaven with songs
Nobody can be so simple
As to stir the happiness of this island with songs

---

[91] 2018 年 8 月 6 日在電視上看到一部影片（四十年），播出校園民歌盛行時期的歌手、作曲家的身影及其音樂演唱會的實況記錄，令我內心澎湃不已；在此特別感謝臺灣著名的音樂家胡德夫、李宗盛及數十位歌手的熱情演出。

What
Can sing our pain and silence
What
Can reveal the memories and joys of the past

Forty years[92] have gone by
Still you embrace the future with ardent hope
Like the flames of burning youth
Singing together the hymn of life

✧✧✧

124 ·

憶梅　　　　　　　　　　　　　李商隱

定定住天涯，依依向物華。
寒梅最堪恨，常作去年花。

Remembering Plum Blossoms

Li Shangyin

Planted in the remote
horizon, yearning for fair

spring view, cold plum
blossoms are to be hated,

---

[92] On August 6, 2018, I saw a film *40 Years* on TV, which broadcast the singers and composers in the popular period of campus folk songs and the live records of their music concerts, which made my heart surge. Here I would like to express my special thanks to famous Taiwanese musicians Hu Defu, Jonathan Lee and dozens of singers for their enthusiastic performances.

for they always open
flowers of the last year.

感謝有您──Athanase Vantchev de Thracy
　　　　　　　　　　　　　　　林明理

　　　你走在星野中
　　　　目光堅韌而溫柔
　手握緊權杖的形貌
　　一邊聆聽著藍山雀和溪流
　　一邊創造世界文學的至寶
　我跟著你前進的足音
　　　　　永不會迷失方向
　你是謬斯之子
　　　　必獲至上的光耀！

　　　　　　　　　　　－2017.7.14 台灣

Thanks to You: Athanase Vantchev de Thracy
　　　　　　　　　　　　　　Lin Ming-Li

　　　You walk in the starry field
　　　With firm and gentle eyes
　Hands clenching to the pole of power
　Listening to the blue tits and streams
　And creating treasures of world literature
　I follow your footsteps
　　　　Never getting lost
　　　You are the son of Muse
　　　To gain the supreme glory!

　　　　　　　　　　—July 14, 2017, Taiwan

❖❖❖

125・

夜雨寄北　　　　　　　　　　　　李商隱

君問歸期未有期，巴山夜雨漲秋池。
何當共剪西窗燭？卻話巴山夜雨時。

Northward Missing in a Raining Night
　　　　　　　　　　　　　Li Shangyin

You ask the date of my
return, which I cannot tell;

autumn pool is swollen with
night rain in Ba Mountain.

When can we together
trim candle wicks against

the west window and recall
the rainy night in Ba Mountain?

時光的回眸：中山大學[93]　　　　　林明理

每當我凝神諦視——
這座校園在碧空下的光與色
　　就有一種盲目的喜悅
那怡人的西子灣
　　常以溫柔來撫慰我

---

[93] 一九八八年五月，我曾在中山大學資管系擔任國科會「資訊管理政策」專題研究的專任助理研究員，當年的計畫主持人黃慶祥博士已退休；任職一年後，我轉往屏東師範學院等校擔任講師，而後，專於文學寫作。二〇一〇年十二月十一日，與美國詩人（非馬）馬為義博士同遊中山大學校園時，回眸已近二十二個秋。－2019.8.8 寫於臺灣

讓我勇往直前——
　　無畏前途迢迢或暗流湧動
讓我把往事……印在月上
而今，它仍矗立在那裡
以莊嚴又略帶笑意的神情
　　給沉默的天空　披上金衣
而我卻一如往昔
　　喋喋地在你耳邊閒言絮語

Looking Back in Time: Sun Yat-sen University[94]

Lin Ming-Li

Whenever I look closely —
The light and color of this campus in the blue sky
　　With a blind joy
The pleasant West Bay
　　Often comforts me with tenderness
For me to charge forward—
Unafraid of the remote road ahead or the hidden surging water
For me to print the past events….on the moon
Now, it still stands there
With a solemn expression and a slightly smiling look
　　To cloak the silent sky with a golden coat
While I remain as before
　　Murmuring and whispering in your ears

---

[94] In May 1988, I worked at the Department of Information Management of Sun Yat-sen University as a full-time assistant researcher for the special research on "Information Management Policy" of the National Science Council. The program leader of that year, Dr. Huang Qingxiang, has retired. After a year of employment, I transferred to Pingtung Normal College and other schools as a lecturer, and then, specialized in literary writing. On December 11, 2010, when I visited the campus of Sun Yat-sen University with the American poet Dr. William Marr, it was nearly 22 years ago. — August 8, 2019, written in Taiwan

126 ·

嫦娥　　　　　　　　　　　　李商隱

雲母屏風燭影深，長河漸落曉星沉。
嫦娥應悔偷靈藥，碧海青天夜夜心。

The Moon Goddess　　　　　　Li Shangyin

Against the screen of carven
marble the candle shadow is deep;

the Silver River fades and morning
stars disappear into twilight.

The Moon Goddess regrets she
has stolen medicine for eternal life:

now the blue sky and green seas
accompany her from night to night.

鐫痕　　　　　　　　　　　　林明理

愛，鐫在波濤裡
就在此一靜沉的時刻
夜雪，帶著白的記憶
輕描舊城……

我倚著樹身
為捕撈一個皺了的
身影
漾過幾回春深

The Engraving Mark Lin Ming-Li

Love is engraved in the waves
In this quiet moment
The night snow, with a white memory
Is lightly delineating the old city...

I lean against the tree trunk
To catch the wrinkled form of
A figure
Rippling time and again with a deep spring

✧✧✧

127 ·

微雨 李商隱

初隨林靄動，稍共夜涼分。
窗迴侵燈冷，庭虛近水聞。

A Drizzle Li Shangyin

Initial movement with
woods brume; it slightly

shares night cool. Distant
window and cold lamp;

rain drip-drop is clear
and near in empty court.

流浪漢[95]

林明理

他，來自花蓮……一個流浪漢──孤單的晃影擋住了我。
疲憊的、無助的步伐，一把雨傘、簡易的背包。哎──怎麼說呢？──
掩翳的傷口，自慚形穢的腳丫，透出惜的神色……
呵，不必多說，這個不幸的人，還有那跋涉的荊棘路，讓我費神許久。
我摸索自己的口袋……只掏出錢包裡的一張大鈔、一罐飲料，
加上一包糧食，甚至不好意思握住那只厚實的手。
「哦，兄弟，我這點心意。別客氣──神會眷顧你的！」
那就是我最後看到他轉身離去、月光照亮在柏油路上的時候。
不過──可能嗎？這天氣是越加寒涼了。遠處，還有狗吠的聲音。
他該回到家中的小屋了吧。今天去應徵的那家果園面試得如何？
「大姐，謝謝妳。但，我想，還是留在這附近再找找工作啦……。」
他靦腆地說道，聲音來自遙遠的一方、有雜訊干擾著。
「喂喂……喂哪兒的話呀。」我急急地回覆。哎他手機沒電了吧。
而我終於了悟，失去一切，對他而言，還不算災難。
因為，他天天思念，那熟悉的牧場，牛羊成群，還有一整片綠原。

---

[95] 今年九月，巧遇了一位因工作九年的牧場突然關閉而失業的原住民流浪到台東求職未成，遂而折回花蓮繼續謀職的坎坷故事，有感而作。─寫於 2014.10.6

The Vagrant[96]   Lin Ming-Li

He, from Hualien… A homeless man — the lonely shadow blocking me.
Tired, helpless steps, an umbrella, a simple backpack.
Well — how can I say it? —
Covered wounds, ashamed feet, revealing a timid look…
Oh, no need to say, this unfortunate man, and the thorny road for further trudging, keep me occupied for long.
I fumble in my pockets… Only to take out a big bill, a can of drink,
And a package of grain in his wallet, and even feel embarrassed to hold the strong hand.
"Oh, dear brother, it's nothing. Don't mention it — God will take care of you!"
That was the last time I saw him turn away, the moonlight shining on the asphalt.
But — is it possible? It is getting colder and colder. In the distance, there was barking of dogs.
I think he should be back in his cabin. How was your interview with the orchard today?
"Thank you, dear sister. But I think I'd better stay around to look for a job…"
He said timidly, the voice coming from the distance, with some noise.
"Hey, hey… hey, hey." I replied urgently. Hey, his phone died.
And I finally realized that losing everything wasn't a disaster for him.
Because, every day, he misses the familiar pasture, the herds of cattle and sheep, and the whole green plain.

---

[96] In September this year, I heard the story of an unemployed Aboriginal who had wandered to Taitung in search of a job after the sudden closure of his ranch where he had worked for nine years, and then returned to Hualien to continue looking for a job. The poem is thus inspired. — Written on October 6, 2014.

唐詩明理接千載
古今抒情詩三百首
漢英對照

✧✧✧

128 ・

夕陽樓　　　　　　　　　　　　　李商隱

花明柳暗繞天愁，上盡重城更上樓。
欲問孤鴻向何處，不知身世自悠悠。

The Tower Basking in Setting Sun
　　　　　　　　　　　　　　Li Shangyin

Dark willows and blooming
flowers incur limitless sorrow;

atop one after another high tower,
again another tower looms. In

the boundless sky a solitary
goose soars, but where? It

dawns on me I am as helpless
as the lonely goose.

白河：蓮鄉之歌[97]　　　　　　　　林明理

每當六月
亭台的嘻嚷笑聲不絕
那王蓮的葉盤，兀自閃爍
在微風中輕顫著
呵，白河
你是安謐的古鎮
有明鏡的水庫

---

[97] 白河區 Baihe District，前身「白河鎮」，位於臺灣臺南市東北端。

流過多少人心頭
流過多少虛無的時空
在這頂山仔脚部落北側
水蓮公園頻頻點頭歡迎我
行棧道、扶疏花樹
涉蓮池、騎單車、其樂融融

白河啊，你北隔八掌溪
哺育了幾代原鄉者
你似一朵大王蓮
昂首與茫茫天空爭雄
想當年大排竹、馬稠後的聚落
先民以擔挑、推車載運
越過白水溪畔
漸漸形成店仔口
自力更生不斷線
白河街道暖心窩
關子嶺流出黑濁泥狀的泉
枕頭山、虎頭山
山山嶺嶺唱白河

望碧雲寺寶塔呵
一草一木都問我
可知道，白河精神是什麼？
這曾是平埔族舊哆囉嘓的番地
從先人開荒地，種雜糧植甘蔗
至今豆菜麵、蓮花餐
店仔口肉圓、廟口春捲
鴨肉羹…滷味均獨到
誰說那王蓮立於耀眼的水面
不是偉大的宣導者
猶如白河溪水呵流不斷

炫耀來自紅蓮朵朵
橫推水波，每當月下流螢四起
它在燈火間燦然
睡了，在這天水相間的幽靜之中

White River: The Song of Lotus Land[98]

Lin Ming-Li

Each June
The pavilion is aloud with endless laughing
The lotus leaf disk, still flickering
Shivering gently in the breeze
Oh, White River
You are a quiet ancient town
With the reservoir of a bright mirror
Flowing through how many people's hearts
Flowing through how much vain time-space
In the north of the mountain foot tribe
The Water Lotus Park is frequently nodding to welcome me
The trestle road and flowery pavilions
Lotus pool, riding a bicycle, so joyful

Oh, White River, to the north you are separated by the Eight Palms River
To feed several generations of native villagers
You are like a king lotus
Head up to vie against the vast sky
Thinking of the settlers with big rows of bamboos and horses
The ancestors carry a load on their shoulders
or by using the cart
Over the White River
Gradually to formthe shops

---

[98] Baihe District, formerly known as "Baihe Town", is located at the northeast end of Tainan City, Taiwan.

Constant self-reliance
The White River street is warm in the heart
Black muddy spring is running from the Guanzi Ridge
The Pillow Mountain, the Hutou Mountain
All ridges and mountains are singing the White River

Oh look at the pagoda of Biyun Temple
All the grasses and trees ask me
Do you know, what is the spirit of the White River?
This used to be the doroko of the Pingpu tribe
The ancestors open up the land, planting cereals and sugarcane
So far bean vegetable noodles, lotus food
Meat dumplings, the temple spring rolls
Duck soup…all with a unique flavor
Who says the king lotus is tanding in the dazzling water
Not a great advocate
Like the water of White River running endlessly
What is showing off is from one after another blossom of red lotus
Horizontally pushing water waves, whenever fireflies fly under the moon
It is brilliant among the lamps
Asleep, in the quiet of the sky and water

✧✧✧

129 ·

天涯 李商隱

春日在天涯，天涯日又斜。
鶯啼如有淚，為濕最高花。

The Horizon   Li Shangyin

Spring sun is in the
horizon, where the sun

is slanting. If the twitters
of orioles are liquid

and wet, the highest
flowers are moistened.

為搶救童妓而歌   林明理

那孩子……
被迫在火坑裡
長大。
她可能來自悲慘的
歲月，來自失去滿臉稚氣的
童年。
那孩子…沒有選擇的
自由；暗夜哭泣於其中，
舔拭傷口於其中，
那孩子吶喊著
　——神的名字，
隨後只有窗櫺的風作伴，
聲音越來越微弱
熄滅於黑暗的角落中。
啊，哪裡有光？
哪裡能更親近神的國度？
那孩子只想在
　陽光下盪鞦韆…
甜甜地一笑。

　　　　　　　　　　—寫於 2018.03.01.

Child Prostitution Lin Ming-Li

The child…
Forced to grow up
In the firepit.
Perhaps she comes from tragic
Years, from the childhood deprived of
Innocence.
The child…has no freedom
Of choice; the dark night is crying,
Licking her wounds.
The child is shouting
  —The name of deity,
Only the wind outside the window is responding,
The voice trailing off…
To die in a dark corner.
Ah, where is the light?
Where can I get near the deity's kingdom?
The child just wants to be there
  Playing on a swing in the sunshine…
Smiling sweetly.

✧✧✧

130・

靜夜相思 李群玉

山空天籟寂，水榭延輕涼。
浪定一浦月，藕花閒自香。

Thoughts On a Silent Night Li Qunyu

The sounds of nature all
die in empty mountains;

waterside pavilion is
suffused with coolness.

No ripples, the mirrored
moon is round in river

mouth; pale, idle, free, and
fragrant are lotus flowers.

短詩兩首   林明理

1. 晨露
那凝，那明眸，我已淺醉——
滿山的星星，妳數著。妳是
聰穎，靜寂，妳是晶瑩的碧翠。

2. 破風車
在荒城邊，我編織著你的故事
你旋轉著我的夢。為了愛的傳說
聽，也是一種唱和

Two Short Poems   Lin Ming-Li

1. Morning Dew
The condensation, the bright eyes, I am slightly drunk —
A mountainful of stars, you are counting them. You are
Smart, quiet, you are crystal green.

2. Broken Windmill
On the edge of a desolate city, I am weaving your story
You are spinning my dream. For the legend of love
Listen, as well as a kind of singing

✧✧✧

131·

引水行   李群玉

一條寒玉走秋泉,引出深蘿洞口煙。
十里暗流聲不斷,行人頭上過潺湲。

Conducting Water   Li Qunyu

A bamboo tube is
running with autumn

water, which elicits
cave spring in the deep

mountain. For ten miles
above the travelers

it is noisy with gurgling
water: audible but invisible.

獻給勝興車站[99]   林明理

一條舊山線,滿眼翠色。
月台下閒坐,
　　遙想當年風華。
喔,灰舊的石碑啊,
　　歷經多少風霜?
客家的先民啊,
　　歷經多少苦難?
陽光親吻的油桐樹,

---

[99] 勝興車站 Shengxing Station,苗栗線三義鄉觀光景點,啟用於 1907 年,是臺灣西部鐵道最高的火車站,是客家先民集資在這裡拓墾,在山林裡製造樟腦,後來也有木炭產業,挑夫往來挑柴以供應炭窯生產所需,所以在車站附近有一條挑柴古道。

年年花開滿山野。
到了這兒，
　　就像日據時代的悠靜自然，
各種小商販，在石階旁，
在擂茶店仔旁，細心招呼。
那難忘的古道和隧道，
　　遊客的歡聲笑語……
這山城使人感到親切溫暖。

Dedicated to Shengxing Station[100]

Lin Ming-Li

An old mountain line, an eyefull of green.
Sitting idle under the moon,
　　Thinking about what it was like.
Oh, the old grey stone,
　　How much wind & frost?
The ancestors of Hakka
　　How many sufferings?
The parasol trees kissed by the sunshine,
Blooming all over the hills from year to year.
Here,
　　It is like the quiet leisure of the Japanese occupation era,
All kinds of small vendors, by the stone steps,
By the rolling tea shops, warmly greeting.
The unforgettable ancient roads and tunnels,
　　The laughter of tourists…
The mountain city makes people feel friendly and warm.

---

[100] Shengxing Station, as Miaoli line Sanyi Township tourist attraction, in service in 1907, is the highest railway station in western Taiwan. The Hakka ancestors raised funds here for cultivation, in the mountains to make camphor, and later there is charcoal industry, porters picking firewood to satisfy the kiln production needs, so there is an ancient road near the station for firewood.

✧✧✧

132 ·

過分水嶺   溫庭筠

溪水無情似有情，入山三日得同行。
嶺頭便是分頭處，惜別潺湲一夜聲。

Crossing the Watershed   Wen Tingyun

The creek water seems
to be affectionate; three

days in the mountain it is
our company. Mountaintop

is the place for us to bid
adieu: with reluctance the

water is babbling and gurgling
throughout the night.

致以色列拿撒勒   林明理

我來了
　　　在加利利山脈的高地之下
　　　千年的回憶轉啊轉
一株古樹棲息著無數野鳥
終至大平原與天空結合
而我立於神的國度
　　　用盡力量呼喚
　　像是獻給懸崖山的風與光

然後，閱讀古城的細細紋理
　　心，竟如此溫暖

To Israel Nazareth　　　　　　　Lin Ming-Li

I am coming
　　Under the highlands of the Galilee Mountains
　　The millennium memories keep turning
An ancient tree is nuring countless wild birds
Finally the Great Plain is combined with the sky
And I stand in the kingdom of deity
　　With all my might I call out
　　Like the wind and light dedicated to the cliff mountain
Then, to read the fine texture of the ancient city
　　The heart is so warm

✧✧✧

133．

早春　　　　　　　　　　　　　儲嗣宗

野樹花初發，空山獨見時。
踟躕曆陽道，鄉思滿南枝。

Early Spring　　　　　　　　　Chu Sizong

Wild trees begin to
blossom, when the

empty mountain
catches sight of it.

Hesitatingly, I walk
on the sunny path,

when nostalgia fills
the southern branches.

寫給未來的我 　　　　　　　　　林明理

沒有什麼可扭轉時空
除非是星震
傷及地球

倘若未來
外星船不再是假象
北極面臨乾旱
寸草不生

倘若地球轉軸失去平衡
荒原的動物不再回應
噢，再會吧

但盼靈魂聳入天庭
我會記起在這個世界
擁有愛情，雖充滿征鬥
卻仍散發出奪目的光彩

　　　　　　　　　　　　　　　－2024.12.17

For My Future Self 　　　　Lin Ming-Li

Nothing can reverse space-time
Unless it is a starquake
Which brings harm to the earth

In the future
If the alien ship is no longer an illusion
And the Arctic is under drought
So barren that not a blade of grass grows

If the earth spins off balance
And the animals of the wilderness no longer respond
Oh, goodbye

But may my soul rise to heaven
I shall remember in this world
There is love, though full of battle
It still radiant with a dazzling light

—December 17, 2024

✧✧✧

134・

退居漫題七首（其一） 司空圖

花缺傷難綴，鶯喧奈細聽。
惜春春已晚，珍重草青青。

Random Poems in Retirement (No. 1)
Sikong Tu

When flowers fade
it is hard to make

it up; when orioles
are noisy it entails

attentive listening.
When loveable spring

is on the wane, green
grass is to be cherished.

向建築大師貝聿銘致上最後的敬意[101]

林明理

你是不朽的巨匠
　安居天庭裡——
　是那麼自在
　享受閱讀的樂趣
或，這就是你想要
帶給敬愛你的人的訊息

Paying Last Respect to Renowned Architect Ieoh Ming Pei[102]

Lin Ming-Li

You are an immortal master
Living peacefully in heaven —
At such a great ease
Enjoying the pleasure of reading
Perhaps, this is the message
You want to bring to whose who love you

✧✧✧

---

[101] 貝聿銘（Ieoh Ming Pei，1917-2019 年 5 月 16 日），華裔美籍建築師，1983 年普利茲克獎得主，被譽為「現代主義建築的最後大師」（the last master of high modernist architecture），享年 102 歲。

[102] Ieoh Ming Pei (1917-May 16, 2019), Chinese-American architect, winner of the Pritzker Prize in 1983, is known as "the last master of high modernist architecture", and he died at the age of 102.

135 ·

退居漫題七首（其三）   司空圖

燕語曾來客，花催欲別人。
莫愁春已過，看著又新春。

Random Poems in Retirement (No. 3)
Sikong Tu

Swallows twitter
as guests come and

go; flowers bloom
and wither in haste:

bidding adieu. Spring
vanishes, no worry:

a new spring, lo,
is around the corner.

夢回大學時代[103]   林明理

穿越洶湧的大海
　　　讓時光停駐——
　　　回到那個青春歲月

---

[103] 1983-1985 年間，我經常獨自一人在大學圖書館專心讀書，也曾利用暑假協助石齊平教授校對手稿，學習電腦課程。印象最深刻的是，感恩曾受業於我的班導師宋健治教授兼所長，係美國科羅拉多州立大學經濟學博士。驀然回首來時路，就像潛入記憶的海洋裡，感悟到任歲月滄桑，曾經走過的路，必然留下痕跡。而今的我，卸下大學教職，做一個作家很自在。未來，亦是如此。——寫於 2019.5.30。

校園的鐘聲靜寂
鳥雀在步道老榕樹上啼叫
啊，飛翔吧，我的心
　　請擦亮我的夢想
　　揮走蒙塵
讓我繼續在字裡行間
　　留下瀟灑自在的印記

Dreaming Back to College[104]　Lin Ming-Li

Across the turbulent sea
　　　For time to pause —
　　Back to the years of youth
　　The school bell is silent
The birds are twittering along the path of old banyan trees
Ah, fly, my heart
　　Please polish my dream
　　To swing away dust
For me to continue to leave
　　Clear marks between the lines

✧✧✧

---

[104] From 1983 to 1985, I have been absorbed in reading by myself in the university library, and also used to help professor Shi Qiping proofread manuscripts and study computer courses during the summer vacation. What impressed me most was that I was taught by professor Song Jianzhi, professor and director of my class, who is a doctor of economics from Colorado State University. Suddenly looking back, I feel like diving into the ocean of memory, to realize that through vicissitudes of the years, there are to be some traces along the road which has been covered. Now, away from my college teaching post, I am comfortable as a writer, which stretches to the future years. — Written on May 30, 2019.

136.

獨望　　　　　　　　　　　　　　　　　　司空圖

綠樹連村暗，黃花入麥稀。
遠陂春草綠，猶有水禽飛。

Solitary Gazing　　　　　　　　　　Sikong Tu

Green trees darken
at the juncture with

the village; rape
flowers are sparse

in the field of wheat.
Green with spring grass

is a pond afar, where
waterfowls are flying.

走在彎曲的小徑　　　　　　　　　　　　林明理

沒有生氣的
　　給他一雙高翔的翅膀
沒有甦醒的
　　給他一顆燃起的雄心

我有意氣
　　也有豪情
前面，已沒有多餘的視線
　　只有無休無止的馳騁

在沒有妳燦爛如夏的日子裡
　　我是個擦身而過的

行者，正待回頭轉身
　　開創命運

Walk Long the Winding Path

Lin Ming-Li

For him who is lifeless
　　Give him a pair of flying wings
For him who fails to wake up
　　Give him a burning ambition

I have ambition
　　And pride
In front, there is no redundant sight
　　Only endless galloping

In the days without you through brilliant summer
　　I am a traveler who
Pass by, waiting to turn around
　　To mater the destiny

✧✧✧

137·

春草 唐彥謙

天北天南繞路邊，托根無處不延綿。
萋萋總是無情物，吹綠東風又一年。

Spring Grass Tang Yanqian

grows by the roadside,
even to the end of

the sky; its roots shoot
here and there. Lush

and green grows the
unfeeling grass, and

another year is blown
away in the east wind.

想當年

林明理

想當年
　　學習是我的目標
　　讀書是我的至愛
偶而
也會想起那些日子裡
一些溫馨的往事
看著窗外細雨
一幕幕回憶……遂成了動畫
有時候想，變老也挺不錯[105]

Those Were the Days

Lin Ming-Li

Those were the days
　　When learning was my goal
　　Reading was my favorite
Occasionally
I would think of those days
Some warm memories of the past

---

[105] 作者於民國 75 年（1986）參加北區大學院校研究生幹部冬令講習會，曾聆聽官員有關翡翠水庫興建工程的報告。就讀法學碩士期間，我曾同三位同學利用下課後，一起搭車到台灣大學選修英文寫作課程。而今已匆匆過了三十二載，凝視著照片中當年的我，誰也沒有料到我要寫下這懷念的詩行。——寫於 2019.05.30.

Looking out of the window at the drizzle
A scene after another scene... into animation
Sometimes I think, it is fine to get old[106]

✧✧✧

138 ·

小院 唐彥謙

小院無人夜，煙斜月轉明。
清宵易惆悵，不必有離情。

A Small Courtyard   Tang Yanqian

Nobody in the small
courtyard veiled in

dark night; smoke
curling, the moon turns

bright. A quiet night is
tantamount to melancholy,

which is unfit for
parting & separation.

---

[106] In 1986, the author attended the winter seminar for graduate students of North District University and listened to the report of officials on the construction of Feicui Reservoir. When I was studying for the Master of Laws, three of my classmates and I took a bus to Taiwan University after class to take an English writing course. Now it has been a rush of 32 years, looking closely at me in the photo, nobody can imagine that I should write such nostalgic lines. — Written on May 30, 2019.

燈塔

林明理

睥睨著潮來潮往
不經意地銜起一塊小貝石
極目眺望
等待每一個遊子
等待船歌和星月
當時間的巨掌
啃蝕莫名的憂傷

我是沙
我是浪
我循著足跡
找尋曾經的疆場
是你
把每個期待的眼神
照得更璀璨

The Lighthouse

Lin Ming-Li

Looking contemptuously at the tide
Inadvertently to pick up a small shell stone
To gaze afar
Waiting for each and every wanderer
Waiting for the song of the boat and the star and moon
When the giant palm of time
Gnaws at nameless sadness

I am the sand
I am the wave
I follow the footprints
To find the field which has ever been
It is you
Who enlighten each look
More bright and brilliant

139.

田上　　　　　　　　　　　　　　　崔道融

雨足高田白，披蓑半夜耕。
人牛力俱盡，東方殊未明。

In the Field　　　　　　　　　　Cui Daorong

Plentiful rainfall
whitens the field,

wearing rain hats,
the farmers labor

into midnight. When
they and the oxen are

exhausted, in the east
the day has not broken.

記憶中的麥芽糖　　　　　　　　　林明理

昔日老村
挑著扁擔的賣糖師傅
長長吆喝聲
　　劃破黃昏的靜默
也有騎著老鐵馬
　　回收紙類或鐵罐
　　　在街頭巷尾的老伯
總能吸引孩童們的駐足圍觀
啊，那歲月留香的

麥芽糖——多麼甜蜜溫潤
它用糯米、山泉水和小麥草
以柴火蒸米、醣化
　　精煉後收鍋
這是記憶中的甜品
　古老傳承的美味

Maltose in Memory　　　　　　　Lin Ming-Li

In the past, the old village
The master carrying a pole to sell sugar
His long shouting breaks
　　The silence of the dusk
And the old man riding an old iron horse
　　Recycling paper or iron cans
　　Along the streets and lanes
Can always attract the attention of children to stop and watch
Ah, the maltose
Scented with the years — how sweet and warm
It uses glutinous rice, mountain spring water and wheat grass
To steam rice with firewood, saccharine
　　Refining before collecting the pot.
This is the delicious dessert in memory
　　The flavor of age-old inheritance

✧✧✧

140．

春日山中行　　　　　　　　　　裴說

數竿蒼翠擬龍形，峭拔須教此地生。
無限野花開不得，半山寒色與春爭。

Walking in the Mountain in Spring

Pei Yue

A few green bamboos
grow like dragons,

which are thin and
high-rising. Countless

wild flowers are timid
to blossom: half a

mountain of cold
color vies with spring.

閱讀布農部落[107]

林明理

關於布農族
在歷史上
曾有許多傳說
特別是兩位傳奇性英雄——
拉荷·阿雷和拉馬他·星星（Lamata sin sin，-1932）
他們為尊嚴而壯烈成仁
他們抗日的鬥志
讓日人懼怕

愈是艱苦
他們愈縱聲高歌
因為，——就是這樣
有了歌
才能製造原鄉的記憶

---

[107] 「海端」是由布農族語「Haitutuan」而來，意指「三面被山圍繞、一面敞開」的虎口地形。日治時期日人稱「瀧下」，是指瀑布之下。

因為，就是這樣，——
讓自己和祖先的土地
有了緊密的聯繫

因為，——就是這樣
他們樂天知命，散居山林
並不孤單
因為，——就是這樣
過去以狩獵為生的人
如今成為平靜祥和的部落
花開了——春來了
豐收了——來舞蹈

啊，漂泊的部落——
勤奮的布農族
敬天而惜物
您們挺過多少風風雨雨⋯
⋯風帶來希望的種子
鳥銜來野花幽草
還有天上的雲　不停地問
你們好嗎？⋯你們好嗎？

Reading the Bunon Tribe[108]　Lin Ming-Li

There are many legends
About the Bunon people
In history
Especially two legendary heroes —

---

[108] The word "Haitutuan" is derived from the Bunun language "Haitutuan", meaning "tiger mouth terrain surrounded by mountains on three sides and open on one side". During the Japanese occupation period, the Japanese people are called "Takiha", meaning to be under the waterfall.

Raho Arey and Lamata sin sin (-1932)
Who died fighting for dignity
Their fighting spirit against Japan
Was feared by the Japanese

The harder it is
The louder they sing
Because — thus it is
With songs
There is a memory of your homeland
Because, thus it is —
For yourself and the land of your ancestors
To be closely connected

Because — thus it is
They are happy by nature, scattered to be living in the woods
They are not alone
Because — thus it is
In the past those who live by hunting
Now become peaceful tribes
The flowers bloom — it is spring
A bumper harvest — dancing

Ah, wandering tribes —
Diligent Bununs
Who worship heaven and cherish everything
You have survived how many storms…
…The wind brings the seeds of hope
The birds come with grass and wildflowers
And the clouds in the sky   keep asking
How are you?…How are you?

✧✧✧

141 ·

閩中秋思   杜荀鶴

雨勻紫菊叢叢色,風弄紅蕉葉葉聲。
北畔是山南畔海,只堪圖畫不堪行。

Autumnal Thoughts in Fujian Province   Du Xunhe

Autumn rain evens the purple
color of a clump after another

clump of chrysanthemums;
in golden wind, red banana

leaves are rustling, from leaf to
leaf. Hills to the north and a sea

to the south: the view makes an ideal
painting instead of an easy walking.

墨竹   林明理

我從畫中出來
夕陽輕輕暈染山頭
一朵雲藏在岩後
帶著一種穿過黑暗直立海心的
獨走,停駐燈塔片刻

漫步老街小巷
晚風正酣
烘乾了我的汗顏
那徐徐的斑斑的瘦影
跟著我細數歸舟
等待破曉,點破天光

The Ink Bamboo Lin Ming-Li

I come out of the painting
The setting sun sweeps gently over the mountain
A cloud hides itself behind the rock
With a kind of solitary walk through the dark to be upright
in the heart
Of sea, stopping at the lighthouse for a moment

Walking along old streets and alleys
The evening wind is at its height
To dry my sweat
The thin mottled shadow
Slowly follows me in counting the returning boats
Waiting for the dawn, to break the light of heaven

✧✧✧

142 •

古離別 韋莊

晴煙漠漠柳毿毿，不那離情酒半酣。
更把玉鞭雲外指，斷腸春色在江南。

At Parting Wei Zhuang

Spring is veiled in
smoky willows; helpless

parting sorrow is drowned
in wine. The wanderer

points his horsewhip
heavenward: the spring

view of Southern Shore
is heartbrokenly fair.

寫給相湖的歌　　　　　　　　　　　　林明理

多美的雲天！在七月的暮影下，
月亮灣沙灘竟羞紅了臉，如同繆斯久久凝視的輕俏戀人。
瀲瀲湖波，一眼看去，總是歡欣雀躍。
漁歌唱晚好像白鷺飛舞。跟搖櫓的吱吱聲不同，此地河道，每每質樸純真。

我向相湖莞爾一笑，是愛，讓我們相親相近，這景象便在我心中永存。
這裡花香流轉，涼風習習。這裡水域廣闊，更有稻田縱橫，濕地之眼為鄰。
在一沉靜無垢的湖畔旁，遙思昔日懷家亭館，我就要扮演揮毫的墨客。
看盡七星鎮穿梭著寬寬窄窄的河道，看盡這裡的一鄉一景。

啊，這是一首甜蜜的戀歌。是誰？在黑夜睡夢時將它哼起？
是誰？在晨靄漫漫時將它隱沒？
啊，這支歌曲，帶我飄洋過海，來到湘家蕩，感受她不朽的面貌！
相湖——我願隨風與妳嬉舞！與妳共呼吸。

每當妙曼的月亮在樹梢，在這塊上蒼遺落在長三角腹地的液體翡翠上⋯⋯
當我把耳朵貼進一灣碧水，我就聽到那百鳥在夢中振羽的旋律，

那些旅人在盡享水上遊樂，那魚米之鄉的故事和遠方──

那不斷眨眼的星子如露水一滴。

A Song for Xianghu Lake   Lin Ming-Li

What a beautiful cloudy day! In the twilight of July,
The Moon Bay Beach blushes, like a Muse gazing at a lover.
The sparkling waves, at first glance, are always rejoicing.
Fishing songs at dusk like egrets flying. Unlike the creaking of oars, the river here is always pristine.

I smile to Xianghu Lake, it is love, let us be close to each other, the scene is forever in my heart.
Here the flowers are flowing with fragrance, cool breeze.
The waters here are vast, crisscross rice fields, the eyes of wetlands are close by.
By a lake which is quiet and free from dirt, remote thinking of the past Huaijia Pavilion, I will play the fluent writer.
Watch the Seven Star Town crisscross with big and small rivers, all the views taken into sight.

Oh, it is a sweet love song. Who? to hum it in the night sleep?
Who? to hide it in the morning mist?
Ah, this song takes me across the sea, to Xiangjiadang to feel her immortal face!
Xianghu Lake — I would like to dance with you in the wind! To breathe with you.

When the beautiful moon climbs atop the trees, on the liquid jade which is dropped by heaven in the hinterland of the Yangtze River Delta...
When I put my ear to a bay of green water, I hear the melody of birds fluttering in their dreams,

The travelers are enjoying the water, the stories of the land of fish and rice and the distance —
The stars that blink constantly like a drop of dew.

✧✧✧

143 •

江外思鄉　　　　　　　　　　　　韋莊

年年春日思鄉悲，杜曲黃鶯可得知。
更被夕陽江岸上，斷腸煙柳一絲絲。

Nostalgia Beyond the River　Wei Zhuang

From year to year my
nostalgia in spring days

is known by cuckoos
and orioles in the trees.

At the sight of the fading
sun over river bank, my

heart seems to be minced
into willow leaves.

自由廣場前冥想[109]　　　　　　　　林明理

為了一個自我信念
　讓這古蹟隨之更名

---

[109] 台北市「中正紀念堂」園區內的「自由廣場」，建築設計者是楊卓成先生，它融合南京中山陵的構型表現，表現出莊嚴恢弘的氣度。

有人欣悅
　　有人懊惱
只有風　為了愛
　　折回廣場
鼓舞這土地
　　合唱福爾摩沙之歌

Meditation in front of the Freedom Square[110]

           Lin Ming-Li

For a self-belief
  The historical site is renamed
  Some rejoice
  Some chagrine
Only the wind out of love
  Returns to the square
To inspire the land
  To sing together the song of Formosa

◆◆◆

144．

驚雪　　　　　　　　　　　　　　　　陸暢

怪得北風急，前庭如月輝。
天人甯許巧，剪水作花飛。

---

[110] The "Freedom Square" in the park of "Chiang Kai-shek Memorial Hall" in Taipei City is designed by Yang Zhuocheng. It integrates the configuration of the Sun Yat-sen Mausoleum in Nanjing, displaying a solemn and magnificent bearing.

Snow of Pleasant Surprise   Lu Chang

The northern wind
is strangely fierce,

and courtyard is
bathed in moonlight.

The heavenly person
is so artful to cut

water into flowers
flying so beautifully.

在後山迴盪的禱告聲中[111]   林明理

願諸神保護你…
…我親愛的鄉親和受難者,
因為正經歷垂死的邊緣和苦痛。
願神拯救你的靈魂於危險之中,
　　從現在到沒有折磨。
願受難者親屬、甚至全島人民
　　都一起來集氣,
讓失去生命的人
　　有神的光引領他們前行之路。
讓存活者能腰身挺直,
　　繼續將夢想完成。
而我只有在後山迴盪的禱告聲中,
為你們虔誠禱告。感謝我的主。

---

[111] 2018 年 10 月 21 日臺鐵普悠瑪發生出軌事件,造成重大傷亡,且罹難及重傷者多為臺灣台東鄉親、卑南國中師生等,令人哀痛與不捨。—寫於 2018.10.22.

In the Echoing Prayers from the Back Hill[112]

Lin Ming-Li

May deities protect you…
…My dear fellow countrymen and victims,
For they are on the verge of dying and suffering.
May deities save your soul from danger,
From now on until there is no torment.
May the relatives of the victims and even the people of the whole island
Gather together,
For those who have lost their lives
To be with the light of deities to guide the way forward.
For the survivors to straighten themselves,
To continue to fulfill their dreams.
And I can only pray for you in the echo
Of prayer in the back hill. Thank you, my Lord.

✧✧✧

145．

農家

顏仁鬱

夜半呼兒趁曉耕，羸牛無力漸艱行。
時人不識農家苦，將謂田中穀自生。

---

[112] On October 21, 2018, Taiwan Railway Puyuma derailed, causing heavy casualties, and most of the victims and seriously injured were Taiwan Taitung villagers, teachers and students in Peinan country, etc., which greatly saddened people. — Written on October 22, 2018.

The Farmer   Yan Renyu

At wee hours he awakens
his son to till the field

before daybreak: the weak
ox labors slowly. People

know not the pains &
efforts of the farmer:

they take crops in
the field for granted.

消失的湖泊[113]   林明理

阿特斯卡騰帕湖的夜
泥水漥，飢餓的小孩
讓明月低頭
滿地的空貝殼和旱地
消失的蟲鳥和生物
還有湖邊遍布擱淺的船隻
唉，沒有收入的百姓
還能有什麼

The Disappearing Lake[114]   Lin Ming-Li

The night of Atescatempa Lake
Muddy, hungry children

---

[113] 媒體報導，瓜地馬拉（Guatemala）西南部湖泊嚴重乾涸，百姓挨餓著，因而為詩。—2017.7.1.

[114] According to news report, there is a severe drought in the southwest of Guatemala, which brings hunger to common people. The poem is thus inspired. — Written on July 1, 2017.

For the moon to lower her head
A grounful of empty shells and dry land
The disappearing insects and creatures
And the stranded boats scattering about
Alas, common people without any income
What else do they have?

❖❖❖

146 ·

感懷   李煜

又見桐花發舊枝，一樓煙雨暮淒淒。
憑欄惆悵誰人會？不覺潸然淚眼低。

Reminiscence   Li Yu

Parasol tree is seen
to open old blooms;

dusk is murky with
chilly mist and cold

rain. Leaning on the rail,
heavy of heart, who knows?

I cannot help shedding tears
while lowering my head.

難忘邵族祖靈祭   林明理

我不知道為什麼
在族人齊聚的祭場
當舂石音叮咚地響

那應和的竹筒聲
也緊貼著我的耳畔
讓我歡愉又感傷

啊,美麗的拉魯島
在自由中騰飛
森林與山也跟著我歌唱
那痛苦的精靈
已不再抖顫
原來臼与杵
可以是這樣融合
原來生 老 病 死
也是一種本然

我不知道為什麼
像隻孤鷹,惆悵而迷惘
那記憶裡的魚姬傳說
已攫走了我的靈魂
把我輕輕地帶過泛紅的潭水
回到溫存的夢鄉[115]

Unforgettable Shao Ancestral Sacrifice
　　　　　　　　　　　　Lin Ming-Li

I don't know why
In the midst of a religious gathering
When the pounding of stone is aloud
The corresponding sound of bamboo tubes

---

[115] 邵族(Ita Thao),聚居於臺灣南投縣日月潭一帶。每年為迎接新年來到,邵族人齊聚杵音祭場舉行祖靈祭。每戶族人帶著祖靈籃 ulalaluwan〈通稱為公媽籃〉置放祭場,再由先生媽(女祭司)吟唱傳統歌謠祈福。

Clings to my ears
And I am happy and sentimental

Ah, the beautiful island of Lalu
Is rising in freedom
The forests and mountains sing with me
The spirits of pain
No longer tremble
The mortar and the pestle
May be fused so that
Birth, senility, illness and death
Are natural

I do not know why
Like a lone eagle, lost and melancholy
The memory of the legend of mermaids
Has seized my soul
And gently carried me across the red pool of water
To the land of gentle sleep[116]

✧✧✧

147 ·

春雪   東方蚪

春雪滿空來，觸處似花開。
不知園裡樹，若個是真梅。

---

[116] The Ita Thao people live in the area of Riyuetan Pool in Nantou County, Taiwan. Annually, in order to welcome the New Year, the Shao people gather at the Zuyin sacrificial ground for the ceremony. Each family brings an ancestral basket, ulalaluwan, commonly known as the Mother Basket, to be placed by the altar, and then the priestess sings traditional songs as a kind of blessing.

唐詩明理接千載
古今抒情詩三百首
漢英對照

Spring Snow   Dongfang Qiu

Spring snow fills
the sky, high and

low; snowflakes
are flowery. Which

is real plum tree
in the garden,

how, oh, can I tell
one from the other?

蘆花飛白的時候   林明理

夜幕從我流轉的眼神中逃離
我的心鋪滿憂鬱
為著翱翔於星宿之間
為著我曾擁有唯一的真實
為著許多編織的舊夢

哦，我親愛的朋友
你為什麼哭了
我可以無視我的孤獨
但無法阻止風躍回每一熟悉的名字
或注滿於流水、山丘中

世界啊，快來丈量我的軀體
為何變得如此輕靈而猶疑
好似雀兒唱著：啾啾啊嗨，呦
在清秋，萬頃原野
蘆花飛白的時候

When the Reeds Are Flying White

Lin Ming-Li

The night escapes from turning my eyes
My heart is covered with melancholy
To fly among the stars
For the only truth I have ever had
For a host of old woven dreams

Oh, my dear friend
Why are you crying
I can ignore my loneliness
But cannot stop the wind from leaping back to each familiar name
Or filling the waters and hills

The world, oh, come to measure my body
Why to become so ethereal and hesitant
Like a singing bird: chirp-chirp-ah-hai-yo
In the clear autumn, thousands of acres of wild field
When the reeds are flying white

✧✧✧

148 ·

春日　　　　　　　　　　　　　　　　宋雍

輕花細葉滿林端，昨夜春風曉色寒。
黃鳥不堪愁裡聽，綠楊宜向雨中看。

The Spring Day

Song Yong

The woods top is laden with
light flowers & fine leaves;

spring wind of last night
brings about morning coldness.

In sorrow, yellow birds' twitters
cannot bear to be heard;

in drizzling rain, poplars
look fresher and greener.

在那雲霧之間 　　　　　　　　林明理

萬物息息相連。
峽谷郁郁青青,
座頭鯨乍現——
隨即沉入海底。
古老的石頭畫
把過去的歷史串連
在天幕之間迴盪……

同樣的雨林,
從來由不得原住民選擇。
而那些盜伐者或狩獵者,
是否也該深思,
動物將定居何處?

Between the Clouds 　　　　Lin Ming-Li

All things are closely connected.
The canyons are green,
Humpback whales begin to appear —
And sink to the bottom of sea.
The ancient rock paintings
Connect the history of the past
Echoing in the vault of sky...

The same rainforest,
Never to be chosen by the indigenous people.
And should the poachers and hunters
Also ponder:
Where for the animals to settle?

✧✧✧

149.

金縷衣   杜秋娘

勸君莫惜金縷衣，勸君惜取少年時。
有花堪折直須折，莫待無花空折枝。

Golden Clothes   Du Qiuniang

I urge you to
cherish your bloom

of youth instead
of golden clothes.

Pluck blossoming
flowers now, no

tarry: only bare
boughs barely stay.

流螢   林明理

穿出野上的蓬草
靈魂向縱谷的深處飛去
群峰之中
唯我是黑暗的光明

The Flitting Firefly

Lin Ming-Li

Through massy grass in the field
The soul is flying to the depth of valley
Among mountain peaks upon peaks,
Only the flitting firefly brings luminosity in darkness

◆◆◆

150·

洛堤步月

上官儀

脈脈廣川流，驅馬歷長洲。
鵲飛山月曉，蟬噪野風秋。

Strolling along the Dyke in Moonlight

Shangguan Yi

A river runs afar: deep
and wide; along a dyke

I ride a horse, at ease.
Crows fly now and

then, at moonset and
daybreak; cicadas shrill

in the breeze blowing across
the field of autumn morning.

致以色列特拉維夫——白城

林明理

那座老城
　　如巨人般

時時兀自聆聽
　　地中海的潮起潮落
並以神的步伐
　　庇護著天空
　那海灘在遠方
　　　夕陽在遠方
而我溫柔地
　　朝向夜晚
讓生命之河開始流動

To Tel Aviv, Israel: the Big Orange

　　　　　　　　　　　Lin Ming-Li

The Old town
　　Like a giant
Always attentive to listen
　　To the rising and falling tides of the Mediterranean
In the steps of deities
　　To protect the sky
　　The beach is distant
　　The sunset is remote
When tenderly I
　　Into the night
Coax the flow of the river of life

國家圖書館出版品預行編目資料

唐詩明理接千載——古今抒情詩三百首（漢英對照）/
林明理 著、張智中 譯 －初版－
臺中市：天空數位圖書 2025.02
面：14.8*21 公分
ISBN：978-626-7576-10-6（平裝）
831　　　　　　　　　　　　　　　　114001275

書　　　名：唐詩明理接千載——古今抒情詩三百首（漢英對照）
發 行 人：蔡輝振
出 版 者：天空數位圖書有限公司
作　　　者：林明理
譯　　　者：張智中
美工設計：設計組
版面編輯：採編組
出版日期：2025 年 2 月（初版）
銀行名稱：合作金庫銀行南台中分行
銀行帳戶：天空數位圖書有限公司
銀行帳號：006—1070717811498
郵政帳戶：天空數位圖書有限公司
劃撥帳號：22670142
定　　　價：新台幣 530 元整
電子書發明專利第 I 306564 號
※如有缺頁、破損等請寄回更換

版權所有請勿仿製

服務項目：個人著作、學位論文、學報期刊等出版印刷及DVD製作
影片拍攝、網站建置與代管、系統資料庫設計、個人企業形象包裝與行銷
影音教學與技能檢定系統建置、多媒體設計、電子書製作及客製化等
TEL　　：(04)22623893　　　　MOB：0900602919
FAX　　：(04)22623863
E-mail：familysky@familysky.com.tw
Https ：//www.familysky.com.tw/
地　　址：台中市南區忠明南路 787 號 30 樓國王大樓
No.787-30, Zhongming S. Rd., South District, Taichung City 402, Taiwan (R.O.C.)